Maya Sharma Sriram is a full-time writer. She was one of the winners of the Elle Fiction Awards in 2010. *Bitch Goddess for Dummies* is her first novel. She can be contacted at: mayasram@gmail.com.

MAYA SHARMA
SRIRAM

RUPA

First published by
Rupa Publications India Pvt. Ltd., 2012
7/16, Ansari Road, Daryaganj
New Delhi 110002

Sales Centres:

Allahabad Bengaluru Chennai
Hyderabad Jaipur Kathmandu
Kolkata Mumbai

ISBN: 978-81-291-2061-8

10 9 8 7 6 5 4 3 2 1

The moral right of the author has been asserted.

Typeset in Dante MT 11/14

To
My father, V S Sarma:
I never got that PhD, but how about this instead?
and
My mother, Radha Sarma:
At least I was less trouble than Mira!

Contents

Who is a Bitch Goddess?

1   Someone who is extremely successful.
2. Someone so good at being a bitch, she has received
    the title of goddess.

Urban Dictionary

'Sometimes you have to be a bitch to get things done.'
—Madonna

'When a man gives his opinion he's a man. When a woman gives her opinion she's a bitch.'
—Bette Davis

'I love to see a young girl go out and grab the world by the lapels. Life's a bitch. You've got to go out and kick ass.'
—Maya Angelou

Goodbye, Good Girl?

*M*ira grimaced and moved her knee away from Paresh's leg. Again. That would make it three times since they had sat down for dinner. She slid a quick glance at her watch. It had been twenty tedious minutes with Mr Jerk.

Mira studied her reflection in the mirror that hung from across their table. She made a face at the solemn-eyed woman who stared back at her. Oval face, big brown eyes, thick dark hair tied in a rather flattering ponytail, and a piquant chin. As for the rest of her, she was well above 5'6" and had a slim figure—everything that should help her get her own man, a Mr Right, or even better, a Mr Perfect.

So why was she spending a perfectly good evening—that too a Saturday—with a boor? She knew just why when the image of her mother crossed her mind.

No more of this matchmaking, Amma. You are not going to talk me into anything I don't want to do again.

She sighed as she considered the man in front of her. She openly stared at him with impunity. The last half-hour had shown her that nothing discomfited this man, because nothing existed in his world except himself. She took in his perfectly gelled hair, his smooth face, his fashionably-pink shirt, his faultlessly creased trousers and his shiny shoes. He was so perfectly made up that she felt almost dowdy in her black mirror-worked blouse, maroon gypsy skirt and matching open-toed sandals. She could bet her new smartphone that he had more make-up on his face than the moisturizer she had on hers.

It was going to be the longest meal of her life. When was she going to learn to say 'no' to her mother? Her mother had gone and done it again—coaxed her into meeting some man because *she* was convinced that he and Mira were a match made in arranged marriage heaven. Paresh was the sixteenth such 'ideal' man she had shortlisted. Sadly he, like the ones before him, had turned out to be a social solecism.

Mira stretched her lips in disgust. She disengaged Paresh's oily fingers from her forearm and tried to focus on what he was saying.

'And then I told my boss, "No, that is not the way to do it. I have it all worked out. One crackling PowerPoint presentation is all we need to clinch the hundred million dollar account…"'

She curled her lips. Of course Paresh didn't catch the signal. Her eyes wandered away from him and took in the Singapore River from the window beside her. The water shimmered every time it caught the lights from the bustling shops on the banks. The Quay was integral to Singapore's nightlife and was one of Mira's favourite places to chill in the city. Bars, pubs, restaurants and roadside cafés dotted the winding sidewalk that ran along the river.

Mira and Paresh were in an Indian restaurant that claimed Tandoori cuisine as its specialty. The Frontiers sat atop a set of curving wooden stairs and had a deep scooped-out interior with wall panels like stone blocks, resembling a cave. Lamps, which sat on little nooks on the wall, lit the room. Discreet waiters hovered around. Mira had eaten here enough number of times to know that there would be a hefty bill tonight.

She chewed on the last of her missi roti; it was quite good. An almost fair return for a miserable evening spent with Paresh. She turned down his offer for dessert and coffee—she was no masochist—and waited for him to finish both his meal and his monologue. Mira cursed herself silently. She should have never asked him, 'So, how's work?'

'Good coffee, huh?' Paresh said, sipping the brew the waiter had served him.

'Oh yes,' she lied. He had not even noticed that she had declined the coffee.

Paresh swirled his cup and studied his coffee like some connoisseur. 'You know, the best coffee I ever tasted was when I was in Seattle, on a business trip. Mind you, we had gone to Redmond to strike a multi-million dollar deal with Microsoft...'

Mira suppressed a yawn and surreptitiously glanced at her watch again. One and a half hours. Was that a decent length of time to make excuses and run? Maybe she should wait until he finished his coffee—if she could last that long. She was a good girl who remembered her manners, after all. Amma would be so proud, she smiled tightly. Mira eyed his coffee impatiently and fantasized pouring the hot beverage on Paresh's shirt.

Damn. There was his leg again, this time against her shin. She kicked it hard, at least as hard as she could with her sandal, hoping he would get the message. Paresh looked a bit startled but recovered soon enough to launch into a tirade over his Employee of the Month award.

Mira scanned her surroundings again. She had to do *something* while she waited for him to finish his coffee. *Ten minutes. That's all I'll give him.*

That's when Mira saw her. Sanya—her colleague and her bête noire. Sanya, who lunched with the boss and wangled all the good projects away from her. Sanya, who changed boyfriends as often as other women changed their underwear. Sanya, who always looked like she could top Cosmopolitan's poll of Singapore's 'Best Dressed Women'. Mira eyed her with a twinge of envy. Sanya was seated across the room from her, and her skin radiated in the afterglow of some exotic skincare routine. She looked so stylish and incredibly poised in her pale pink blouse, white capris and a broad vintage-inspired brown belt that accentuated her curvy figure. Mira gave a silent groan. Sanya always came out on top—everywhere. Bet her mother would not be able to or even need to hook her up with complete losers over weekends. Sanya was capable of landing hunks all by herself, thank you. In fact, her current companion seemed a case in point: lean, clean-shaven, with a face that showed a strong jawline and an eminently kissable mouth. His raffish ponytail and silver-rimmed glasses added to his yummy quotient. And, more importantly, he seemed a gentleman who kept his hands and legs to himself.

Mira edged her chair further away from Paresh who was moving too close for comfort. She smelt his spicy breath on her face and felt the beginnings of a headache. *Time to get away, girl.*

'Eh, Paresh,' she ventured. 'This is clearly not working, is it?'

He went silent for a minute and then inched forward.

'I guess not. Maybe not marriage,' he shrugged.

Another inch forward.

'Next weekend I am off to Langkawi. I was wondering if you would be interested in…er…getting away?'

Mira's eyes widened. 'If your hand moves another inch, you won't be going on that flight or any other for a long time.' She reached under the table and flicked off his hand that rested high on her thigh. She surged to her feet, her eyes flashing. No matter what, she was not the kind of girl who made a scene. Sanya would have crushed him, she thought irrelevantly.

'I think you have my answer,' Mira said, through gritted teeth. She placed a hundred dollar note on the table. 'My share of the bill.' She swung her bag on her shoulder and stalked off, leaving a stunned Paresh with his mouth agape. Out of the corner of her eye, Mira noticed that Sanya and her date were observing the scene with great interest. Super. Now Mira knew there would be snide jokes from Queen Sanya and her faithful coterie of hangers-on in the office on Monday.

Damn. Damn. Damn. Mira was shaking. She wandered down the quay and sat on an empty stone bench near the water. She took a few deep breaths and stared at the tiny waves caused by the boats cruising the river. She should have slapped Paresh, or at least thrown the glass of water on his face. Or she should have definitely cursed him loudly. She blinked back the tears that threatened to roll down her cheeks. She, Mira Iyer, was a wuss. What kind of self-respecting woman walked out with just one angry retort in the face of an unsavoury and demeaning proposition? Stupid, stupid Mira! What was she doing? Training for sainthood? She rose from the bench feeling disgusted with herself. First her mother bamboozles her into meeting men and then Paresh walks all over her. When was she going to learn to fight for herself? Learn to say NO?

Unsavoury memories swamped her. Memories of the million times when she wanted one thing but had done the opposite, because that was what 'nice girls' did. The 'nice girl' malady had started as early as when she was in third grade—like when a new girl, hugely popular for her dimpled cheeks and imported hairclips, wanted to join their bench and all the other girls forced Mira to move out. She had meekly complied and sat on the floor, swallowing the words of protests that formed in her mouth. Or that time in the seventh grade, when the class hero, on whom she had a huge crush, befriended her to send messages to *her* friend, the prettiest girl in class. All along, she had wanted to say, 'Go give them yourself' but instead, found herself playing courier to the two of them for a whole year. She had remained angry at herself for a long time after that— especially when the boy began ignoring her once he hooked up with Mira's friend.

Mira swallowed hard. She recalled the many times she had wanted to charge over to her father's new house and demand that he explain his behaviour. But nice girls never caused scenes, did they? So she had, predictably, never confronted him in all these years. This 'nice girl' malady sucked. She slung her bag on her shoulder and wandered down the riverside.

Christmas was just fifteen days away and the whole place twinkled with fairy lights. It was, thankfully, not raining now, though it was the monsoon season in Singapore. Mira was happy she could enjoy a late evening walk. She loved this time of the year. The city usually wore its festive best, starting from Hari Raya—as Ramzan was called here—through Diwali, into Christmas, and all the way past New Year, up to mid-January for the Chinese New Year. Of course, it was crass commercialisation at its best, and Mira unabashedly bought into it.

But today, the lively scene did not cheer her up. The laughing, chattering people irked her, reminding her of what was missing in her life. Everybody seemed to know where they were headed. Even Oily Paresh. Mira felt like that pet hamster she had once seen with a little boy on the Mass Rapid Transport. It had been pedalling furiously on this wheel in its cage, but was going nowhere—much like how her life was panning out. Another new year was coming and twenty-seven-year-old Mira still had only one friend in the city (the ever-dependable Vinay), she still met all the flotsam and jetsam her mother threw at her and she still lost all her prime assignments to Sanya.

Still pondering over her life, Mira began walking towards the taxi queue. A pub announced a New Year deal for couples.

Mira felt a quick stab of pain at the thought of being alone on New Year's Eve and then her thoughts moved on to resolutions. Bright new resolutions were part of the New Year, weren't they? Well, the coming year she needed to make one. And fast. It was something she had been toying with for the last couple of years, and she felt that if she didn't do it now, she would never be able to get off that hamster wheel.

It was time for her to change, to take on a whole new avatar. But...but into what? And more importantly, *how*?

The word 'avatar' triggered off images from her childhood— of stories of gods and goddesses she had heard from her grandmother. Mira closed her eyes. She had a brief vision of herself astride a lion, wearing a skull necklace, her tongue hanging out and wielding a bloodied trident. Nah, she didn't want to be Kali. What she wanted was something more urban, something more sophisticated, something more subtle—but just as lethal.

Mira sighed at her whimsy and joined the taxi queue. Then she noticed a woman stride past her. She was not beautiful or physically imposing in any way, nor was she dressed in a slinky outfit that barely left anything to the imagination. But she still looked impossibly sexy; the sexiness reflected on her face and in every line of her body. The woman appeared to say: I dare you to mess with me. A light bulb popped in Mira's head. *This* is the persona and attitude that she wanted—the new avatar. Her current persona had a 'come-walk-all-over-me-I-am-a-wuss' sign plastered on her forehead in bold capital letters. She was going to act on her New Year's resolution, and how.

The queue moved and it was her turn to get a cab. She was lost in her thoughts and barely noticed the passing scenery on her ride back home. The minute Mira stepped into her two-bedroom apartment that was off Holland Road, the phone rang.

'Hello Amma,' Mira said. She eased out of her sandals, padded softly to her camel-coloured stuffed chair and sat down.

'So, how did it go?' her mother sounded worried, as if inquiring about a prolonged root canal. And that, in comparison to her evening, would've been a walk in the park.

Mira sighed tiredly. Why couldn't she have chosen to live in America instead? The time difference between the US and India would have given her extra hours to prep for her mother's barrage of questions.

Mira made a face at the phone, angry at her mother, at herself.

'Oh, very well, Amma.'

'Really?'

'Yeah. He liked me so much that he has invited me to Malaysia for a weekend.' Mira gushed, knowing her exaggerated tone won't be lost on her mother. She paused for effect and trailed off in a wounded tone, 'Only, he does not think marrying me is such a good idea...'

A sharp intake of breath was heard down the line from Chennai. Mira pictured her mother, phone in hand, lounging on the sofa in one of her brightly flowered nighties, getting ready for watching the 9 o'clock Tamil soap on Sun TV—it must be on its two-thousandth episode now, the heroine still weeping about her conniving sister-in-law and adulterous husband. Mira figured that this phone call was probably squeezed between her mother's dinner and the soap.

'Oh,' her mother said. Mira wasn't sure if the reaction was one of shock or of repentance.

'Maybe you misunderstood him, Mira?' Mrs Janaki Iyer, a mother who had single-handedly raised her daughter, was not one to give up that easily.

Mira rubbed her tired eyes. 'There was nothing to

misunderstand, Amma. This Paresh guy was very specific, very "focused in his approach to life", like his twenty-page Tamil Matrimony profile reads.'

There was silence from the other end. 'I hope you...you didn't agree, Mira,' her mother finally spoke.

Of course I jumped and said, 'Yes, Yes, YES!' Do you think I would say no to such an exciting and romantic offer from so charming a man?

'No Amma, what did you think?' Mira replied wryly. She was itching to end the conversation.

'Hmm...never mind.'

Wonderful. Her mother seemed to have recovered from the shock instantaneously. She had dismissed Paresh, his indecent proposal and Mira's excruciatingly unpleasant experience in two words.

'I met Lalitha aunty at Spencer's yesterday. She was talking about her sister-in-law's son.' Mira's mother had truly moved on. 'Engineer...working in London...'

Mira shook her head disbelievingly as her mother extolled the virtues of Bharat—IIT topper and Carnatic virtuoso. Last week it had been Chetan. Next week there would be an Anand or an Arun, and so on and so forth till the list would dry up and the world would be bereft of any 'eligible boys'. Mira knew that her mother was very capable of going and finding a Zack or a Zohab, even while she was in the midst of meeting some other potential groom. She had found her mother's approach bizzare, and had said so many times. But obviously, who was listening?

'You are joking—right, Amma? You seriously don't think I would meet anybody again after what happened today, do you?'

'Why? So Paresh did not work out. But there are other men out there. He is not the last man in the world and anyway—'

Why had she thought her mother would understand?

'Amma, please, not again,' Mira interjected, her tone laced with annoyance. 'I *don't* want to meet anybody. Ever. And I mean it.' Her mother went quiet. 'So you are going to remain single all your life?'

Mira exhaled and counted to ten. This was her mother's offensive act.

'I'll get married someday, I suppose. But not yet.'

'You are twenty-seven years old, Mira. After a year or two, nobody will be ready to marry you.'

I should be so lucky.

Her mother's tone softened and became a little mournful. 'I am not getting younger, don't forget that...'

Mira rolled her eyes. This was the Maudlin Mother Act.

'Amma, you are only fifty-nine.'

'Almost sixty.'

Mira was sure her mother was sniffing. She rolled her eyes again.

'A marriage completes a woman...' her mother's voice quivered.

'*You* are saying this, mom?' said Mira, immediately regretting her words. They lapsed into silence for a few minutes.

'Forget I said that,' Mira said quietly.

'Such things—like what happened to me—don't happen to everybody,' her mother said in a hurt tone.

Mira pictured her mother's face as it would be now—her features drawn and her eyes sad. She hated it when her mother became sad. Damn emotionally manipulative mothers.

'Look Amma,' she said gently. 'I will get married. But not right now.'

Silence.

She spoke into the silence about the only thing that would make her mother forgive her.

'I've got my travel dates to India finalised. I'll be there in April.'

This should surely make her mother happy.

'Have you bought your tickets?' Her mother's voice registered some cheer.

Mira smiled, despite her dark mood. 'Not yet. I have given the travel agent the dates. He should have a reservation for me in a couple of days.'

'How long will you be here?'

'Not sure. Let's see how much leave I can manage.'

'Hope you can come for more than three weeks.'

Phew. Mira exhaled the breath she had holding like she were a diver surfacing for air. Amma *had* forgiven her.

'I think I can manage three weeks,' Mira said slowly.

Her mother followed her cue and dropped the marriage discussion. She made some approving noises about Mira's travel plans and brought her up to speed on the family gossip. Then, a few cousins, a miserly uncle and a couple of spend-thrift aunts came in for serious censure.

Fifteen minutes later, Mira put the phone down and wondered, not for the first time, what the extended family was saying about them behind their backs. Something on the lines of: 'God knows what this Mira is up to, living alone in Singapore. She is a nice girl, but...'

Or it might go something like this: 'Mira has been given so much freedom to live alone. But what can you expect; after all, her mother separated from her husband, even in those days...'

Mira's mind wandered over to her past. It must have been tough for her mother back then, soon after her separation. People didn't do such things in Myalpore back then in the 1980s.

Mira now wondered, for the first time in her adult years, if her parents were merely separated or divorced. Shouldn't she be told the truth after all these years? Maybe she should ask her mother? Or her father? Mira closed her eyes to block the memories that threatened to seep in. No, not her father, she thought with conviction.

She felt her stomach clench. *Deep breaths, Mira, deep breaths.* She needed chamomile tea to calm her. Pronto. She went to the kitchen and made herself a cup. Twirling the tea bag idly in the hot water, she pulled her mind out of the cobwebs of the past and thought about her mother's desire to see her married.

Her mother might have dropped the marriage discussion for now, but she would not have completely abandoned her plans. Knowing her mother's modus operandi, there would be a long line of men, ordered according to some exacting criteria, waiting to meet Mira when she went home in April.

Mira went out to the living room with her tea. She stood near the window and looked out at the darkness enveloping the apartment complex. She had a soothing view of the pool from her thirteenth floor window. The pool was lit and she could see a few late night swimmers doing their laps. Even in the darkness, she could make out the neat little playscape near the pool, and beyond that, the busy Holland Road. She lived alone and was glad she could afford to. Most importantly, she was glad that the safety of this island nation made it possible for her to live all by herself—being a single child had made her somewhat of a loner and she didn't feel the need for apartment mates.

Mira's mind went back to the phone call with her mother. She shuddered as she thought about her mother's untiring matchmaking efforts. She sat on the sofa and sipped her tea. She knew her mother would use every weapon in her arsenal to make her meet all the 'eligible boys'. Before her vacation was over, Mira would find herself married to someone entirely unsuitable. She shook her head, as if to ward off the impending doom. Truth was, she did not trust her mother's judgement when it came to men. She had good reason not to, as her mother always claimed it was love which had gotten her own life into the mess it had become. Over a period of time, Mira had started questioning the purpose of love because of her mother's unfortunate experience and notions.

She got up and dumped her mug in the kitchen sink. She had to find a way to stop her mother from finding more matches for her. She began pacing her living room, her forehead knit in a frown. But it all came back to the same thing, didn't it? What the Universe had been trying to tell her: get a new personality, get a new avatar.

Learn to say NO, Mira. Stand up for yourself. Learn to fight.

Yeah, right. Muttering to herself, Mira crawled off to bed and fell into a deep slumber as soon as her head hit the pillow.

Winds of Change

$\mathcal{T}$he first thing Mira saw as she walked into her sleek glass and steel office, Network Systems, the next day, was Sanya coming out of their boss, Gerard's cabin. The smug look on Sanya's face should have warned her, but Mira dismissed it as the woman's usual man-eater-on-the-prowl smile.

Only Sanya would think of teaming a dark chocolate shirt with a black suit and know how to carry it off. Mira would have paired black with something unimaginative like white or cream and looked, well, ordinary. But she refused to succumb to envy. She gave Sanya a cursory nod and disappeared into her cubicle. She dumped her bag on the desk and grabbed a folder. She flicked her ponytail off her shoulder and it hung straight down her back. The plain blue long sleeve shirt and the perfectly creased black pants gave her a smart, efficient look. Her fuss-free appearance was accentuated by her flat black shoes.

She peeped into the next cubicle. Her friend and comrade-in-arms, Vinay, was not in yet. Mira had a morning meeting with Gerard so she took the folder and went to his room with some trepidation. This was an off-schedule meeting, and she wondered what he was going to discuss. Perhaps the Elcard project?

Gerard was poring over a file and he absently waved her in. Mira caught her breath. He had the best view on the floor—the entire wall behind him was made of glass and it overlooked the harbour. A large ebony, glass-topped table dominated the room's decor; Gerard sat on a sleek black leather chair behind it. A couple of plush chairs were on the other side of the room where Mira stood patiently, staring at the Japanese prints that hung on the walls.

Gerard looked up after a few minutes.

'Yes, Mira. Do we have a meeting?' he said. 'Oh, and sit down.'

'Thank you.' She sat down and tucked her legs under her chair. 'I thought you had called me to discuss the...the Elcard project...' she trailed off, unsure of how to continue.

'Ah, yes. Are you doing that project?' he looked at her briefly and glanced down at his iPhone.

'No...but—'

'Right. I thought it was not yet handed over to any team.' Gerard gave her a fleeting glance and jabbed a text message.

'Yes...but...' she began again.

'So what are we meeting for?' He looked up again, faintly impatient. He put down his phone on the table, next to a roll of mints.

Mira sat up taller in her chair. 'You wanted some preliminary figures and projections for the Elcard project, so here they are.' She put down the folder on his large gleaming table, but he barely glanced at it. He leaned back on his chair. 'Hmm...' He flashed her a toothy smile. 'A great job as usual, I am sure.' Gerard distractedly viewed his computer screen. 'Why don't I go over it later and we can talk then?' His tone indicated mild dismissal.

'But we were supposed to...'

He picked up his phone again, and pointedly looked at his watch. 'Of course,' he said crisply. 'But surely this is not that urgent, is it?' Mira resisted the urge to drop the folder on his head.

He tapped it. 'I shall mail you about this soon,' he said. The meeting was over. She got to her feet, politely nodded, thanked him, and left as unobtrusively as she had come in.

But Mira walked back fuming. She was so angry that she missed the breathtaking view of the sea that framed the entire passageway.

I should have pulled out all the stuff from the folder and showed it to him. I should have forced him to discuss the project. How could he dismiss me like that?

Nah, he was probably busy. He did have his own deadlines, after all. Today was probably a tough day for him. And he did promise to get back to me soon. I know he would.

He should have made eye contact though. That was a bit rude.

But then, again, bosses often behaved like this. Mira shrugged. She had heard some pretty horrible stories about bosses from her friends. It would be alright; such things happen in offices, she mused.

'Yo, Mira!' Vinay greeted her as she entered her cubicle. She was bursting to talk to him. Vinay and she had met five years ago at the fresh recruits' orientation programme and they had instantly hit it off and become thick friends.

'Where to, this early?' She studied his lean, almost boneless frame perched on her table. He slid off and stretched his 6 foot frame. She critically eyed his blue jeans and black shirt.

'I swear you have been wearing the same jeans all week, and that shirt...' she reached out and pinched it between her forefinger and thumb. '...has it even seen an iron? Like...ever?'

He ignored her remarks with a grin. 'Where were you?' he demanded, his eyes dancing with curiosity.

'Meeting with Lord Gerard,' she said shortly.

'Ah, Elcard.' He shot her an understanding look. 'He dismissed you again, didn't he? Took your file and swatted you away like a bug.'

'He said he would get back to me,' she said defensively. 'He usually does...' Mira looked away.

Vinay gave her a 'don't-tell-me' look. But before he could speak, somebody called for him and he left in a rush.

Mira exhaled in relief; she was spared a lecture. She opened her project blueprints and got to work.

A few hours later, Vinay called out from his cubicle, asking Mira to check her mail. She peeked into his office, around the wall they both shared. He was staring at the monitor, his tall frame fitting awkwardly in the tiny cubicle, his grim face making him look like a slightly worried giraffe stuffed in a toy box.

'Wassup?' she said.

He didn't reply but simply gestured to his computer screen.

Curious, Mira went back to her desk and clicked open her mailbox. It was a new mail from the boss. Her forehead creased. She read the mail, blinked rapidly, and read it again. She rubbed her forehead. The significance of Sanya's smile that morning suddenly hit Mira. She shut her eyes tight and felt the onset of a headache.

'I can't believe this.' Mira stabbed at her tofu. She and Vinay were at lunch in the office cafeteria that was buzzing with activity. This was the first time they had gotten a chance to talk about the morning's email.

'Gerard has given Sanya and her team the Elcard project. All because their current project finishes,' she made quotes in the air with her fingers, 'a day before ours does. Pah.' She sipped water from her glass. 'One bloody day. Twenty-four hours! Can you believe that we lost the project because of a measly twenty-four-hour lag? Arrgghh!'

She put her glass down and picked up some tofu with her fork. 'After practically promising it to us, Gerard gives Sanya's team the project.' She laid her fork back on her plate, the morsel on it uneaten. 'So this is why the bitch was smiling when she walked out of G's office.'

'What? When?' Vinay asked. He noisily slurped the noodle strand dangling from his mouth.

'Eww...don't do that,' she waved her fork at him. 'Yeah, I saw her this morning, looking all gung-ho.' Mira tilted her head up to meet his gaze. Sometimes, she got a kink in her neck by just looking up at him the whole day. Vinay had gifted her a tube of pain relief cream when she had complained about this for the five hundredth time. 'She came out wearing one of those cat-getting-the-canary smiles.'

'Bitch.' Vinay ran his fingers through his hair, disturbing an already unruly mop of curls. Mira had threatened that she would put a hairband on his head if he didn't have regular haircuts. 'Elcard's the biggie of the year. So she made sure she got it.'

'Totally! And I had even made some preliminary notes... and...' Mira pushed her plate away. She looked so gloomy that Vinay gave her a friendly nudge. '...and stupidly handed it to Gerard this morning. The folder would have reached that woman by now,' finished Mira.

Vinay jabbed his chopstick in her direction. 'I think you should go and talk to Gerard,' he said. 'Ask him why we didn't get it after all those initial discussions we had with him. Tell him about the prelim work you have done. Brag about our successful projects. Use management jargon and talk about our team's USP and our specific strengths and anything else you can think of. Tell him we can work on two projects simultaneously, till the current one is done. This won't be the first time we would be doing that. Do whatever it takes. *Fight* for Elcard. You are the only one who can, I can't, the others can't either. You are the senior player here. I think the team deserves it.'

Seeing Mira hesitate, Vinay ploughed ahead, 'Mira, you know how bad the market it. You know how, at every meeting, there is always a talk of downsizing. It's simple maths—the team that performs, stays. We have had just one big contract this year. Win this two-million-dollar contract and we are safe; lose it and we may be the ones looking for new jobs.'

Mira pondered over Vinay's words. Then she shook her head. 'It's clear, the email. Elcard pushed up the dates, so the company needs to hurry up on it. Hence, the first free team gets it.'

Vinay smirked. 'Get real, woman.'

Mira shook her head again, this time more firmly. 'Let it go. There will be others.'

Vinay did not reply. Neither spoke through the rest of the meal.

As they walked back to the office, Vinay gave Mira a long look. 'You know what, Mira?' he said. 'You need to stand up for yourself. Learn to say, "No, I won't take shit." Become more aggressive, fight for what you want. That's the stuff winners are made of.'

Mira was so surprised that she stopped short in her tracks. This was the third time she had been road-rolled in three days. There *was* something wrong with her and she hadn't known it all these years! Fancy Star Wars and LOTR obsessed Vinay going all Dr Phil on her.

'Learn to say no. NO.' She robotically repeated after Vinay.

'Yeah, baby,' he said, patting her. 'Don't let people get away with taking advantage of you or treating you badly.'

She nodded and entered her cabin.

Back at her desk, Mira opened her screen. But she wasn't

really looking at what was in front of her. Her mother, then Paresh and now Sanya. Maybe it was karma. The Fates were telling her to change. Become a fighter, learn to go after what she wanted, be firm and say 'no' to what she did not want and become brave. *Don't be a pushover, Mira.* Even Vinay, the most non-confrontational person she knew, was saying it.

She closed her software programmes and then opened them again. That was the problem, wasn't it—becoming brave. She shook her head and tried to go back to work. But the numbers and letters on the screen didn't make any sense. She played with the pen on her table, her eyes fixated on the screen.

Maybe that had been the problem with Amma, too. Maybe she had not fought hard enough for what she wanted; had not been aggressive enough.

Mira was no relationship expert, but she figured that in a marriage, sometimes, you had to *fight* to make it work. Her mother should have, perhaps, pulled out some feminine tricks or something. Like the women in her Tamil soaps did to win their man back. Instead of trying to be a 'nice' woman and stepping aside for some other woman to walk off with her husband, her mother should have put up a big fight.

Mira clenched her fist. *I won't be like Amma. I will not be a pushover.*

Footsteps clicked past Mira's desk. She turned around and watched Sanya walk by, brimming with confidence. People like *her* won. Women like Sanya and the Other Woman. Mira flinched at the memory.

The first and the only time Mira had seen the Other Woman was thirteen years ago. Mira had been fourteen years old and enroute to her maths tuition class on her cycle. It was hot and humid, which was the default weather for Madras anyway, and the clogged-up traffic was not making it any better.

She had stopped her cycle to let the other vehicles go past. That was when she did a double take. Her father and the Other Woman were in her family's silver-grey Ambassador that was coming from the opposite side of the road. He was driving and staring straight ahead. She was sitting beside him and talking. There was a vibe between them that even young Mira could sense. And even after all these years, she remembered the woman's stylishly cut hair that fell in soft waves on her shoulders, her long curved pottu, and her sheer blue and yellow printed sari. But it was the sleeveless blouse that had remained with Mira all these years. Somehow, its image had embedded itself in her memory, maybe due to her largely conservative upbringing. Most women in the prim, 1980s Madras didn't wear sleeveless blouses. In her impressionable young mind, only vamps wore sleeveless blouses. Mira felt like the woman was almost using the blouse as a weapon to lure her father away from her mother.

Mira had watched them drive past without noticing her. When the light had turned green, she had almost collided with an auto rickshaw.

'Have you said your goodbyes at home?' the auto driver had snapped crudely in Tamil.

But Mira hadn't replied; she was too busy brushing the tears from her face. She could barely see because the road and the traffic had all blurred.

'Amma, why don't you ever wear sleeveless blouses?' she had asked her mother that night at the dinner table.

'Po di, my arms are too fat,' her mother dismissed the idea.

Mira looked at her mother's arms carefully. They were no bigger than the Other Woman's.

'Other women your age wear them.'

'North Indians,' her mother said, a little disdainfully.

Ah, the Other Woman was one of *them*, a North Indian. Now Mira knew. She slowly chewed her vegetables.

'Amma, you don't understand...' Mira's voice was pained. She felt agonized and confused.

If only you had worn sleeveless blouses and cut your hair short, then, maybe, we wouldn't be living like this. And I wouldn't be without a father...

She didn't say it aloud—that would have been disloyal to her mother.

Her mother looked concerned. 'What's got into you today?'

'Nothing.' Mira pushed her plate away and rose from her chair. 'I am not hungry.' She charged into her room, nearly in tears.

Mira's phone rang on her desk, snapping her back to the present. Of course she remembered the past and the Other Woman. And of course her mother had not changed her look—that had been the conservative Mylapore of the eighties. Sleeveless clothes were scowled at and short hair was mostly an anti-lice measure for pre-schoolers. But this was the 2000s and Singapore was a long way from Chennai's Mada Street in the Mylapore neighbourhood. Mira was today's independent woman and could do as she pleased with her wardrobe and appearance. She could—and was going to—change. Even the idea set her heart racing. She was going to learn to say 'no' and fight for her space under the sun. She had had enough of being a pushover and was going to transform into a woman even *she* wouldn't recognize. But the question still remained: *Into what do I transform? And how?*

Bring on the Bitch Goddess!

*I*t was 3.30 p.m. and Mira was still lost in thought about the image change she craved. She knew future projects would be hers if she played her cards right. But first, the transformation. She looked away from the pie charts on her screen and at the view from her cubicle's window. Though it was not as spectacular as that from Gerard's office, it was always nice to look at Singapore's cityscape splayed over the skyline. She looked past the tall office buildings, onto the distant glint of the waters that peeked from between the concrete structures. She watched the sun play hide and seek with the skyscrapers as she pondered over her question.

She sighed. The answers would come, she thought. Her inbox pinged. She clicked on the new mail: some query from the software testing team that needed a quick response. As she sent off her reply, she noticed her chat image, as if seeing it for the first time. She was a little appalled that she had chosen a cute piglet with a cherubic smile as her profile picture. What was she thinking? Mira most certainly didn't want to be a pig, however cute it might be. She wanted to resemble something more vicious. That was the persona she needed to project, she mused with her newfound wisdom. Maybe a tigress, a feline on the hunt. Hmm... She liked the idea.

She gave a few experimental growls. Grrr...grrrr.... More menace. Ggrrrrrrrrr...awogrrrr.....

Nah. Not working. She needed something with more

panache and spunk. Sanya's husky voice floated down the corridor. It came to Mira instantly. She snapped her fingers. A bitch. No, a Bitch Goddess. Yes, that's what she will be. She vaguely recalled coming across the phrase in some women's magazine and, somehow, it had stuck in her sub-conscious. The article had not explained its meaning, though.

Mira racked her brain. So who was a Bitch Goddess and what did she do? She surmised that she crushed her enemies under killer stilettos, didn't let her mother blackmail her into embarrassing situations with loser suitors. And she played with men. Yes, *played*. Mira's lips curled into a thin smile. A Bitch Goddess was what she was going to become. And she was going to rock her new avatar! Only, how did one become a Bitch Goddess? Mira figured some were born that way, and others learnt it the hard way. Option one hadn't happened and option two, Mira decided, was just the way she was going to do it.

Google should have some pointers. Wasn't there like a manual or something on this? Mira typed search options furiously:

```
How to become a Bitch Goddess in thirty
days
Bitch Goddess for Dummies
Bitch Goddess 101
```

She shook her head in dismay. Even omniscient Google didn't know. She wasn't going to find these titles on library bookshelves either. And who else could help her with this? Certainly not Vinay! She was going to have to do this on her own, from scratch. She knew one thing, though. If she was going to be a Bitch Goddess, then she had to be one all the way through. No half-measures would do. But before that, she had to find out what the heck made a person a Bitch Goddess.

Mira was aware that a Bitch Goddess was neither a nice girl, nor an out-and-out bitch. The persona was something more than that. She pondered over it for a few minutes. Oh yes! She snapped her fingers. She knew what kind of a Bitch Goddess she was going to be: a bitch with class, a bitch with a purpose.

First order of business: change the chat image. Now, immediately. No more cute and cuddly animals. What she needed was an all new sexy, hard-hitting, don't-mess-with-me image that men will lust after and women will loathe.

She was almost dancing in her seat with excitement as she began an image search. A tiger? No, not stylish enough. How about red lips with a burning cigarette butt dangling from it? Nope. Too moll-like. A black lacy bra? She was a Bitch Goddess, not a hooker for heaven's sake. Red-tipped long nails? Nope. Too noir-ish.

Then she found it. A shiny pair of red, killer stilettos. She stared at the six-inch heels that looked like ice-picks. They could literally be Killer Shoes. She fantasized crushing Paresh under it. Yeah. This was it. Even an idiot who looked at the image would get the message. Sometimes, clichés could be so handy.

Click. Copy. Paste. She studied her new chat image with satisfaction. She was already feeling like a new person. Go, Bitch Goddess. Go, Woman Power! She banged the desk with her fist.

'What's up, Mira? All well?' Vinay called out from his cubicle.

'Nothing, just tried some desk yoga.' Mira stiffled a giggle and got back to work with renewed vigour. But the rest of the afternoon went in a daze, she couldn't concentrate on her work. She pondered over how she was going to make the Bitch Goddess transformation. Changing the chat image had been easy; if only the rest were just as simple.

Mira had to deal with her appearance first. The attitude will follow, she surmised.

She decided to start with a physical makeover: wardrobe, make-up, et al. All that jazz which will make her look like a Bitch Goddess. Then she would start behaving like one. What was that someone said: You are what you wear? She didn't know if it was really possible, but she had to start somewhere, and a physical makeover was as good a beginning as any other.

Mira finished work and shut down her computer. It was late evening and it had started raining again. The roads would be glistening with the moisture and the shrubs lining them would look verdant, she thought. But from where Mira sat, all she could see were steel and glass buildings and a darkened sky. She sat back in her chair, pen and pad in hand.

Alright. If she was going to construct the Bitch Goddess avatar ground up, then what she needed was a List. Mira chewed on her pen. Ground up meant that on the top of the list was underwear.

1. Bitch Goddesses don't wear ordinary underwear. They wear provocative lingerie that hint at sin...

She continued chewing on her pen and resumed writing.

2. Shirts: sleeveless, slinky and feminine.
3. Trousers. Were they vastly different from the ones other women wore? She thought of Sanya and sighed. *Everything* was different about her—she set a very high sartorial benchmark to follow. But a nagging sensation told Mira that this had more to do with the person and her attitude, than with her clothes.
4. Skirts? Short and tight with a slit or two thrown in.
5. Shoes: stilettos, gladiators, pumps and anything with heels that can come in handy on a bad date.

6. Make-up. Here Mira looked lost. She would have to go and find out from experts. She had better visit one of those make-up counters at the department stores.
7. And of course, a killer haircut. 'Give me a Bitch Goddess haircut, please,' she'd say to the elderly Chinese lady at her regular salon.

'Hey!' Vinay called out, startling her. 'Ready?'

She looked up at Vinay's thin, long bespectacled face peering over the cubicle wall. They had an offsite meeting to go to, she then remembered.

'Yeah, getting there,' she replied, smiling at her secret joke.

'What's with the grin?' Vinay looked at her suspiciously.

'Nothing. Can't a girl grin, Vinay?' She stuffed her pad and her pen into her handbag, slung it on her shoulder and got to her feet.

She was not going to tell Vinay about Project Bitch Goddess—at least not yet.

'Come on, let's go,' she said, and they left.

Born-Again Woman

*T*he next day was Saturday but Mira was up early. She had an appointment to keep and a shopping list to attend to. She finished her breakfast and did her chores, idly wondering if Bitch Goddesses did their own chores. Surely they had people to do the cleaning and tidying up after them?

Then, with a cup of lemon tea to go with her perky mood, she picked up her list. Mira's eyes widened as she went over it. In the calm of the morning, it looked like a lot. Did she really have to buy so many things? Fortunately, she had lived frugally all these days and knew her bank balance to the last cent. Good girls usually did. Maybe, if she were lucky, after today, she would be clueless about what good girls did.

She was determined to get out now and seize the day, before her other, more angelic self, made her change her mind. She hurriedly finished her tea and left the cup unwashed in the sink, resisting every urge to rinse it. Then she picked up her bag and checked all the debit and credit cards she owned. They glinted in the morning light, ready to be swiped by gleeful shop attendants. Satisfied that she had all that she would need, she slipped into her shoes and stepped out of the door.

In twenty minutes, she was at Orchard Road, Singapore's ultimate shopping destination.

Her first stop was for clothes. A few hours later, Mira stepped into the changing rooms of Robinsons to study her list. She sat on the upholstered bench and trailed her pen down her notebook's page.

Underwear: Check. Sexy lingerie does maketh a bitch. Who knows when they will come in handy to make an impression? Shopping for it had been harrowing, though. She had braced herself for lace, colours, and embroidered flowers. She had been prepared to give up her Code Name Beige and go in for the coloured stuff. But diamantes? Cami-knickers? Demi bras? And that thing that sounded like a part of a house—balconette? Now she knew so much about underwear that she could probably do a doctorate in Women's Lingerie.

Mira smiled, remembering the bewildered expression on the face of the young shop girl at Triumph. She must have wondered why Mira was so confused about garter belts and thongs, and took three hours to choose. Finally, Mira had picked up silk thongs in pink and lots of lacy underwear and even one that had embroidery all over the front!.

Mira moved down the list: Shirts, skirts, dresses and trousers. She had spent a lot of time mulling over this last night. After much reflection, introspection, and research about everything sartorial—thank God for Google—Mira decided that women who wore their clothes with panache, whether they were saris or power suits, had supreme confidence and a ready acceptance of their bodies that reflected in their persona. They wore clothes that suited their body types. The more stylish women she knew never settled for the easy or the safe or the conventional way out, unlike Mira did. She took a deep breath. Now, all that was going to change. No more going blindly for flat-front, polyester-blended black pants or pleated skirts or collared shirts in dark colours. She was going to look for pinstripe pants, pencil skirts and bright sleeveless blouses with V necks, and God knows what else. From now on, she will buy only those clothes that made her feel powerful, and strong, and classy—it was adieu Ms Bland and hello, power dressing.

By the time she left the store a few hours later, her shopping bags were filled with pin-striped black pants (wide at the leg); two chocolate 'cigarette' pants (new word learnt), blazers in white, red and deep purple; a couple of sleeveless tops in v-neck and ruffle-neck; a red pencil skirt; a braided brown belt and sheer leggings.

It had taken her twenty-seven years to derive joy from shopping. Talk about late bloomers. But now that she had experienced every shopaholic's bloodsport, she knew she would be back; in fact, she had already mentally made a note of all the things she would buy on her next visit to the mall.

Next stop: Shoes. Mira should have felt burdened with the weight of all the bags she was carrying as she walked out of the store and hit the street outside. But instead, she found herself practically skipping down the five-minute path and across the busy street to the shoe store. She stopped at its entrance and stared at the imaginative window display that had all sorts of footwear dangling from a gigantic Christmas tree. Bright shoes, dull shoes, tall ones, flat ones, boots and moccasins beckoned her to try them out. The cautious and prudent Mira had planned to get only two pairs, but the Bitch-Goddess-in-training figured that a Bitch Goddess was probably a shoe hoarder—after all, pointy heels were her trusted weapon. So in went Mira, with no idea of what she was going to buy, or how many.

Mira felt like a little girl playing dress-up. She stood there dazed, as the shop assistant trotted out pair after pair: golden ones and brown ones; roman sandals; knee-high boots; kitten heels and flats; flip-flops and closed shoes. She tried them all and, finally, bought a pair of dark brown wedges, a fancy alternative to her regular black office sandals. She also picked up a pair of red slingback kitten heels, the mandatory pair of stilettos, and one black with silver heels, which the stylish shop assistant called a d'Orsay pump. Mira wondered what she was going to pump up with it, but bought it anyway because it screamed 'Bitch Goddess'. She picked up the shopping bags and strode out of the store, poorer in the pocket but stronger in the Bitch Goddess quotient.

Mira paused on the sidewalk, trying to remember what else she needed. Now there was something she absolutely *had* to get, though she had not written it down on her list. The one thing every fashion consultant urged women to purchase, the one thing that every fashionista worth her Jimmy Choos owned: the Little Black Dress. She didn't find the perfect Little Black Dress in any of the stores she had just visited in the mall. But somewhere in the world there was one with her name on it and she was going to get it. She crossed her fingers and hit the next mall with a vengeance.

But when she came out of the fourth store empty-handed, she wondered if the Little Black Dress was even meant for her. Despite her slim figure, she could hardly compete with the petite, size zero women who inhabited the changing rooms.

Was this a sign?

If it was, she chose to ignore it and continued going from store to store, lugging around the shopping bags. Some ten or eleven stores later, just when she was ready to call it quits, she spotted *it*. The perfect Little Black Dress that screamed her name. It was draped on a mannequin, and made her eyes shine with lust. A few seconds later, the shop assistant disrobed the mannequin and the gorgeous dress was in Mira's hands.

She tried it on, studied her reflection in the mirror, and then a slow smile spread on her face. This was exactly what she had fantasized about. It was a one-shoulder dress that ended just above her knees. The cut was snug, but flowed just enough for it to swirl a little when she turned around. She startled at seeing how sexy she looked in this dress. Sexy, but elegant. Rock on, Bitch Goddess.

With that smug smile intact, Mira went off to the salon for her appointment. An hour later, she was staring at a near-stranger's face in the salon mirror. When she had walked in, all she had said was that she wanted a stylish but fuss-free cut. Now she had shoulder-length hair, shorter in the front, with some wisps framing her forehead. Her eyes looked bigger and her features sharper. She liked the hardness that the haircut added to her face. She smiled. The Bitch Goddess was slowly emerging.

Mira was so pleased with herself that she decided to lunch at the food court in the mall's basement. She sat down at a corner table and started on her meal.

'Is this chair taken?'

Mira looked up from her plate. Her eyes travelled up a T-shirt clad muscular chest, took in broad shoulders and stopped at a pair of dark eyes that were studying her. She raked her memory; the face was familiar to her. Ah, he was Sanya's dinner companion at the Frontiers that night. But the rakish ponytail and glasses were missing. He had a friendly smile on his face and was pointing to the empty chair across from hers. Why did she feel weak in the knees? It was Sanya's boyfriend, for God's sake! But did he know who she was? He cocked an eyebrow, making her flush. Did he read her thoughts?

'No, please sit,' Mira replied, giving him a friendly smile.

'Thanks,' he said and sat down.

'I know you are Mira, a software engineer, and that you

work with Sanya. She mentioned it once. I am Rohan.'

Mira was so surprised that it took her a few seconds to shake the hand he was extending.

'I noticed you that day at Frontiers, ' she said. 'But didn't you have a ponytail that day?'

He grinned. 'I chopped it off. I was ready for a change.'

Me too. 'It looked cute.' She had almost said "hot". 'You also had glasses...'

'Now I wish I hadn't visited the barber, or put on my lenses.'

They both laughed. The crowd around them ebbed and flowed, the noise was a steady hum in the background.

'Are you also in IT?' she asked after a while. Mira searched for something to say. Bitch Goddesses should know how to strike up effortless conversations with good-looking men—especially if they were dating a rival Bitch Goddess.

'Nope,' he shook his head. 'Professor of Physics, at the National University.'

'Oh.'

'Mira Iyer, TamBram, huh?'

'Yep, the name says it all. If it doesn't, my profession does,' she said dryly.

He laughed. 'I'm also a TamBram. Rohan Bhardwaj. Last name, of course, being my Gothram.'

She wasn't sure what to make of this extra information. Was he also caught in the TamBram arranged marriage trap? Then she remembered he was Sanya's boyfriend. Damn, why did she keep forgetting it?

'Of course,' she said. Mira and Rohan exchanged a knowing glance that spoke of common roots and collective history.

They ate in silence until he asked, 'So, you are going for that next weekend?' He pointed at a flyer that lay next to Mira's tray. It announced the opening night of the *Madame Butterfly*.

'No,' her tone was wistful. 'I picked this up just now at the booth in the foyer. This was one opera I badly wanted to see. I called them, but apparently it's sold out. I called too late, I guess,' she shrugged.

Rohan looked thoughtful 'Hmmm...should be good.'

They finished their meal and got up.

'Can I drop you somewhere?' he said.

'Um... I am going home, Holland Drive?' Mira said. She was dead on her feet—prep work for a metamorphosis was so exhausting! She was too tired for 'I am today's woman who can hail a cab, thank you'—and, hell, the guy *was* good looking.

'That is on my way, I am going back to my campus too,' Rohan said. She knew he would have to drive past Holland Drive to get to the university. She nodded and followed him gratefully to the car park.

He asked for her business card as she was about to get down at the apartment building's foyer. National University of Singapore (NUS) did a lot of business with her firm. Maybe he would give them a project and her team would get more work? Mira thought this over. Vinay was right. It was tough times in this economy and if they didn't find enough projects, her team might be in trouble. They exchanged cards and waved goodbyes, with vague promises to meet up later.

Only late that night, when she was lounging in front of the TV, did it hit her. Stupid, stupid Mira! What kind of a Bitch Goddess was she? She had the boyfriend of her rival all to herself, for almost three hours, a part of that in the closed confines of a darkened vehicle, and what had she done? Nothing, nada, zilch. No flirting, no invitation for a late nightcap, no attempt to lure him away from Sanya. Instead, she had exchanged—not passionate kisses—*business cards* with him. She slumped her shoulders in self-disgust. Her future as a Bitch Goddess looked dismal. Very, very dismal.

At that moment, as if to add to her gloom, the phone rang.

She knew it would be her mother, nobody else called her anyway. But hadn't they spoken just yesterday? This was not going to be good.

Damn. Damn. Damn.

With practice, she ought to get to more colourful expletives soon.

'Hello.'

'How are you, kanna?'

'Amma, we spoke just yesterday.' Mira was exasperated. 'No, no. We spoke two days, ago. But I wanted to know if you were okay today.'

'Why would I not be okay tod—' She looked at the calendar on the wall. For the first time in many years, she hadn't woken up saddened on this day. She had been so caught up in the excitement of Project Bitch Goddess that the date had completely slipped her mind. She was filled with a sense of lightness. Yes, she punched the air.

But now that her mother had reminded her, she felt weighed down by memories.

'Mira, I knew you would've remembered your father's birthday. I thought you...you would be sad...'

Mira frowned. 'Actually, Amma, I never even noticed the date today. I was out doing so many things and having fun, that I never even thought of *him* once.' *Until you called and spoilt it all.*

Her mother fell silent. Mira knew her mother did not believe her.

'It's time to let him go, Mira. For your own sake.'

Where do we have him, Amma? When did we have him last? Hold onto what?

'I am not the one who brought this up, Amma.'

'Seventeen years is a long time, Mira, to carry this around.' It was as if her mother had never heard her.

Mira bristled. 'This is my father's betrayal you are talking about, Amma. How is there a time frame on that?'

Her mother sighed. 'I wish you would forgive...and forget.'

'I had forgotten, until you called and reminded me.'

'Not that kind of forgetting. The kind that comes from laying ghosts to rest.'

Mira didn't reply.

'That's why I have been asking you to meet him. At least once.'

'Amma, you promised,' Mira was suddenly ten again—sad, lost and bewildered. She paused and took a deep breath. *Hold on. Bitch Goddess, remember?* 'Amma, we have already discussed it and you said you would wait until I was ready.' She hoped she sounded mature and rational.

'Everybody's growing old, Mira. Time doesn't wait for us. When you are ready, it might be too late...'

Mira had underestimated the mother of the Bitch Goddess.

She closed her eyes and counted to ten. She didn't want to prolong this really painful conversation. 'Amma, let's talk about it when I come home. Anyway, I can't meet him unless I am in India, right? So until then, no discussion.' She kept her voice bright and chirpy.

Her mother sighed in resignation. It was amazing how much her mother could pack in a simple exhalation of breath.

'Okay, kanna, call me later, when you are feeling better.'

Mira agreed and disconnected. She got ready for bed. Later, she lay on her bed, staring at her ceiling in the muted light of the bedside lamp and thought about her mother. Some things about her mother puzzled her. She knew that she was in touch with her father because she got periodic updates about him—even when she didn't want them. But why was her mother still in touch with this man? Did they call or did they meet? Did they talk about old times or were they stiff with each other? Did they still have...feelings?

A knot formed in her stomach. *Calm down. You are a Bitch Goddess, remember?*

She turned over and switched off the light. But it was a long time before she fell asleep.

Hello World

*T*he next morning, Mira startled at the person who looked at her from the bathroom mirror. It wasn't the hard working woman with a practical ponytail that she was used to seeing, but a sultry woman with hair that looked like it was mussed after a wild night of sex.

A slow smile spread on her face; today was the first day of her new avatar.

After a shower, she stood before her wardrobe and flipped through the hangers. Her pulse quickened at the thought of wearing the gorgeous clothes she had wiped out her bank account for. The pinstripe trousers and the white blouse with the ruffled collar were pulled out. She tucked in the short blouse, buckled the belt around her slim waist and slipped her feet into the new brown wedges. Hmm…what else did the dress need? She wondered what accessory Sanya would wear. Possibly a scarf or a stole. Or, perhaps, a garter belt, Mira thought wickedly. She thrust her chin forward. No, she won't be a Sanya clone. The understated diamond flowerets on her ears were enough to complete the look.

She moved onto make-up and mentally recited the instructions the sales assistant had given her. First the moisturiser, then the foundation and then the compact—the cardinal rules in the art of applying make-up. She twirled the eyelash curler (new addition) over her eyelashes and lightly brushed on some blusher to bring colour to her cheeks. A dab of bronze lipstick and brown eyeliner later, she was done. But when she picked up her brown tote, it struck her—she had forgotten to buy *bags*. How *could* she have omitted them from her list? No self-respecting Bitch Goddess could be seen carrying the same handbag every day of the year. Sadly, she'll have to wait for payday now.

Think Bitch Goddess. Be Bitch Goddess. Mira recited the lines like a mantra and stepped out of her apartment.

She felt weighed down by her make-up. The light bounce of her freshly shampooed hair made her feel a little under-dressed. The narrow cut of her pants seemed to restrict her movement when she walked, and she was sure the short top would come untucked very soon. She stepped into the lift.

'Good morning,' the suit-clad man inside said when the door opened. 'Morning,' she replied and stepped in beside him. He seemed to be in his late thirties, and not at all bad-looking. Mira didn't remember seeing him in the building and hoped he lived here. It wouldn't hurt to run into such a handsome man everyday. She found him studying her from the corner of his eyes. Mira smiled inwardly, pleased with the impact her appearance had had on him. When she got off the lift, her stride had a zing to it. She flagged a cab and got in. When she paid off the cabbie in front of her office, even he was eyeing her appreciatively.

Yes. The physical makeover seemed to be a success. Now things could only get better from here.

'Whoa! You got laid?' asked Vinay as soon as Mira stepped inside her cabin.

'Good morning to you too, Vinay,' she chirped and dropped her bag on her desk.

'Whatever. Well, did you?'

She had to admire the man's gall. But she was not surprised at their easy banter. What had begun as a casual friendship in their Chennai office had grown into a deeper bond when they both moved to Singapore together on the same assignment. Their friendship had reached a point where they had become each other's sounding boards, confidantes and best friends.

'No, not that I know of. And why am I even answering such a rude, personal question?' she took her own time in replying.

Vinay stared at her for a long minute. 'But there *is* something…an air about you. Something has happened,' he said.

Atta boy, good observation.

Mira flicked her hair back and sat on the edge of her desk. 'Maybe it's my new haircut…' she tilted her chin at him.

He shook his head. 'Could be, though I think there is something more. This sitting on the desk, leg swinging thingy you're doing… What's up?' His eyebrows wiggled up and down.

'Maybe it's your overactive imagination,' Mira breezily replied. Mentally, she punched the air. The makeover *was* working.

'No. I have known you for five years and have always seen you sitting primly on your chair, legs tucked in, back stiff. And here you are—suddenly, this woman who has discovered some new secret about her body. So, I repeat, what's going on Mira Iyer?'

And she had thought Vinay was unobservant! But before she could speak, somebody called out:

'Hey, Mira! Boss wants to see you. Now.'

For a fleeting moment the timid and servile Mira surfaced, but was deftly overpowered by the Bitch Goddess. She waved at her co-worker in acknowledgement.

'He is calling you for a progress report?' Vinay wondered absently, still dazed at his friend's overnight transformation.

'Who knows?' Mira muttered and left. She could barely suppress the impish smile playing on her lips. She knocked tentatively on Gerard's door and took a deep breath. *Act cool, you are now officially a Bitch Goddess.*

Her boss waved her in and pointed to a chair. Mira smiled and sat down. She studied him as he spoke on the phone. Gerard was a Caucasian with a British accent. Mira, Vinay, and most of the office had a pool going, trying to guess his nationality. He had been living in Singapore, like, forever. Mira was sure he held a British passport, though some people in the office claimed he was Aussie. That was because he often spoke about the cricket he had played for his college in Melbourne. Vinay maintained that he was Singaporean, the local version of the Anglo-Indian. Mira wasn't sure if such a thing existed. Though they had been working for him for three years now, they were no closer to knowing about his nationality than they had been initially. All they knew was that he was married with no kids; they had even met his wife. But that hadn't helped in cracking the puzzle—she was from Japan.

Gerard put the phone down and placed his arm on the table. That brought him a little closer to Mira; she could smell the aftermints he constantly ate the whole day. He ran an eye over her. 'You look different today. But nice...very nice.' He raised an eyebrow. 'New boyfriend?'

Should I just punch his nose or bean him with my $150 wedges? Are we women so pathetic that we get a new look only if we had sex or a new man? This has to be one of those male-propagated myths.

Bitch Goddess Rule #1: A Bitch Goddess always uses her charms.

Mira shot a lingering smile at her boss. 'Thank you very much, Gerard, but no boyfriend, I'm afraid.' Her tone was appropriately mock-sorrowful.

'Are the men blind around here?' he said, meeting her gaze. Wow, Gerard was a flirt. She would have never known.

You didn't notice me until this morning, bucko.

'Maybe they are,' she said.

'So, Mira. I wanted to talk to you about this new project,' he said, assuming a business-like tone. 'The one from NUS.'

Mira frowned. 'Oh? But…I mean, our group doesn't handle them.'

'That's right. But this is a new one and…and they sort of asked if *you* could handle it.' He watched her, obviously trying to gauge her reaction.

Mira was surprised. 'Asked for *me*? Are you sure?'

Gerard shrugged. 'Must have heard or seen your work somewhere.'

Rohan. 'Does this have anything to do with the physics department at NUS?' she asked.

'No. Admin work, really.'

'Oh.' Why was she disappointed that her hunch was wrong?

'Yeah.' Gerard took out a folder. 'Here, take a look. All the details are here.'

Mira's mind raced. The NUS project was a poor substitute for Elcard, but it was still work. How had Rohan managed this? She took the folder from Gerard.

'It's a six-month long project that requires upgradation of their employment payroll system. See if you can give me an early report soon.'

Mira nodded and got to her feet. She paused at the door, her hand on the handle, and looked over her shoulder at her boss. 'Sure, Gerard. This doesn't really fit in the same league as an Elcard project, but it is a good start,' she shrugged.

She relished the stupefied look on Gerard's face, and walked out. She did a little dance on her heels. Was the change happening or what?

Mira reported the meeting to Vinay and dropped the folder on his desk.

'Read through and share your thoughts,' she said. Mira rummaged through her bag and pulled out the card she was looking for. She picked up her phone and punched in the number printed there.

Hi, this is Rohan Bhardwaj. I am unable to take your call now. Please leave...

Mira disconnected.

What was with that accent? Ro-aan Bar-ad-waj? Why did Indians acquire an accent the minute they cleared customs and entered a new country? She had to get to the bottom of this cultural quirk.

'Vinay?'

'Yep?' Vinay's eyes were glued to the computer, his hair was messed up and his shirt was spilling out of his pants' waistband. And it was only ten in the morning. Really, Vinay was like a grubby school kid sometimes.

'Do I put on an accent when I talk?' she said.

'To non-Indians? At work? Of course, we all do.'

Mira mulled over this. 'But why?'

'Because we are all terrified of sounding like Ranjit from *Mind Your Language*. "A thousand apologies please",' he said, mimicking the actor perfectly.

Mira laughed unpretentiously for the first time that day.

'At least somebody has free time here to laugh and joke.' Sanya breezed into Vinay's cubicle, her hands on her 36" hips. Mira and Vinay exchanged knowing looks and turned to face her. Mira grudgingly admired her bête noir's impeccable dress sense: lavender blouse teamed with an olive-green skirt and nude pumps. The blouse flattered her dainty neck and the skirt showed off her toned legs. How does this woman nail it each time? Every bloody time? Sexy and stylish. Mira suppressed a sigh. It looked like she had a lot of learning to do from the original office bitch.

'Know what? I just got off the phone from the Elcard people,' Sanya tittered.

'Oh?' Mira knew what was coming.

'They are very happy with my initial proposal.' Sanya flicked her streaked-to-perfection auburn hair over her shoulder. 'The firm's bigwig said he would write a letter of appreciation to Gerard.' She gave them a cat-ate-the-cream smile and flicked her hair again. 'Well, I would love to chat with you guys, but I have work to do,' she said.

Yeah, yeah, so we've heard. 'Then, what are you doing at my desk?' Mira said, flashing a saccharine smile. It was time to bring out the Bitch Goddess.

Sanya's eyes widened in shock.

'Hmm...unless this is a ploy to distract me from my work?' Mira was on a roll.

'Your work can't be that good, if G had to give *me* the Elcard project.' Mira might be good but Sanya was better—she had more years of practice after all. She gave Mira an even sweeter smile.

Ouch.

She wiggled her fingers at a tongue-tied Mira and vanished in a whiff of Eau-de-Wang.

Mira worked her jaw closed.

Bitch Goddess Rule #2: A Bitch Goddess should never mess with the Master.

Vinay had been watching the exchange like a spectator at Wimbledon. He stared at Sanya's receding figure until it was out of sight. Then he turned to Mira. 'Whoa. What was *that* all about?'

'Exactly what you saw, dahling.' Mira recovered fast and went back to her desk.

'Yeah, but what *did* I see? Told you, something was different about you.' Vinay narrowed his eyes and looked at her suspiciously.

'I am relieved. If nobody noticed, then it means it is not working.' Her eyes twinkled.

Vinay walked to her desk. 'Okay, what is happening here? C'mon, spill the beans.'

She swivelled her chair and faced him. 'Meet Mira, the Bitch Goddess.'

'The...the...what?' Vinay looked puzzled.

She was almost purring when she spoke. 'It's exactly what you think it is. No more Ms Nice Gal, no more Ms Pushover. No, siree. From now on, it's going to be Bitch Goddess all the way.'

Vinay snorted and hastily covered it up with a cough.

'Something behind this...this...umm...avatar?' he said.

'Nothing. Everything.' Mira pushed back her chair and crossed her legs.

Vinay adjusted his glasses and waited.

'You could say I had a Revelation...Siddhartha-like,' she said enigmatically. 'And I am beginning to do all the things *you* said I should do—be aggressive, learn to say no, stand up for myself—all that.'

Vinay went still. 'Uh-huh. I think I said too much.' He ran a hand through his hair. 'Forget what I said. Are you sure this change is a good idea? I mean, is this what *you* want?'

Mira shrugged. 'Maybe it is, maybe it isn't—who knows? But anything would be an improvement over the old me.'

Vinay was about to say more, but Mira had turned back to her screen. He watched her for a few minutes and then returned to his cubicle.

Mira tried Rohan's number again when she was about to

leave work. He was still not available, so she left a message. *Hi. Mira here. Just called to thank you for that project. Bye.*

When she walked into her apartment that evening, the phone rang. Mira rushed to get it.

'Oh. It's you, Amma.' Her mother had the uncanny ability to get her on the phone each time she returned to her apartment. It was almost as if she were monitoring Mira's movements from a telescope fixed on her Chennai apartment's terrace. On some days, Mira felt that she and her mother conducted their relationship only over the phone. Which, on second thoughts, wasn't a bad deal at all.

'Why, were you expecting someone else?' Mira felt her mother should have been a psychic.

'Er…no…I didn't expect your call today, that's all,' said Mira, keeping her tone casual.

'That day…our conversation did not end well. So I wondered…' her mother explained.

I am over that hurt, Amma. As much as I can be.

'I am okay, Amma, don't worry about me,' Mira said. *I have now become a Bitch Goddess and can deal with it.*

'Hmm…'

'How are you, Amma?' Mira asked gently, bracing herself for a melodramatic outburst.

'It hurt that day, kanna.'

Mira winced. Bitter memories of her father insidiously crept into her thoughts.

Her mother added softly: 'Now I am okay, don't worry about me.'

Mira immediately felt guilty for not worrying enough about

her mother, for not calling her enough. She switched the topic to her relatives and sundry topics to avoid further discussion.

'How long will you be here when you come in April?' her mother asked.

Mira tensed. She knew what her mother was getting at.

'Told you, Amma. Three weeks max.' Mira was anxious to hang up. 'I'm ravenous and am dying to make myself some pasta.'

This ought to derail her mother.

'Pasta? That is just maida, where is the nutrition? All that cheese will make you fat.'

'Amma, it's the whole wheat kind, but never mind.' Mira bit back a smile.

'I was wondering what I should tell the families of these boys I have been talking to...'

Mira sank into the couch. Her mother was not going to stay derailed for too long. She resisted the temptation of being rude. The whole arranged marriage subject was becoming a sore point between them these days. She inhaled sharply. 'Amma, I am not going to meet any boy or his family when I come there.'

'But you have to get married some day. Or don't you want to, at all?' her mother's tone was matter-of-fact.

Mira did not reply.

'Have you found somebody, Mira?'

Mira could have sworn her mother sounded so eager that she would have landed at her door with the priest and mangalsutra in tow.

'No Amma, no such luck. Wouldn't I tell you if I did?'

A long sigh. This was her mother's see-how-much-trouble-my-daughter-gives-me sigh.

Then the dam broke.

'Why can't you be like other girls of your age? They all get married. Or at least find boyfriends. Why, some even manage to find two! But look at you: twenty-seven and no boyfriend. Worse, you don't even want to *meet* all these nice boys that I have found for you. What do you think—'

'Amma, please…', Mira cut her off, too tired to carry on. 'I'm not sure you remember, but I have met *only* sixteen boys till date.'

But her mother continued unabated. 'Mira, just meet some more when you come here. Then decide. You may like someone from the boys I have short-listed…'

Yes, that's what the most important decision in my life whittles down to: shortlists, like the bloody projects at work.

She may not be the Bitch Goddess with her mother but she could surely be firm.

'Amma! I don't want to get married, okay? I want to be left alone,' Mira snapped.

Silence.

'I feel I may never get married,' she added in a mournful voice.

It was a nice touch. If she could get away with it, that is. She was not sure if what she heard on the other side was a sigh, a sob or a smothered cough.

'Somehow, these men, relationships, commitments; I don't want any of those. I have my job, I have you, and I have my friends. I am okay—okay?'

'I won't be here forever…' Oh, how her mother loved this trump card.

Mira sighed exaggeratedly. She could never win against her mother.

'Amma, let's not go there again. Not today. Please, I am tired and hungry.'

Her mother tried another track. 'Don't you want children,

kanna? Women should have kids before they turn thirty.'

'No! Aishwarya Rai had her's when she was thirty-eight. And I can't deal with kids when...when I am myself such a mess.'

Besides, I am not sure if the husband would stay...

Her mother's silence was intimidating. Mira began counting and reached till twenty when the dam broke again.

'I knew it! It's all my fault. Just because you heard those stories about your father and me, and saw me cry....I'm not a good mother... Why can't I get anything right? Why must this...'

'Amma, you are the world's best mother and this has nothing to do with you. Any other mother would not have raised a happy child. See? I am happy.' She tried to infuse cheer in her voice.

'I have failed you as a mother, Mira.'

'No, Amma, and this is about *me*, not *you*. I just don't want to get married. There are lots of women like me out there nowadays.'

Mira sensed that though her mother would not have bought it, she was going to let the topic be. For now at least. Retreat and attack when the enemy least expected it—her mother would have done Sun Tzu proud.

'Okay Amma, smile now.' Mira felt like she was talking to a toddler.

'I am smiling,' her mother said. She probably was; army strategists were resilient people, thought Mira. She gripped the phone receiver. This time *she* was going to strategise like a pro. This time *she* was going to win by ending the call before her mother could extract difficult promises from her.

'I am going to put the phone down, Amma, because *Kolamgal* is going to start and I know you want to know what happens to that Abhi woman.' *Checkmate Amma.* 'Bye, Amma. I love you.'

'Me too. Come home soon, kanna. Bye.'

Mira hung up and mentally thanked Tamil television soaps for coming to her rescue. Her mother was difficult and demanding, but Mira couldn't imagine life without her.

She felt tired to the bone. The brush with Sanya, her meeting with Gerard, Vinay's reaction, and now, this conversation with her mother—everything had exhausted her, all the planning and plotting for the day. The transformation seemed like a struggle, not a pleasurable experience. It was just Day One, and she already felt drained. Hats off to Sanya for the consistent behaviour. But then again, it was probably in her DNA coding.

Mira entered the kitchen to rustle up some pasta. She set the water to boil and mulled over the day. She crossed her fingers. She was going to make the Bitch Goddess transformation happen. At any cost.

Thrust and Parry

The doorbell was ringing. Mira knew who it would be on the other side. She hopped out of bed, her bedclothes tangling in the rush. She kicked them off and raced to the door. Nobody was there—where was her dad? He had promised… It must be because of the teddy she had refused to take from him on his last visit. She knew he had left it behind. Would he come if she took it now? But where was it? She ran through the house, opening and closing cupboards and shelves, but the teddy was nowhere in sight…

Mira's eyes flew open. For a minute she felt disoriented. She got up and stood at the window and peeped through the gap in the curtains. But she didn't notice the paved path that ran around the apartment complex, or the kids cycling there. She was still caught in her dream, something she hadn't dreamt in a long time. It was ironic that it should come to her after her first day in her new avatar. Bitch Goddesses steered clear of emotional entanglements, didn't they?

Mira had a quick shower and studied her new wardrobe. She carefully selected what she would wear today. It was only Day Two of her Bitch Goddess persona at work.

When she was done, she studied her image in the mirror. The blood-red sleeveless chiffon blouse ended precisely at her hips, accentuating her curves. The grey slim-fit trousers flattered her figure. They made a good combination. She had lined her expressive eyes with kohl and her lips shimmered with 'Barely Nude'. She spun around and peered at herself over her shoulder, her legs slightly apart, and her hands on her hips.

Well, she *looked* like a Bitch Goddess, until she noted the shadows that still lurked in her eyes. Being depressed didn't help the Bitch Goddess cause.

Think Bitch Goddess, Be Bitch Goddess was getting to be her regular mantra. Maybe if she said it 108 times, like other Hindu prayers, the day might bring better things.

But things didn't get any better when she reached office an hour later. Her inbox was flooded with emails that needed action *yesterday*. And the first question Vinay asked when he wandered into her cubicle a little later was, 'Do you realize what day it is today?'

He sipped coffee from his Dilbert mug that Mira had gifted him on his last birthday. 'Work is Worship', it said. She had deliberately engraved it with the very Indian office slogan, knowing it would irk him.

'Er...what day? Other than Thursday, I mean?' she asked distractedly, typing an email.

'It's the *last* Thursday of the month, silly. Duh-huh.' He punched her arm.

'Oh, right. Thanks for the reminder, Vinay.' Mira made a face at him.

On the last Thursday of every month at Network Systems, someone was identified as the best performer, the Employee of the Month, and was given five hundred dollars by the management. The amount was not much, but there were about fifty programmers competing for it every month. And more than the money, it was the recognition that came with the title.

'I could use the money,' sighed Vinay, who seemed perpetually broke.

'Me too, though I could use the morale boost even more,' Mira said.

Her inbox pinged. She scanned the new email distractedly.

'Bosses,' she muttered. 'Let me see...there was the CONROM project, and then we finished that financial one for Bank of America last month and the one we will be doing now for NUS will be our third for this year. And all our projects have been successful so far. Network Systems earned a revenue of $200,000 from the BANKAM project alone.'

She crossed her fingers. 'May one of us get the Employee of the Month award.'

'Amen,' Vinay intoned, raising his mug. 'No coffee today?'

Mira shook her head and pulled out a tea bag from a wooden box near her window.

'Lavender tea to calm you down,' she announced like the voiceovers in TV ads.

Vinay made a funny ridiculing sound, making Mira laugh.

Mira rose to her feet. 'But you can get me a cup of hot water, slave, while I go and find out what it is that Gerard wants to see me about.'

She jaunted off before Vinay could get her for the slave comment.

Gerard waved Mira in when he spotted her through the glass panel of his office.

'Morning, Gerard. That's a wonderful view of the harbour you have here,' she said, admiring the cityscape that stretched beyond the large bay windows. Not that she was surprised; he did have the Corner Office, after all. But every time she walked in, the view took her breath away. More so on clear days like today.

'Morning Mira. Perks of my job,' he said. 'Sit down. Here, want one?' He held out a packet of mints.

Does this man eat anything else? 'No thanks,' she said politely and sat across the table from him.

'Ah, Mira, I was just going over your work.' He leaned back on his plush chair and studied her for a moment. 'Good job, so far. First the CONROM project and then the Bank of America financial project.'

'Thanks, yes, my team did well. We worked really hard on those projects, Gerard.'

He nodded. 'Now I hope to see good progress on the university project too.'

'Of course, Gerard. Our team won't disappoint you, we are on top of it.' After ten more minutes of project discussions, she strode out of the room confidently. She gave herself a silent high-five—the new Mira knew how to take compliments and remind her boss about her worth.

Maybe this month's award would be hers?

Mira had barely sat down at her desk when there was the sound of footsteps on the other side of her glass panel. The now familiar, slightly overpowering fragrance of Truly Pink, hit Mira's nostrils. It had to be Sanya.

'So, what did Gerry want?' asked Sanya, coming around the panel and standing next to Mira.

Gerry? Mira gave her a stare. 'Gerard talked about work,' she replied brusquely and got back to work.

Sanya flicked back her shoulder-length dark hair; the movement caught the coppery highlights that went well with her burgundy shirt.

'Of course he would,' she sniggered. 'But what *else* did he want from you?'

Mira bristled at the implication but forced herself to keep

her cool. A Bitch Goddess needs to pick her battles with care. She turned back to face her screen and started working. The hiss of the other woman's in-drawn breath warmed Mira's soul.

'So, did you enjoy the lunch at the Sun Tech food court?' Sanya asked nonchalantly, unwilling to give up so readily. She had, after all, been at this game for a lot longer than Mira. 'I personally don't like food courts, too crowded for my taste,' she crinkled her nose.

Mira turned to face Sanya. 'I'm sorry, I don't get you.'

Sanya flashed a feline and predatory smile. She straightened a non-existent crease on her shirt. Her olive green skirt was a snug fit, four inches above her knees. 'Rohan and I met over the weekend and he was telling me about the lunch you guys had at the food court.'

Mira itched to wipe off the smug smile on Sanya's face by giving her a whack.

She mentally recited the Bitch Goddess mantra; she needed time to gather her arsenal.

'Oh, did he? How nice,' Mira shrugged. 'You don't like food courts? I love them; just think about it—the seating is so causal and not stiff and formal like in pricey restaurants.' She wore a dreamy look. 'Food courts let you sit close, huddle together and...you get the drift, right?'

Not to be outdone, Sanya shot Mira a meaningful look. 'Rohan is such a fun guy, really knows how to show a girl a good time.'

'Good for you! Terrible if the guy you are with is a bore,' countered Mira.

Sanya glared and walked away. Mira resumed her work with a low chuckle. A few more rounds, and it might have turned into a physical cat fight.

'More Bitch Goddess display?'

Mira jolted at the sound. Vinay was standing behind her.

'How much did you overhear?' she said.

'Enough to ask you why you never told me about this Rohan guy. Were you stupid enough to make out with a guy you met for the first time?'

'Vinay, I didn't make out with him. I just let Sanya *think* I did.'

Vinay nodded brusquely. 'I am telling you, Mira, stop this Bitch Goddess thing before it becomes dangerous.'

'Come on, Vinay. Nothing dangerous here. Just life lessons,' Mira said airily.

Vinay put up his hands. 'Fine, do what you think is right. Don't tell me later that I didn't warn you.'

Mira watched him leave with some misgiving. Was Vinay right? She shook her head. Nah, he was just being a man. Men didn't like Bitch Goddesses, they preferred doormats.

But this is Vinay, your best friend, a voice in her head said. She ignored it and got back to work.

Then things got only worse after lunch. Mira had been a little apprehensive about the lunch itself, expecting a stiff lecture from Vinay. But to her relief, he let the subject drop. They ate with their usual camaraderie and went back to their cubicles. Mira was going through her project reports in a mellower mood when she heard Vinay grimly call out from his desk, 'Check your mail.'

'What's in it?' she asked.

'Let's just say that you're going to need another cup of your lavender tea,' was all he would say.

Mira opened her Outlook to find an email from the admin team. She read it and then re-read it. *Shit.* Hard work and dedication didn't always pay. Life was a bitch, she thought with feeling.

Vinay entered her office.

'How the hell did she manage it?' Her voice shook with anger.

He shrugged and sipped his coke loudly.

'It is not fair. Not. Fair.' She thumped the desk, making a pen jump out of the penholder.

'No it is not,' repeated Vinay quietly.

'What is it about Sanya that she got the best projects in the last few months and now, she gets this month's best performance bonus? The Employee of the Month award. Bah.'

'Gerard likes her, I suppose,' said Vinay in a matter-of-fact tone.

'Damn, damn, damn. I worked very hard for it this month. Slogged my butt off.'

'We both did.'

Mira banged her fist on the table again. But things did not change by banging desks. She shook her head sadly. There was no way anybody in the organization could question the award. The employees had to just accept the management's decision without protest.

Vinay piped, 'Hey, but look at the bright side; she won't get it again this year.'

The organization had a rule that an individual could receive the award only once in a year. Going by that, Sanya was now out of the running for the rest of the year.

'Pssssssssss,' Mira made a dismissive sound. 'But she has already won it, right?

Vinay shrugged and drained his coke can.

'Either you or me should have got it, before she did,' Mira said. 'I mean, our BANKAM project brought in more revenue than most other projects in the company. And it was also so difficult to pull off…'

'Hey relax, Mira. You will get it next time.' Vinay patted her shoulder.

'What's with you? First you tell me I have to start standing up for myself, and when I do, you say I am being stupid. Now here is a situation where we both need to stand up for ourselves and tell the management that we have been unfairly overlooked for the award. But you lack courage, Vinay. You know what, *you* need to figure out what exactly you want before you start doling out advice to *me*.'

'Whoa, hold on. This is just a stupid award and sooner or later, everybody gets it.'

Mira glared at him. 'Just an award? I don't think so. You know what will happen now? She will be more unbearable than ever. I will KILL her if she comes here and gloats!'

Vinay wisely did not respond.

'I hate my life. Why is everything going wrong? My projects are getting tougher; I am slogging, but guess who's on a winning streak?' She rested her head on the table. 'I think I'll push off to some desolate part of the world, a mountain or forest, or something. So bloody much for becoming a Bitch Goddess. Looks like it takes a long time to work—if it does at all.'

Bitch Goddess Rule #3: A Bitch Goddess needs cunning and chutzpah to win.

Mira was so angry and upset that she decided not to work for the rest of the day. Didn't do much good—did it, anyway? She clicked open Solitaire and idly moved the cards. An unknown number flashed on her mobile screen.

'Hello.'

'Mira? Rohan here.'

'Hi Rohan, what's up?' Mira made an effort to sound peppy.

'Nothing much, I am returning your call,' he said.

'Oh, yes. Our team has got a project from the NUS, so I thought I should call and thank the person responsible for giving us some additional work.' She mechanically clicked on the cards. 'Extra work is terribly important in these competitive times, you see.'

'Don't thank me. I had nothing to do with it,' he disclaimed.

'Of course. Your admin department googled and found me on the net,' she said wryly.

He laughed. 'I think I might have mentioned your name in passing, or something.'

'Thanks, and may you do more of the same,' she said.

They chatted for a while and then Rohan said, 'So...that opera you were mentioning? *Madame Butterfly*? Are you still... um...interested in seeing it?'

'Is the Pope catholic? What do you think?' laughed Mira.

'Well, I happen to have two tickets. Want to come along?'

Mira hesitated. Then she fantasized about Sanya's reaction to this invitation and felt victory wash over her.

'Thanks, Rohan. I would love to,' Mira purred. A Bitch Goddess doesn't—cannot—pass up dates with her adversary's boyfriend.

'Great. Will pick you up tomorrow, say, around seven? The show begins at eight. That should give us plenty of time to get there.'

Mira kept her voice casual, 'So, how did you get the tickets, Rohan? I thought they were all sold out.'

'Somebody I know couldn't go and offered them to me.'

'What a stroke of good luck.' Her tone was dry as dust.

'Yes, isn't it?' he laughed easily, completely unfazed by the fact that Mira had seen through his ploy. Mira smiled as she disconnected the phone. The day was looking less gloomy now.

Soprano and Bass

*T*he next evening, Mira stared at the contents of her wardrobe and tried to work out the perfect look. Classy chick meets sultry seductress. Suddenly she became unsure. What was she doing? Why did she want to lure away Sanya's man from her? What would it prove? That she, Mira, was better? She rifled through the hangers, and sifted through her thoughts. Why would a man like Rohan date a woman like Mira, if he already had a girlfriend like Sanya? Or had she got the plot wrong? But if she had, how did Sanya know about all her meetings with Rohan? Something did not fit the puzzle. A series of scenes, as if from a movie, played in her head: Sanya smirking at her, Sanya taking away her project, Sanya getting the award, Sanya cozying up with Rohan, and...Rohan telling Sanya about this poor lost girl called Mira he had lunch with. The last scene jolted her: Rohan and Sanya laughing at her.

Mira sat down on her bed, her hands tightly gripping the bedsheet. Inhale. Exhale. Inhale. Exhale. Count to ten. More deep breaths. At this rate she should enroll in a yoga class, Mira thought. She paced the room to make the images go away. She didn't know why Rohan had offered to take her to the opera, but she decided on using the evening as an opportunity to further her plans.

She went back to her wardrobe and pulled out the black cigarette pants. She slipped it on and matched it with a sleeveless raw silk kurti in rust. The blouse had mirrors and sequins sown around the deep v-neckline, accentuating its depth.

Mira stared at her reflection and wondered what Sanya would have worn with black trousers. She visualized her bête noir in the mirror: hands on hips, her slim legs in skinnier pants, some sexy clingy top with no back and, no doubt, hardly any front either. A look that would complement her glossy and stunningly perfect highlighted hair, her gorgeously made-up face and her 6" sandals. Mira realized with a pang that though this would make Sanya look like a million dollars, she herself would, on the other hand, appear like a hooker hitting the streets.

The gloomy forecast made her peel off the trousers and opt for a red ruffled skirt that ended just above her knees. Thank God her legs were soft and smooth. And thin.

Mira looked herself over in the mirror and grimaced. Maybe she *did* look like a hooker in her red and black heels. The blouse, too, didn't seem to be working. She took it off and slipped on a black sleeveless kurti with a vibrant Kutchi patchwork yoke. She applied kohl and glided on her new Wildberry & Cocoa lipstick. She clasped her hair at the nape with a broad leather clip, and then took it off as an afterthought. Her hair fell in soft cascades down her shoulders. She let her gold hoops remain and sprayed on some perfume. She studied her reflection and decided that the east-west fusion look suited her much better. She picked up her purse when she heard her phone beep, and left the house wiping her suddenly clammy hands on her skirt.

Mira spotted his silver Honda Civic in the foyer and got in beside Rohan after exchanging cheery hellos. In the dim light, she could barely make out the colour of his jacket, but the tangy lemon of his cologne hit her hard, and for a second she felt light-headed. They spoke little through the journey and Mira was surprised at how comfortable the silence felt.

She got a proper glimpse of Rohan only at the opera house's brightly-lit lobby. She knew he was attractive, but today, in his crisp white shirt and black trousers, he actually made her catch her breath. She took in the warm appreciative glint in his eyes and enjoyed the little spurt of satisfaction she felt. When the usher showed them to their seats, she realized that Rohan had bought the most expensive tickets to the show. And she guessed, at a premium. She ought to offer to pay for hers. But a Bitch Goddess would treat it as her due. Then again, there was this thing as the New age woman who goes dutch. She would offer it to him, she finally decided. But before she could speak, the lights dimmed and the show began.

The female lead made a heart-rending Madame Butterfly, the man playing her love interest, Pinkerton, had a rich baritone. The costumes were beautiful, and the backdrops stunning. But Mira was most aware of the man beside her; she could feel the strength of the shoulder that rested casually against her. By the second act she was convinced that it was not by accident that his leg was brushing against hers, and in the third act, when he placed his hand lightly upon hers, it was all she could do to not link her hands with his. She was saved by the curtain call, which forced them to stand and applaud.

'That was wonderful,' Mira said softly as they drove back after the show. 'Thank you, Rohan,' she said sincerely.

'The pleasure is mine,' he said in a deep sexy baritone that rivaled Pinkerton's. 'Dinner?'

She almost said yes when the indefatigable Bitch Goddess kicked in. Pace was everything. *Take it slow.*

'No, thank you. I am stuffed with the sandwiches and coffee we had during interval.'

He inclined his head and met her gaze. A hint of a smile played on his lips. They drove on in companionable silence, Jim Brickman's 'Valentine' washing over them.

'Er…Rohan,' Mira said. 'The tickets must have been very expensive. Please let me pay for mine.'

He looked shocked at the suggestion. 'You've got to be kidding!'

'But I feel awful. I made you spend all that money…'

'Well, if you really feel that way,' he changed into a higher gear and looked straight ahead, 'you can take me out to dinner—maybe next Friday?' Mira knew it was more a command than a question.

Smooth. She laughed. Her pulse quickened as she unobtrusively feasted her eyes on his cut-glass cheek bones and chiselled jaw. 'Friday it is,' she answered before she could stop herself. 'I'll tell you the time and place later.' He nodded.

They reached her building and the car pulled over near the lobby. Rohan gripped her hand as she alighted. There was that light-headed feeling again. She looked at him nonchalantly, it wouldn't do to let him know how much he affected her.

'Thanks,' his low voice rumbled over her skin. 'I had a great evening, too.' She read sincerity in those dark eyes.

Mira smiled and gently extricated her hand from his. She waved him goodbye and stood in the still dark night till she saw his car exit through the gate. It was only then that she realized Rohan had moved so close to her when saying goodbye, that her lips were warm from his breath.

Her face flushed at the thought as she rode up thirteen floors to her apartment. She got home, flung her handbag on the couch, and then herself on it. She was miffed with herself for not playing hard-to-get with Rohan. She had so readily—like a lovelorn teenager—agreed to a date. How could she be so desperate? A fine Bitch Goddess she was turning out to be, letting the first handsome man make her flushed and breathless!

She fell asleep muttering to herself and woke up the next

day, still affected by her reaction to Rohan's obvious charms. She felt a dull pain in her head and her stomach was all knotted up. Damn. Why did he have to be so nice and interesting? As though those drop-dead good looks weren't weapon enough to destroy the female of the species.

The phone rang and she knew it would be her mother. Nobody else called so early on a Sunday. Mira ran to pick it up and came back to the couch.

'Hello, Amma,' she said, idly staring at the glow-in-the-dark stars she had stuck on her ceiling. She braced herself before every telephonic chat with her mother. The world feared Bitch Goddesses and they, in turn, feared their mothers. That was the Universe's way of maintaining equilibrium.

'Yes Amma, I am fine,' Mira tried to sound chirpy. 'Oh, and I got the India tickets.'

'Very good.'

'Yes, I'll be home on 23 April, but the thing is...' Mira paused, 'I get only two weeks off.'

'But, Mira, two weeks is too short!' her mother predictably lamented. 'I mean, have you thought about those boys?' *Ah, that's why Amma was upset. And why did she insist on calling fully-grown men, 'boys'? Must be an indication of the level of their maturity.* Mira suppressed a giggle at the thought.

'Amma, I told you. No marriage discussions on this trip, please. I just want to spend time with you and Patti, and relax. No bride-viewings and horoscope business.'

Uncomfortable silence. Mother of the Bitch Goddess was displeased.

'Look, Amma,' Mira assumed a placating tone. 'When I come to India next December, I'll be home longer. Then we can talk about marriage and these *boys*.' She was happy to live so far away. If she had still been in Chennai, she might have by now been sitting in the wedding mandapam and planning her honeymoon.

Mira picked up the day's newspaper from the center table and went to the kitchen to make herself some tea. She was only half-listening to her mother's arguments as she cradled the phone in her ear. She spread the newspaper on the counter and gleaned the headlines. She hoped that at least before next December's India visit, the Bitch Goddess would have developed into a fully-grown persona and nobody would be able to push her around and mess with her—her mother included.

Mrs Iyer's voice cut into this fantasy unfolding in her daughter's mind. 'But two weeks is long enough to meet him, at least?'

Mira grit her teeth. If not the 'boys' then it had to be about '*him*', her estranged father. Why, oh why, was her mother so infuriating sometimes? She wondered if true-blue Bitch Goddesses felt pain. Who knew, but wannabes definitely did.

Mira strained the tea and carried her mug and the newspaper to the living room. The early morning sun streamed in through the gleaming glass doors, the rays bouncing off the jade Buddha that sat on her center table. She settled down on the recliner beside it.

Mrs Iyer was used to her daughter's silences and simply said, 'He wants to see you, kanna.'

'So, he is still alive,' Mira said tightly, immediately regretting her nasty crack. She could never bring herself around to calling him Appa. Frankly, she did not care or rather, she did not *want* to care. But most importantly, she did not want anybody to know she might actually care.

'Please, Mira.' Her mother's tone was part-admonishment, part-resignation.

An uncomfortable silence stretched between the mother and daughter.

'Why now, Amma; after all these years?' Mira finally spoke. 'Why is he suddenly oozing this paternal love?' She curled up on the chair and sipped her tea.

'Nothing sudden, Mira. He has been asking to see you for a long time,' her mother sounded weary, like one would if they had to carry the cross of someone else's wrongdoings for half a lifetime. 'He cares, he truly does. It's just that I never told you. You…you were not ready. You were angry, sad and…'

'And whose fault was that, Amma?' Mira interrupted her harshly.

There were memories, shadowy images of her father visiting them, lots of bags in his hands, calling out to her, arms wide open for her… But Mira never ran into them, never took the brightly gift-wrapped parcels he always left behind. Because the first time he had come home, she had run into his arms, laughed at his jokes and joyfully hugged the teddy bear he had brought for her. She even told him that it was the happiest day of her life. But when he left a few hours later, she had felt devastated and betrayed. Even worse was when her mother later asked her in a pained voice which parent Mira loved more. Something had shifted within Mira that day. She knew she had to choose between her parents if she wanted to keep her life peaceful. Her choice had been a natural one: her mother.

Mira placed her empty tea cup on the center table and looked at the wall clock. It had been half-an-hour on the phone. Her mother sighed, 'Don't forget I was young and deeply grieved when your father left us. Those early years I used to feel vulnerable and easily threatened. I am not making excuses, Mira. I am simply asking you to understand…as a woman.'

Mira began pacing the living room. 'Think about this,' she

said in a harsh tone. 'For a long time, you didn't like it if I spent time with my dad and discouraged my seeing him. Your needs were greater than your daughter's happiness. And I guess he found the situation so convenient that he decided to stay away and, eventually, stopped visiting us. I *am* thinking like a woman, Amma. Maybe he didn't try hard enough to make Mira, the little girl, like him. To me, it seems like he just took the easy way out.'

'Mira, it is not so simple...' her mother began.

Mira laughed mirthlessly. 'Amma, nothing in our life has been simple. But I am not done yet. Then suddenly, when I am sixteen or seventeen, you sit me down and tell me my father wants to see me. To "get to know me again" were your exact words. That was the day I discovered that you both had been in touch for the last so many years, ostensibly to keep him as a shadowy presence in my life.'

Mira paused and took a deep breath. 'Do you even know how it felt to discover that you two had been in touch, and because of your ego clashes, I had lost him forever? Do you know how betrayed I felt that day?' Rage and tears made her voice wobbly. She was pacing at a furious rate and yelped when she stubbed her toe against the tall potted plant that stood in the corner.

'I am sorry, I didn't realize how much we...I...have hurt you...' her mother's voice trailed off.

Mira wiped her tears with the back of her palm, too choked to respond.

Her mother spoke into the silence: 'I think it's all the more important that you meet your father now. If I caused this rift, I need to make amends and set things right between you two.'

Mira sat down on the sofa again. 'It's not just that, Amma. I also find it hard to accept what he did to you as a woman.'

'You are an adult now, Mira. All I can say is, learn to separate the parent from the man,' her mother said.

'Why are you like this—nice and understanding and wise? Why can't you be angry and…and revengeful like your Tamil soap heroines?' Her lips twitched to laugh but nothing happened.

Her mother's sigh swept down the line and made Mira's heart heavy. 'I was angry for a very long time and see the damage it did, kanna.'

'Amma, don't be sad. I am fine now,' Mira relented.

'So you will meet him this time?' her mother rushed in.

Mira had made a big mistake; she had forgotten how resilient her mother was.

'I don't think so. I am not ready for that,' Mira replied crisply.

'Maybe waiting for *you* to get ready had been a mistake. I am no longer going to wait until you are ready to meet your Appa,' her mother said firmly. Mira could envision her mother, probably sitting at their dining table, clad in one of her cotton saris, a tumbler of coffee at her elbow. It was just seven in the morning in Chennai and her mother would have her second coffee after breakfast.

When Mira remained silent, her mother pleaded: '*Meet* him, Mira. You must, only then can you be happy.'

And you too, Amma, thought Mira, putting down the phone gently. She wiped her damp cheeks, horrified at her tears. Bitch Goddesses never cried. They made *others* cry.

Bitch Goddess Rule #4: A Bitch Goddess should never have a family. It makes her act out of character.

Only much later into her Sunday did she realize that she still didn't know if her parents were divorced or just separated.

The Plot Thickens

Work was busy the following week and Mira gratefully immersed herself in it. The result was a fragile inner peace that was, however, severely challenged. It was Wednesday and she was deep in the final stages of one of her projects. She was eager to finish this and begin working on the NUS assignment. She tried to push Rohan—and what she would wear for their Friday date—away from her thoughts.

The telltale heels click-clocked into her cubicle. Sanya.

Mira's gaze remained focused on her computer screen—if she had to win the next Employee of the Month award, she couldn't afford to get distracted.

'Mira, where are you?' a throaty voice drifted toward her.

Mira clenched her teeth. 'In Mars,' she muttered under her breath. She looked at Sanya who was looking especially ravishing today. Fuchsia and plum? Wow. With a cream scarf that was tied cleverly to accentuate her lovely neck. And Mira had thought *she* looked elegant in her skyblue shirt and charcoal gray trousers.

'Mmm…what's that you said?' Sanya asked, raising her eyebrows.

'Nothing,' said Mira.

Sanya leaned over Mira's cubicle wall. 'How's work on the NUS project shaping up?' Her deep purple lips were perfectly painted.

Mira frowned. 'I think only Gerard can ask me that question?'

Sanya's eyes briefly flashed. 'So, how was the opera?' she smiled smugly at Mira's startled expression. 'Rohan always tells me what he does and who he goes out with—we're quite close you know.'

'Really? How nice.' Mira's eyes wore a cold look. 'Rohan never mentions you when we are together. But then I suppose it's because he and I have *so* much to say to each other, that we don't talk about other people...' *Ha.*

Mira heard the heels click-clock away and she punched the air in triumph.

Bitch Goddess Rule #5: Practise, as in everything else in life, makes a Bitch Goddess perfect.

'You went to an opera without *me*?' Vinay popped out of his cubicle. He had obviously heard the whole exchange.

'Rohan invited me,' Mira mumbled.

'Rohan,' Vinay repeated slowly, 'And who pray is this new player in our game of Life?'

Mira stretched her limbs and curtailed a yawn. 'Long story. Rohan is actually Sanya's friend.'

Then she told him the whole story from when she had seen him at a restaurant with Sanya to their evening together at the opera.

'You have been keeping secrets from me,' Vinay wagged an accusing finger at her.

Mira patted his bony arm placatingly. 'No, nothing of that sort. It's just that things are a bit messed up here.' She gestured at her head.

'You like him,' Vinay said in a teasing voice.

Mira looked thoughtfully at the view outside her window. 'He is...nice.'

Vinay pulled out a granola bar from his pocket. 'Want some?' He tore the wrapper and bit into the bar.

She shook her head. 'Must you always eat, Vinay?'

'So you really dig this guy, huh?' he said, munching the snack.

'Eeee...not like that!' she exclaimed. 'He is just a nice guy, that's all.'

He cocked an eyebrow at her. 'Is he good-looking?'

She shrugged. 'Fine. I find him attractive. Happy?'

He hoisted himself onto the corner of her desk. She automatically moved the crystal ballerina paperweight out of his reach. The last time, he had toppled a glass of water on her BANKAM project folder and ruined it.

'I hear a "but",' Vinay said. He rolled up his granola bar wrapper and aimed it at her wastepaper basket. It missed the target.

'Sanya,' she sighed.

'Ah, it always comes down to our resident bitch. What about her?'

Mira made a face. 'Rohan might be her boyfriend.'

'Ah, the plot thickens. Okay, two questions for you: one, why do you think they are involved and two, what the heck are you doing with somebody else's boyfriend?'

Mira winced. 'I don't know if they are involved, but... umm... they seem to have an equation. He tells her things. Look, she even knew about the opera. Since your first question has no clear answer, the answer to the second one is moot.'

Vinay ran a hand through his hair, messing up an already tousled head. 'He is attracted to you.'

'Oh, please,' Mira said.

'Trust me, I'm a man. I would know. But why do *you* hang out with him? Something to do with our resident bitch?'

Damn him for being smart. 'No,' Mira denied flatly.

'A little romance never harmed anybody, as long as you are sure you are in it for the romance,' said Vinay, looking pointedly at her. Mira chose not to respond.

He heaved himself off her desk. 'Well, I need to go find some more grub. Bye,' he waved and loped off.

She loathed to think what Vinay would say if he discovered that she was encouraging Rohan to make Sanya jealous and maybe even 'steal' him away from her. There would be fireworks and Mira would be badly singed. She didn't want to dwell on it today. But Mira also felt unsettled when she thought about the Rohan-Sanya equation. Why was she so affected by the fact that Rohan had been sharing details of every meeting of theirs with Sanya? But, again, hadn't that been her plan—to date Rohan and make Sanya jealous? So why was she so affected by the fact that Rohan had been giving Sanya hourly updates? Clearly Sanya was upset, and Mira's end was achieved.

Mira's mouth set in a firm line. But if *he* could share everything with Sanya, then it was time to pull out the Bitch Goddess horns and dig her talons deep. The game had just about begun.

By evening, she had come up with a brilliant plan, one that even Sanya would have to admire.

As soon as she got home, Mira dialled Rohan's number and disconnected at the fifth beep. For all her newly-acquired vixen image, she was too chicken to talk to him. She suddenly didn't trust herself to speak. She was afraid that she would either come off sounding like a siren or too needy—as if she was desperate to spend time with him.

She chewed her lips till her lipstick wore off. Then she picked up her phone to send a text message. This wouldn't give away her true feelings.

```
Hey. Remember that dinner? How do you
fancy a home cooked meal? Sat. My place
@ 8.
```

Mira read it again and clicked the 'send' button.

She smiled at the response she received within seconds:

```
You're on, ☺ see you there!
```

Saturday morning arrived with Mira flying out of bed and going into a cleaning frenzy. She cleaned the house till her limbs ached from all that vacuuming. She took out the unused cookbooks from the bookshelf and frantically searched for recipes she could whip up in a flash. But she finally decided to stick to those dishes she knew best. Her entire culinary repertoire extended to five dishes, and she made them all: Bisi bele bath, potato curry, dal makhani and vegetable jalfrezi. She would toast some tortillas instead of chappatis—can't subject cute men like Rohan to leathery disfigured chappatis. There would, of course, be a salad. Bitch Goddesses *lived* on salads, for God's sake! And then the piece-de-resistance, the only dessert she knew how to make—pineapple upside-down cake. She only hoped it wouldn't go all topsy-turvy on her today.

After a marathon session of cleaning and cooking, Mira fluffed the cushions, dimmed the lights, lit some scented candles and went off to shower and change. Half an hour later, she studied her reflection in the mirror. What she wanted to see was a smoky-eyed woman, hair in suggestive disarray, dressed in a slinky kaftan or some other lounging gown that whispered secrets when she walked and had clever slits that hinted at long legs.

But what she saw, instead, was a slightly anxious woman in

black Capris and a white sleeveless top. The woman in the mirror looked smart without looking over-dressed, and that was the nicest thing Mira could say about her. She had deliberately opted for a casual, understated look. She put on her pearl earrings, slipped on her open-toed black sandals, and went off to wait for Rohan.

At exactly seven fifty-nine, Rohan was at her door, a large bunch of assorted flowers in his hand. His hair was still damp from the shower and curled a little above his ears. Today, he was dressed casually in an open-neck white tee and shorts. His legs were well-toned and long, like the rest of him. It was obvious he worked out regularly. She stepped back before his lemony cologne hit her nostrils and disarmed her.

'Hey, nice piece,' he said, running a hand over her Buddha. 'How much do you techies get paid, anyway? This guy must have cost a bomb.'

Mira laughed. 'My only indulgence. Please make yourself comfortable. I need to find a vase for this,' she held up the flowers.

Mira came back to find him at the balcony, his back to her. She placed the vase, spilling with flowers, on a corner table and joined him.

He turned around and leaned against the railing. The wind played with his hair, making her yearn for him even more.

'It's a great place you have,' he said, running an eye over her. He reached out and gently tucked an errant strand behind her ear.

Mira edged away shyly. 'What will you have to drink, Rohan?'

He was looking at her slightly parted lips. Mira flushed and looked away.

'Come on, let's go inside,' she said. Frank Sinatra's magnetic voice filled the room. 'That old black magic…' he crooned.

'This is one of the most romantic songs of all times,' Rohan said as she handed him the glass. His fingers brushed against hers.

Rohan moved away to the sofa. 'So, tell me. How do you like this city?'

Mira was grateful for the change of topic. She occupied the chair across him. 'I like it quite a bit, especially the fact that it is quite multicultural.' They talked some more about Singapore and sundry matters, and Mira was pleasantly surprised to discover more common ground with Rohan. Then they moved over to the table for dinner.

It was a table for four, though now it suddenly seemed to have shrunk for two. Mira's skin tingled. Rohan felt too close for comfort. The sexual tension she had felt earlier was back. Their fingers brushed while passing the dishes and she was surprised that the air in the room didn't arc. By the time they started dessert, she could barely meet his glance without flushing.

'Coffee?' she asked, after they had moved back to the living room.

'That would be great,' he replied, settling down on the sofa and flipping TV channels.

She escaped to the kitchen and plugged the coffee machine on, her mind in a swirl of thoughts.

'What can I do to help?'

Mira startled and turned behind. Rohan was grinning at her. She gripped the counter to keep from collapsing on her knees. It was true what they said: an attractive man can make the knees go all wobbly.

'Can you please grab two mugs? They are there,' she pointed to the cupboard above her head. Rohan leaned over to open the cupboard. Though they did not touch, the air between them warmed. Mira stole a sidelong glance at him while he rinsed the mugs. The machine hissed and poured out the brew. She picked up her sugar jar. 'Oh, it's empty,' she laughed nervously, opening another cupboard overhead to get a new packet of sugar. She felt his eyes glide over her body, watching her tiptoe and stretch to reach the bag. She hoped she smelt as good as he did.

'Let me get that,' he said, stepping close to her.

Before she realized, he had tipped over and fallen over her. She leaned against the kitchen counter to break her fall. This was not the romantic, gently-falling-amidst-swirling-snowflakes kind of a fall. This was more the slipping-on-a-banana-peel, arms flaying, grabbing a handy support fall. Rohan's hard body was pressed against hers, his warm breath on her face. She closed her eyes and flowed into the moment.

Rohan wrapped his arms around her waist and pulled her closer. He lifted her chin and pressed his lips against hers. Their bodies moulded and the kiss became deeper.

'I can't believe this,' she murmured, her eyes half-closed. 'I can actually hear bells.' She tried to steady herself against the kitchen counter.

'I am sorry, sweetheart, but I am afraid that is the phone,' he said with a chuckle.

Mira's eyes popped open. *Amma.*

'It's your landline. Do you want to answer it?' he said.

She shook her head. She can't talk to her mother after the most passionate kiss she had had in her life! Mira gently detached herself from him and stepped back. She felt dazed; her brain felt short-circuited. The Bitch Goddess had given the invitation and hosted the evening. Then he kissed her and the Bitch Goddess had vanished, leaving behind one confused Mira. Who knows what would have happened if the phone hadn't rung? Would the Bitch Goddess have triumphed over Mira?

Rohan was looking at her with concern. 'You okay?'

'I think I'd like to sit down,' she said faintly and hastily left the kitchen.

Rohan turned off the television. He sat down beside her on the sofa and trailed his fingers along her arms.

'I am not sorry this happened,' he said, after a few moments.

'Why should you be when it was my fault.'

He blinked. 'Your fault? Whoa, hold on. I kissed you because I wanted to.' He traced his index finger on her lips. 'I wanted to kiss you, Mira, it's as simple as that.'

She nodded and snuggled close to him. Elvis played in the background, trying to lure his lady love away for a moonlight swim.

Mira knew she should move away. But it felt so good sitting like this with his arm around her, her head on his shoulder, the room dimly-lit by the tall lamp in the corner and romantic music flowing around them. She ought to be alarmed or concerned because she was not sure what was going on here. The Bitch Goddess had left the building. And Mira didn't feel the urge to bring her back.

'Your first kiss?' he smiled tenderly.

She looked away. 'Can we please not talk about it?'

'Why? It's quite sweet.' Rohan's eyes danced mischievously.

'Not when you have to wait for nearly thirty years for it!' Mira groaned and covered her face with her hands.

Rohan looked mock mortified. 'Wow. But I hope it was worth the wait.'

She needed to bring back the Bitch Goddess if she wanted to avoid giving too much of herself to him.

'Rohan, don't you think this is...going too fast? I...we... need more time.' She shot him a questioning look.

Rohan waited for her to continue.

'What I mean is,' Mira added quickly. 'I don't want to regret anything I might do...*we* might do...in the heat of the moment.'

Rohan got to his feet. 'I guess you are right. We have all the time in the world.'

Mira eyed him suspiciously. He was giving in too easily.

He pecked her on her cheek. 'Tomorrow, I am off to Johar Bahru for a faculty picnic. So see you soon,' he said and walked to the door. Mira tensed. The evening was suddenly drawing to a hasty and abrupt conclusion. He gave her a wave and let himself out.

She stood at her door for a long time, thinking about the evening she had just had. She might have wanted to end it, but he didn't have to be so eager to comply! She shut the front door and went inside.

When Rohan had kissed her, he had made her want. Even worse, he had made her *believe*. She stretched out on the sofa and closed her eyes. The kiss had been unbelievable. What exactly had happened tonight? Why had the Bitch Goddess vanished? The idea had been to lure Sanya's boyfriend away from her. But that hadn't happened, had it? At some point, she fell asleep, exhausted.

Snakes and Ladders

*M*ira entered her office the next day, still heavy-lidded due to lack of sleep, and walked straight into people talking in huddles. She went through the corridor wondering what the buzz in the room was all about, when Vinay appeared and blocked her path.

'Guess what?' he asked.

'What's the excitement all about?' she said, keeping her handbag on her desk.

'It's Gerard,' Vinay spoke excitedly.

Mira frowned. 'What happened to him? Hope all is well?'

'He got a promotion; now he's heading the whole department!'

'Oh, good for him,' said Mira, booting her computer. 'Is he in? Did you meet him?'

'No, not yet. But you know what this means, don't you?' He narrowed his eyes at her.

She shook her head impatiently.

'Think, Mira. Part of all *this*,' he waved an arm over the room, 'is about THAT.'

At her puzzled look, he clucked his tongue impatiently. 'Our team will now have a new leader. There is a vacancy for the project leader position.'

He looked at her expectantly. She stared at him blankly.

'You *still* don't get it? The new leader could well be—*you!* It has to be either you or Sanya, and we all know you have done more challenging projects than she has.'

Mira couldn't help smiling indulgently at Vinay. Trust him to have faith in miracles. 'You can rule me out of the reckoning, Vinay. Who are we kidding? The boss likes her better.'

Vinay sighed. 'That's what *she* says, but I—'

'Hey guys!' the all-familiar husky voice called out.

'Well, well, speak of the devil...' Mira said.

'Our in-house bitch,' Vinay muttered under his breath.

'Heard about Gerry, guys?' Sanya said, standing next to Mira's desk. She was the only one in the office who called Gerard that. Vinay and Mira had often debated if she did it to his face, too. Sanya was resplendent today in her charcoal grey skirt and black blouse, a thick string of pearls around her neck. The message couldn't have been clearer; she was already dressing like a 'manager'.

'He told me about his promotion last week when we were lunching at Graze,' Sanya smiled, her perfect teeth blindingly white.

'Uh-huh,' said Mira, wondering if she could take aim at Sanya's smooth forehead with the paperweight on her desk.

Sanya lowered her voice, 'He also sought my opinion— off-the-record, of course—about how I felt about the post. But nothing is decided yet. Ta!' She wiggled her fingers in her characteristic style and left.

'Well, now you have the answer to your question, Vinay,' Mira shook her head dispiritedly. She had visions of Sanya barking orders at her from the plush corner office Gerard occupied presently. 'I don't think I'll be made the project head.'

'You are so mistaken, my friend,' said Vinay.

'Let's get down to work. Never mind who will be made the new project leader. We will anyway have to slog for the company,' she said flatly.

Vinay shook his head. 'Why are you always so pessimistic?'

'That way, you brace yourself from getting hurt,' she replied evenly and resumed her work.

'But—' Vinay began.

Mira held up a hand. 'Close your mouth and get to work, Vinay.' She turned away from him, her gaze back on her computer screen.

'Ouch,' Vinay yelped.

'What happened?'

'I snapped shut my mouth too hard.'

Mira laughed. She could count on Vinay to cheer her up.

Mira scrolled up and down her monitor in a desultory manner. She should be working; there was a deadline to meet. It was important to stay on task, now more than ever. But she could not get last night out of her mind—the Night of the Killer Kiss. She shook her head in disgust. She was almost thirty and too old to be sweating over a kiss. One measly kiss. *Definitely not measly*, her voice of justice spoke. Okay, the kiss had been a bit...unsettling. Unsettling? What kind of a red-blooded Bitch Goddess used a tame word like this for something that knocked the ground from under her feet?

'Oh, shut up,' she said aloud.

'You okay?' Vinay hollered.

Mira grimaced. Great. She had now become like her great-grandmother who was known for talking to herself.

'Nope, all messed up,' she tapped her forehead.

Vinay came over. 'You need a strong shot of caffeine,' he said.

Mira was tired with all the battles going on in her head: office politics, Rohan, her mother—and her estranged father—were taking a toll on her, weighing her down. Only, Bitch Goddesses never buckled under pressure.

She pushed back her chair and got up with resolve. 'Yes, I want caffeine...and lots of it!' she declared.

The coffee in the office cafeteria looked like ditch water and tasted like acid. Just what she needed, to add to her gloom today.

Barring the coffee, the cafeteria was the brightest aspect of the office. It was painted in vibrant colours and pop art hung on its walls. The place was always crowded; it looked like her office was on a perpetual break. Today was no exception. Mira and Vinay had to deal with a long queue and outsmart another couple to snag a table.

'So what's up with you?' Vinay asked after they sat down with their drinks.

Mira slowly stirred the sugar in her cup. 'Nothing.'

Vinay dipped a cookie in his coffee. Mira always teased him about this 'nursery schoolboy' habit but was in no mood to do so today.

'Of course,' he said. 'Nothing is the reason why you have been muttering under your breath all morning and making all sorts of interesting faces at your computer screen.'

Mira giggled. 'I have not!'

'Have too.'

Mira sighed. 'Men.'

'What have I done now?' Vinay protested.

'Not you, silly. Rohan.' She was often surprised at the ease with which she could confide in Vinay, something that she couldn't bring herself to do with even her mother. She would be lost without him.

Vinay sat up. 'What is it now?'

'Dunno…everything.'

Vinay waited as she sipped some coffee.

'He was home for dinner on Saturday.' Mira spoke into her cup.

'Okay, so did he get food poisoning?'

Mira made a face and rapped Vinay's knuckle. 'Hey, he praised my vegetable jalfrezi, thank you very much.'

'Wow, the man is polite,' Vinay removed his glasses and wiped them on his sleeve.

'He kissed me.' she mumbled, looking away.

'He...what? Can't hear you,' Vinay's voice was full of suppressed laughter. He put on his glasses and gave her a deadpan look.

She put her cup down. 'Go ahead, laugh at me,' she remarked dourly.

Vinay wore a serious look. 'Sorry. So he kissed you, so what? It was bound to happen. He finds you attractive, you like him, both of you are single, unattached, yadi-yadi-yada. So the next natural step will be a kiss.'

Mira grimaced. 'No, it is not *just* the kiss that is bothering me.'

Vinay leaned over conspiratorially. 'You mean there is more?'

'Oh, shut up. Even if there was, I am not telling *you*!'

Mira played with her stirrer. 'Rohan is a nice guy...but—'

'I gathered as much, go on.' Vinay cupped his chin in his hand, his eyes intent.

'Will you please let me talk?'

Vinay pressed his finger to his lips.

Mira thought about Sanya, the Bitch Goddess role and Rohan. She threw her hands up in the air.

'I don't know what I'm doing...' Though she felt guilty for withholding vital information from Vinay, she was not ready to reveal her gameplan at this stage.

Vinay shrugged. 'No one ever does. Relationships. Isn't that how they work? We just let them happen, right?'

'How would *I* know? I've never had any boyfriend, or

experience in this department.' Mira's face fell. 'In fact, come to think of it, I've never had too many friends either.'

Vinay studied her for a moment. 'Well, now you have an almost boyfriend in Rohan. Make him a real one and see where this goes.'

Mira smiled. Vinay always simplified the most complex problems.

'But what if I get hurt?' That's how it was with her mother and this is how it might be with Rohan.

'Maybe you won't get hurt, Mira,' said Vinay. 'You know what? I think the reason for your fear is because this is going to be your first relationship with a man. So you feel unsure of him, of the situation, of everything.'

Vinay was right in a way. She did feel unsure about the reasons why she was encouraging this relationship. But Vinay didn't need to know that, right?

'Okay, Dr Freud. But what do I do about it then?' said Mira.

'Take charge,' he said, thumping his fist on the table. 'That would work for you. Force the relationship to the next level, lure him into bed.'

She spluttered on her coffee, spewing the liquid everywhere. She wiped the table, her dress and his arm. 'Look what you made me do, Vinay. I've become a clumsy oaf like you.' He chuckled.

'But I never said anything about luring him into bed!' she said, looking around to see if anyone could have heard their conversation.

'I agree. No need to lure the man, he is already allured.' He laughed at his own joke.

Mira groaned. 'When will you get better at jokes, Vinay?'

'Go to bed with him, c'mon, make it happen,' Vinay continued. 'Perfect solution to conquer your fear. Get him out of your system, Mira. If it is anything more serious and lasting, it will evolve naturally. You don't have to try so hard. So chill.'

Mira stretched her lips. 'You men know only one way of resolving issues—by hopping into bed.'

Vinay got to his feet. 'Think about it. C'mon, let's go back to our desk lives.' They walked back in silence through the maze of cubicles, bathed in pasty white light. Mira stole a look at the bulletin board hanging on Sanya's cubicle wall. It was crammed with her photographs taken on exotic vacations—Bali, Ladakh, Sydney—and several with Fido. Everybody, down to the office cleaning boys, knew about Fido, her green-eyed Persian cat whom she fed dates and toned milk. Yes, Sanya was definitely a cat person, Mira smirked.

The rest of the day passed in painful slow motion. Mira could not keep her mind on her work and resorted to Solitaire as a stressbuster. She kept replaying her date with Rohan and all that was connected to him. At some level, Vinay made sense—this was the first time she was navigating murky boyfriend—no, he wasn't that yet—territory.

She randomly moved her cards on the screen.

Men. She couldn't figure them out. They made her feel... insecure. They had the uncanny ability to mess up her life. First her father, and now the most good-looking professor she had laid eyes on. Except for Vinay, who was funnily enough like the best female friend she had never had, Mira was wary around men. But Vinay was worse than her as far as the dating scene was concerned. She knew that he had nursed the longest crush on his neighbour's daughter who had also been his batchmate at college. For all his daring advice to Mira about getting laid, he had not yet put the moves on the girl. Mira minimized the Solitaire window, thinking she would return the favour and prod Vinay in the right direction before his next trip back home to Bangalore.

She resumed her work, her mind replaying Vinay's suggestion to seduce Rohan. It was positively outrageous! She didn't think she could pull it off. But it was a typical Bitch Goddess thing to do and would be a litmus test for her. Did she want to take such a drastic step and lead Rohan on? She crinkled her nose and shrugged away the thought. Only much later did it occur to her that she had not outrightly rejected Vinay's idea either. It had been left to simmer in her mind.

Mira was heading for the office cab queue that evening when a familiar-looking silver Honda Civic cruised by and slowed down near her. The window slid down.

'Cab, madam?' the good-looking man behind the wheel asked.

'What are you doing here?' Mira was taken aback to see Rohan. Her cheeks flushed remembering the awkward moments they had shared at her place.

Rohan grinned and opened the passenger door. 'Hi, I just decided to swing by your office on the way home.'

They were beginning to cause a line-up, so Mira slid in without protest and they began to move.

'I was keen on seeing you,' his voice was low and smooth. Even sincere. A slow smile lit up her face. But she should not feel happy to see him. That would upset her plans! Darn, darn, darn. Why was he so likeable?

'But,' he held up a warning finger, 'no hanky-panky today. Because I have to go back for an evening class. I can't afford to face my students with an afterglow.'

Mira's face heated up. She couldn't help laughing. 'You are outrageous, Rohan.'

He turned to look at her. 'I love compliments. But before

you feel compelled to give me more, I want to tell you that I am taking you out to dinner tomorrow. Be ready at seven-thirty.'

Mira opened her mouth to protest but felt tongue-tied.

Rohan continued, 'I will be busy rest of the week—some profs are visiting from MIT, then there are late evening seminars, exam paper corrections, and other stuff. So mine is an offer you can't refuse.'

Mira suddenly felt emboldened. 'But I don't *want* to refuse.'

He smiled and turned into her apartment complex. 'I am sorry, I really have to rush.'

'Sure, no issues,' she said, opening the car door. He suddenly pulled her close and briefly kissed her on her lips. Before she could react, he had waved and sped away.

Mira went up the lift thinking that Rohan was a nice guy. She felt guilty about leading him on just to get at Sanya. Then she frowned, recalling something.

Remember, he reports things to Sanya. Everything.

Bitch Goddess Rule #6: A Bitch Goddess never feels guilty. Ever.

Even Bitch Goddesses Get it Wrong

*B*y next evening, Mira had not only accepted Rule 6, she had even internalised it. She did not merely prepare for the evening, she had painstakingly plotted it. By the time their date ended, Rohan would not know what had hit him.

She stood before her open wardrobe and, as always, debated on what to wear. She pulled out a sleeveless lime-coloured T-shirt and khaki shorts. She had bought this on a whim before her Bitch Goddess avatar, but had never gathered the courage to wear it till date. She slipped it on, deciding it was just perfect for a sexy night out with a boyfriend.

Mira applied some lip gloss and kajal, opting for a natural look tonight. She rummaged through her cupboard, looking for the perfume she knew she had somewhere. She bended and probed her hand inside her wardrobe's bottom-most shelf and fumbled around. Her fingers closed around a small bottle, and she pulled it out. She opened the stopper and winced. No, she did not want to smell like she had rubbed crushed petals of every available flower in the world. She closed the bottle and put it on the dressing table. She wanted to smell desirable, yet subtle. Maybe a hint of something spicy and seductive? Unfortunately, she didn't have the right kind of perfume that met her stringent Bitch Goddess standards. She will have to do with the lame deodorant she had used after her shower.

She paced up and down the living room, her stomach in knots. When Rohan called her a few minutes later, she went back to her bedroom to touch up her lip gloss and brush her hair. She took another few minutes emptying the contents of her brown tote and transferring them into a white sling bag. Then she took the lift downstairs.

'Hey.' Rohan opened the car door and gave her an approving look.

'I am so sorry, did I keep you waiting?' Mira said, sliding into the passenger seat.

'Nope. Just got here.'

She was annoyed with herself as soon as she had uttered these words.

Bitch Goddess Rule #7 (learnt a bit too late): A Bitch Goddess never apologizes for keeping men waiting, or for anything else.

The car began to move. She shifted in her seat and stole a glance at him.

'You know, I haven't seen any other man look so good in that particular shade of red.'

Her voice was low and flowed into the space between them like whisky.

His eyes widened in surprise. 'Thanks,' he said. 'This is the first compliment you have given me.'

She caught his gaze and held it. 'And it is not going to be the last.'

He smiled and asked about her work. She told him about the new vacancy for a project leader position in her company, arising from Gerard's promotion.

'So you could be the new project leader, huh? That's fantastic,' he said.

'Or it could be your friend,' she shot him a pointed look. 'Sanya.'

An uncomfortable silence ensued.

'Sure, she is a friend,' he said easily. 'But you are not just a friend, are you?'

Mira blushed and her poise slipped. *The man knows how to speak.*

Rohan grinned, somewhat smugly. Gotcha, his look said.

He took her to Original Sin, a vegan place, off Holland Road. The maitre'd greeted him like a friend and showed them to the table Rohan had booked. How many women had he brought here, Mira wondered as they were seated. The restaurant was elegant without being intimidating, and the instrumental music that was playing in the background relaxed her. Since Rohan seemed to be familiar with the menu, Mira let him order. Then she put her seduction plan to work.

The starter was baba ghanoush with hummus and pita bread. Mira tore off some bread and dunked it into the dip, leaning closer to him. She casually brushed against his fingertips.

'Thanks,' he said, inching away a fraction and piling his plate with the food the waiter brought. 'Do you like vegan food? Sorry, I should have checked first.' He looked sheepish.

'I am learning to be adventurous,' she drawled, 'about food and other things.'

'Good,' he said briskly, and continued eating, completely missing her signals.

She swallowed her disappointment and picked on her bread. He had opted for a quinoa dish for their main course, and it was delicious.

'You know your food, don't you?' she told him huskily.

'Hmm...' was all he said and kept his eyes on his plate.

Mira decided that it was time for another move. She slipped one foot out of her sandal and shifted in her chair, slowly stretching her leg, trying to reach his feet under the table.

'What's wrong, Mira? Why are you sliding down?' Rohan looked a little alarmed.

Heat rushed to her face. 'My sandal has come undone and I think it's somewhere near your feet,' she mumbled, sitting erect.

Rohan stooped to check under the table.

'No worries, I found it,' she said hastily, slipping her foot back into her sandal.

He resurfaced, a glint in his eyes. Mira averted her gaze and wordlessly concentrated on her dessert.

'You look beautiful,' he said after a few minutes. He reached out and put his hand on hers.

Mira inhaled sharply. 'Thank you,' she said and dabbed her mouth with a napkin.

He leaned towards her. At last, she thought in satisfaction.

'Something on your nose,' he said, dabbing at it with his napkin. When he moved back, she was sure it was laughter that lurked in his eyes.

Mira suppressed her annoyance and finished her dessert. The place had filled up and it was getting noisy. The music was almost inaudible now.

The stars were out when they stepped out of the restaurant. They walked to the car park that was a street away. He slid his arm around her shoulders and she leaned towards him.

Kiss him. This is your chance. But how do I do that? Do I stop him in the middle of the road? Try something—anything!.

She tried slipping her other arm around him, and stumbled. She would've fallen if he hadn't caught her.

'Clumsy today, aren't you?' he remarked.

'Maybe you are making me nervous?' she replied stung.

She tried to shake off his embrace but his grasp just tightened around her.

'Come, I'll drop you home,' he murmured in her ear.

The journey back was taken over by some unnaturally chirpy RJ. Rohan spoke about random things and charmed her back into good humour. The traffic was smooth and the city glowed beneath all the bright night lights. He drove up to her building and stopped before the foyer. She took a deep breath. *This is it, girl. Now or never. Ask him to kiss you.*

'Mira,' he called her name softly. He reached out and tugged her into his arms. He took her mouth in his and they kissed fervently. It was a long time before they came up for air.

'And that, my sweet innocent Mira, is how you put on the moves,' he said, his voice laced with mirth. 'Not that I didn't enjoy watching you attempt entertaining moves in the restaurant.'

Mira flushed and buried her face in his neck. This would have been the perfect moment to disappear into the deepest bowels of the earth. 'I could die now,' she said.

'Don't be silly. It was the one of the best evenings of my life and I was hugely flattered.' He dropped a kiss on her forehead and turned the key in the ignition. 'I need to go, it's getting late.'

'Sure,' she muttered, and he drove off. He called out saying he will be in touch.

Mira stood at the entrance to the lobby for a long time, wondering what had just happened. She was mortified. What was she going to do if this story of her gaffes reached Sanya? As she rode the lift, Mira battled with images of a triumphant Sanya shooting her withering looks.

But Rohan is a decent guy, he may not tell her. How easily he had seen through her! God, she must make a pathetic Bitch Goddess. Add to it the fact that even after sharing a kiss that had rocked out of the Richter scale, he had turned around and… left! It looked like her Bitch Goddess needed work—a lot of it.

She stretched out on the couch and flicked the TV on. She stopped at some channel showing *Notting Hill*. Bah. Romance between a movie star and a regular guy—like that was ever going to happen in real life! She flipped more channels. *Sex and the City*. Everybody was talking about it. She began watching the episode with interest, trying to keep the characters and their stories straight. She sighed. In her case, it was all city and no sex.

On the Rocks

$\mathcal{G}$erard called Mira in for a meeting the next day.

'Good luck,' Vinay showed her a thumbs-up sign. Mira smoothed her hair and ran her eyes over her attire: a fuchsia shirt and narrow gray skirt. She gave Vinay a small wave and confidently strode towards Gerard's office.

'So Mira,' he said, once the pleasantries were out of the way. 'Any idea what this meeting is about?' He pushed a roll of mint towards her.

'No thanks,' she said. *Some men love fast cars. My boss loves mints.*

Mira might not know much about being a Bitch Goddess, but she was very clued-in about her work. If Gerard had to ask a question like this, there was only one answer.

She sat and almost crossed her legs. Then she remembered Queen Clarisse Renaldi from *Princess Diaries* saying, 'Royalty never cross their legs.' Mira uncrossed her legs and straightened her spine. She could see what Clarisse had been talking about.

'This is about the new group head, I suppose,' she said.

Gerard smiled, his tiny eyes crinkling. 'Bingo.' He sat up a little taller. 'So who, in your opinion, would be the ideal choice?'

'You mean, excluding me?' she asked, not really thinking about her response.

Gerard laughed and Mira realized what she had just said. But she was unapologetic.

Score one for the Bitch Goddess. She flicked her hair back and tried to flash a sultry smile like Sanya's.

'So, do you think you are a good choice?' said Gerard.

'Yes, I do.' she nodded.

'Why?' Gerard fixed his gaze on her.

'I am smart, hard working and have always shown initiative in my work.'

'Hmm...how about we discuss some specific cases?'

'When the Bank of America project came to me, I figured out a way to cut our costs and fixed snags in the system. The project, if you remember, was the highest grosser for the company last quarter.' She could have added that, despite her remarkable output, she was not given the Employee of the Month award, but she held back.

Bitch Goddess Rule #8: A Bitch Goddess does a cost-time benefit before she whines.

Gerard steepled his hands. 'But the telecom project ran into some glitches. What do you think happened?'

'Yes, we did fall behind schedule by almost a week,' she readily agreed. 'But the fault was not my team's. The biggest problem there was the lack of direction from the client. They didn't know what they wanted—until the last minute.' She then listed a few other issues they had faced. Gerard heard her out, his face bland and emotionless. Mira wondered what thoughts were running through her boss's head.

He dropped his hands on the desk and leaned forward. 'If you were asked to pick somebody—other than you—who would you pick?'

Mira hesitated, and then looked him in the eye and said, 'Sanya.' She did not want to say it, but then she couldn't help being scrupulously honest.

'Hmm…' Gerard kept his eyes trained on her. 'What would you say if I told you that when Sanya was asked this question, she said no one matches her caliber?' Ouch. So that was the correct Bitch Goddess response. But then she, Mira, was a different kind of a Bitch Goddess.

Mira gave a sweet smile. 'I would say our answers reflect a certain attitude, and that might be something you want to keep in mind while making the selection.'

Gerard returned her smile, this time openly appreciative. 'Thank you, Mira. We should have a manager very soon,' he said as they shook hands.

Mira came out less confident than she had been going in. She had the feeling that the odds were not in her favour—despite her smart answers.

'Quick, give me the dirty lowdown,' said Vinay, rushing to her desk. 'Was it about the project lead position?'

'Yes, Gerard grilled me a bit,' said Mira, resting her hips against her desk. 'Come, let's get some coffee.'

'Later,' Vinay was impatient. 'First, tell me about the meeting.'

Mira knitted her brows. 'Hmm…I'm not sure…I was not like before, you know, mouse-like, but then again, I didn't give Sanyaesque answers either…'

'Not bitchy enough?' Vinay mocked. He didn't entirely approve of her makeover, after all.

'I just hope I haven't goofed up my chances—'

'Saw you with G this morning.' Sanya's perfectly made-up face appeared over the wall, startling Mira and Vinay.

'Sanya, Vinay and I are busy with something,' said Mira in a cold tone.

Sanya came around and stood beside Mira's chair, her pageant-worthy hair streaked a deep bronze. Mira ran her fingers on her temple. She was hoping to compete with *this*? Well, she was going to try.

'Do you mind? We are trying to work here,' Mira said, hoping her voice had the right snap.

Sanya coolly ignored her. 'So what did Gerry say, Mira? Who is going to get the top job?'

'I can't believe anybody can be so rude!' Mira snapped again, her eyes flashing anger.

Sanya flinched. But she recovered soon enough to give Mira a condescending smile. She placed her hand on her hip and tilted her head insolently. Her hair picked up the light in the room and glowed.

You had to give it to the woman; she knew how to groom herself.

'So, did Gerard tell you about who is going be the new team lead?' Sanya widened her eyes innocently at Mira.

'Unbelievable,' Mira said, shaking her head incredulously. She was not going to fall into Sanya's trap.

'Damn. I was hoping Gerry would break it to you gently,' Sanya sighed dramatically. She shot Mira a pitiful look. 'Poor thing, now you will hear it only when the others do.'

Mira's mouth flew open but Sanya had already exited the room. Mira wondered what the punishment for murder was in Singapore. Everybody, at least in her company, would agree she had good reason to kill Sanya.

Bitch Goddess Rule #9: A Bitch Goddess works like a student of Kung fu. She has to lose to the Master several times before she earns the title.

Mira went back to her work, but her mind was buzzing. She *had* to bring Sanya down. What would a Bitch Goddess do? Hmm…something bitchy, naturally. But what? She chewed on her lip and opened Google.

'Ten bitchy things to do' she typed and hit the search button. Mira was surprised that this was a legitimate search option and garnered 103,000,000 results! Most links were boyfriend related and many pertained to how to get even with your boss. 'Ten bitchy things you can do to your colleague'—she refined her search. Thousands of links. She scanned them; there seemed many angry people out there. She squinted her eyes as she read through the link descriptions. There were some involving dog poo and other organic matter, which Mira immediately decided was not for her. Some others were related to pornography and to objectionable junk mails. Mira hastily closed the page—she didn't want the Bitch Goddess research to cost her her job.

What she fiercely desired was not to just get even, but to destroy something in Sanya, something deep and permanent. Mira came across a page that listed insulting things to say to people. She pondered over it and then printed it off. She wasn't really sure if anything would come in handy, but wanted it anyway—just in case. She spent the next few minutes browsing through the other links that involved witchcraft and voodoo dolls. She felt dismal; none of these options would work for her. It looked like she would have to come up with her own plan, something lethal that would guarantee results. The alarm on the computer went off. Her fifteen minutes of goofing off was up and she got back to work. That was a good thing because almost immediately, Vinay's giraffe-neck appeared over her cubicle. 'Hey, don't forget you need to get the papers for this afternoon's conference ready.'

Mira groaned. She had forgotten about the programming conference she was going to later that day. 'Thanks, Vinay,' she said, and clicked open the presentation she had to finalize.

The minute Mira entered her apartment later that night, she was swamped by it all—Rohan, the childhood memories and her nightmares. She made herself a cup of chamomile tea and sat down with her phone in hand. She had to call Amma, ostensibly to tell her about her tickets and travel plans.

'Mira? What happened? Are you okay?' her mother's concerned voice came down the line.

Mira grimaced, how could she have forgotten? An out-of-schedule phone call to her mother meant that disaster had occurred. If her mother had worked for the Chennai Meteorological Department, she would have called for Cyclone Warning No. 10.

'Nothing, Amma. I came back early from work today and just felt like speaking to you.'

'Thank God, I was worried,' her mother audibly sighed. Mira smiled. Like most Indian mothers, her mother too could only imagine the worst—either a terrorist attack in her office or a rapist at large who was at her door.

'I have got my India tickets and thought I'd tell you about it.'

'But I think you told me this the last time you'd called?'

She had? Oh lord, she should probably start maintaining a diary for chronologically recording her lies.

'Really? I...I thought I hadn't,' said Mira.

'Never mind,' her mother said, 'In a way, it's a good thing you called. I wanted to ask you something.'

'Sure, what is it?' Mira was automatically on her guard. That was her natural state whenever her mother wanted to 'ask' her something.

Her mother cleared her throat. 'Did you think about that... that other thing?'

'What thing?' Mira asked innocently.

'Your father wanting to meet you...' her mother trailed.

'I will, when I get the time,' she replied evenly.

'Mira, please kanna. Just once, that is all I ask. You can't continue pretending he does not exist. You need to overcome your trauma. Three weeks is long enough for one small visit?'

Mira fell silent and withdrew into a secluded space in her mind that nobody, not even her mother, could enter.

'So how is Vinay? And your project?' Her mother knew when to back off. Mrs Iyer had briefly met Vinay at the Chennai airport when he had flown in with Mira last time. He was enroute to Bangalore and had come across as a perfectly nice boy—but not good enough to be son-in-law material. In her mind, Mira's husband was tall, fine-boned and masculine, with multiple degrees from Ivy Leagues and a (US) dollar salary that ran up to six digits. Not to mention the stellar horoscope he must possess with the most propitious stars foretelling a king's future for him.

Mira gratefully clutched onto the change of topic and chatted about work and sundry matters.

Just as her mother was about to hang up, Mira's voice dropped a notch. 'Amma?' She gripped the phone tighter. 'Do you remember that teddy bear, the yellowish-brown one? Do we still have it?'

There was a long pause. 'Yes, it's in your cupboard—exactly where you left it.'

A melancholic smile formed on Mira's face.

'You were so possessive about it as a little girl, remember?' her mother gave a short laugh.

I am still attached to it, Amma.

They both fell silent, remembering the teddy bear with the sad brown eyes that had been one of her father's last gifts to her.

'Mira?' her mother cut into her thoughts.

'Hmm?'

'He loved you...loves you. He is your father, after all. He cares about you. You can't pretend he doesn't exist.' For the first time, Mira heard a hint of firmness in her mother's voice. She gathered her thoughts, unsure of what to say.

'Have you...could you...forgive him for what he did to you?' said Mira. She needed to know the answer to the question that had plagued her all her adult years. She heard her mother take a deep breath. She could visualize her staring blankly at nothing in particular—she always did this when confronted with uncomfortable questions, as if the answers lay somewhere in space.

'I don't know Mira. I loved him once—more than anything. What he did hurt. Worse, it devastated me. It was years before I became whole and felt a sense of fulfillment at anything in life. Forgiving is not easy.' She paused. 'But I think I have finally let him go.' She gave a short, brittle laugh. 'Now I can see him and not feel the pain or the anger. I won't say I think of the good times and become happy or nostalgic—because he took the good times when he left. All that had happened before the divorce has become a lie in my life.' Her mother's voice turned mellow; Mira knew she was fighting tears. 'But he gave me you. You are my true blessing.'

'Amma, I'm sorry. It's not your fault,' Mira said quietly. She would have forgiven her mother anything then. A part of her brain was assimilating what her mother had just revealed. So her parents were legally divorced, her mother had made a clean break from her past. Mira realized how tough everything must have been for her.

'No. I am happy you asked, Mira. It's the first step to letting it go, which is why I want you to meet him.'

Mira clicked her tongue in impatience. Her mother's words made sense, but she needed time to think things through.

Such resolutions don't happen overnight, like in the movies.

'He loves you Mira,' her mother repeated her words, her voice coming from a faraway place. 'You were always his princess. By the time I was ready to share all this with you, you had developed this...this anger, this bitterness.'

'I am no angel, Amma. After what he did to us, I can't help having so much anger in me.'

'I am not blaming you for your feelings, Mira,' her mother responded. 'All I am trying to say is you need to bury your past and try and meet him. He is your father, after all.'

'Amma, I said I would, didn't I?' Mira was already terrified at that thought. What if he found her wanting once they met? What if he rejected her? Again.

'Thank you, kanna. Now about those boys...'

'Amma! Don't push your luck.' Mira smiled despite herself. 'And they are grown men, not boys!'

'Fine, then,' her mother said in a tight voice. 'I won't say anything after today. It's for your own good. You can't stay this way forever, you know. I won't be around—'

Mira sighed. 'Bye Amma,' she said and disconnected the line. She had been hasty in thinking earlier that she could forgive her mother anything; she had forgotten her mother's obsessive hunt for a son-in-law.

Mira wandered out to her balcony and indulged in her favourite passtime of watching the apartment complex's swimming pool from her window. The pool lights reflected in the water and she could make out the families splashing about. The December sky was clear and it hadn't rained today. She leaned on the railing and reminisced about the conversation she had just had with her mother. Though she was mentally fatigued, oddly enough, she should have expected this difficult topic to come up long ago. She and her mother had trod softly around this for years—seventeen, to be precise. Almost two decades of playing hide and seek! Mira knew that this was a long time to keep feelings bottled up, and build up resentment towards her parents, her father in particular. Though she was aware that this was toxic to her sense of well-being, she felt helpless. She knew no other way to react than with knee-jerk anger, frustration and reticence. But some things never went away, like bad odour that lingers even after the garbage has been emptied. Some days she wished she had been younger at the time her father had abandoned them—there would have been fewer memories to battle with. On other days she wished she had been older at the time, for she might have coped with the betrayal better. Any which way she looked at it, ten was the wrong age for this to have happened to her.

The sky darkened and the pool area was emptying out. She moved away from the railing and walked into the house. She pulled the French doors shut and drew the curtains. Then she entered the kitchen and took out some cauliflower from the refrigerator for preparing curry. But she put it back in, no longer in the mood for dinner. She poured herself some coffee left over from the morning, and barely registered its bitter, stale taste.

Mira plonked herself on the loveseat in the living room and started channel surfing. Almost all channels were showing soaps, whether they were Tamil, Hindi or English. She settled for a Tamil soap where a heavily made-up woman with medusa-like hair was plotting the angel-faced heroine's downfall. Mira rolled her eyes. Anything that happened in real life was less traumatic than the things that happened to these heroines, she mused with a shudder. She suddenly realized that these villains were mostly female and acted way beyond bitchy. They were downright *evil*. She switched to a Hindi soap. Same story: more bitchy, evil women, wearing snake-like bindis and chunky jewellery. For a while Mira watched them manipulate and scheme. Then an idea flashed in her head. She picked up her handbag and dumped its contents on the sofa. She found the business card she was looking for. It was a neon lime and white. 'LC Stewart, Elcard Corp.', it said. She had met Stewart at the conference she had gone to earlier that day. They had gotten talking and she had learnt that he was the project head for the one that Sanya was working on. Mira tapped the card against her palm, a plan slowly forming in her mind.

The next morning Mira walked into her office to find Sanya sifting through the papers on her desk.

'Just what do you think you are you doing, Sanya?' Mira glared at her.

Sanya jumped, her cheetah print wrap dress adding to her feline movements. She straightened her shoulders and gave Mira a cool look.

'Here, take this,' she thrust a plastic folder towards her. 'Gerry wanted me to give it to you.'

Mira snatched the folder and tossed it on her desk. She was livid. *Wait till I raid her desk and rip out Fido's photographs from her bulletin board.*

Mira crossed her arms. 'Of course. Every time there is a folder to be handed over to a colleague, one has to rifle through that colleague's personal correspondence. Office etiquette 101. Forgive me if I forgot.'

Sanya shot her a venomous look. 'Oh, please. Your projects are hardly top secret and NUS is hardly the top client.'

Mira met Sanya's gaze with a long, considering look. 'I wonder if the client would like to be described like this.

Moreover, what would *Gerry* say if he heard you talking about a client like this? Not something they would like to hear from the potential project leader, surely?' she said.

Sanya opened her mouth but Mira wagged her finger at her. 'I am not finished. Talking of top-of-the-line clients, I met LC Stewart of Elcard at the TECH-PRO conference yesterday.' She paused dramatically and was thrilled to see Sanya's face blanch. Oh, the benefits of being a Bitch Goddess.

Mira continued, 'Well, we got talking and he spoke about his project—*your* project. It was a very interesting discussion and in the end he said, and I quote him here, "I would've loved to work with you, Ms Iyer. A pity, maybe next time."'

Mira was amazed at how smoothly she had lied. Stewart had, of course, said nothing of the sort. The only reference he had made about the project was that he was working with her company on it. He had been polite but aloof, but Sanya didn't know that, did she? Moreover, there was no way Sanya could check on Stewart's conversation without sounding like an idiot.

Mira watched questions creep into Sanya's eyes. She knew Sanya would have gladly traded her Hermes bag and Burberry sunglasses to find out what else had passed between Mira and Stewart. Mira bit her cheek to keep from laughing out loud. She sat down at her desk and got to work as if nothing had happened. A minute later, Sanya's heels clicked away, their angry click-clocks making Mira deliriously happy. She gave herself a mental high-five. The Bitch Goddess had struck gold. When Sanya stayed away from her the rest of the day, Mira's sense of well-being grew. She was so jubilant that when the day ended, she decided she wanted to celebrate her achievement. Rohan had told her about some meeting with professors that evening, so she didn't bother calling him.

At six she shut off her machine, turned to Vinay, and

snapped her fingers. 'Right, that's it. We are going out now, for a drink or dinner or something. I know, let's go to one of your pubs and get drunk.'

Vinay blinked rapidly. 'You want to get drunk? It's only Wednesday. But I know where we can go—it's a fancy place with fancy wine. Iggy's. They serve the best Burgundies, from fancy glasses, too!'

Mira dismissed his idea with an impatient wave of her hand. 'No fancy place for me, please. I want to go to a pub or a sports bar where I can get regular food and drinks.'

'Since when did you want to go out for a drink?'

'I do drink, you know.' Mira said defiantly.

'Ah, yes, let me see.' Vinay pretended to think. 'There was this half-a-glass of wine at last year's New Year's do and then—'

'Are you coming with me or should I go on my own?' Mira demanded.

He stared at her, part-amused, part-bewildered. Mira smiled; her Bitch Goddess ways seemed to be in fine form today.

Vinay got to his feet. 'Fine, let's go. That way, I can at least keep an eye on you.'

Mira made a face at him.

Vinay took her to a quaint—though popular—pub on the Quay. Mira felt it looked like a tavern. There was a lot of wood: on the walls, on the floor and even the tables were made of rustic log wood, and the whole place wore a rugged look. Mira loved the carved lanterns that were placed on every table. Vinay and Mira occupied water-facing seats at the deck, where most of the crowd hung out. She felt that if she reached over low enough, she might actually touch the water.

The booze, Vinay assured her, was good here. The sky had darkened and the water was just inky ripples reflected in the lights from the banks or from some passing tourists' boats.

The music at this distance was just a hum in the background. Mira let Vinay order the food, and despite her earlier claims, she chose the house wine. Vinay ordered tequila.

She finished one glass and got herself another. She lazily scanned the crowd around them. For a Wednesday, the place was pretty packed. The majority were casually dressed, in shorts and sandals. It seemed to be a popular watering hole for westerners, though there were also a fair number of locals in the crowd.

Suddenly, her spine stiffened. 'I can't believe this,' she whispered, her palm clamping on her mouth.

'What?' Vinay asked uninterestedly. He didn't really care, he was on his third tequila.

'They are here. The *bastard*. He told me that he would be busy with some visiting professors and look who he is with instead. Oh, I bet I know what *she* is the professor of.' Mira was frothing at the mouth.

'Who? What?' Vinay was startled out of his semi-drunken state.

He followed her gaze to the far corner of the pub. Seated at a table near the entrance were Sanya and a good-looking man in a grey polo neck shirt and jeans. Vinay frowned and looked at Mira.

'Yes, that's him. Rohan,' said Mira, her voice flat.

Sanya had her head close to Rohan's and the two were having, what appeared to be, an intimate conversation. Mira tried not to notice Sanya's flawless olive skin that glowed in her simple white linen dress.

'What did you say you were having?' Mira asked Vinay.

'Tequila.'

'Is it strong?'

'Oh, very. Deadly stuff,' he answered rashly.

'Good, get yourself another.' She snatched the glass from

his hand, and downed it in one gulp, the sharp liquid burning her throat. She signalled the waiter. 'And another for me, too, please. Better still, make that two.'

'God, look at the love birds,' she hissed viciously. 'He is probably telling her all about our last meeting. In graphic detail.' She took another slug. 'Good, this is why I am using your boyfriend, Sanya—to serve my ends. Burn, bitch.'

Vinay stared at his glass. 'Tell me this. From your periodic rants in the last few weeks, I have gathered that you are going out with this Rohan guy to make Sanya jealous. Right?'

'Bingo. Also to take him away from her.'

'Er…why?'

Mira shrugged. 'Dunno, just seems appropriate.'

'But why?'

She waved a hand at herself. 'I'm a Bitch Goddess, remember?'

He shook his head. 'You are serious about this new avatar, aren't you?'

'Dead serious,' she slurred. 'I think this might even be my destiny.'

Vinay gazed into the waters and fell silent.

'Getting back to Rohan, if you are using him just to make her jealous, then why are you so upset to see them together?'

Mira blinked a few times, as if trying to weigh the import of his words. She leaned forward conspiratorially. 'I know that I am using him. But *he* doesn't know it, does he?'

She sat back. 'So what business does he have, going out with two women at the same time? The two-timing reptile,' she spat and guzzled down her drink. 'All men are bastards.'

Vinay, very prudently, refrained from commenting further. One does not argue with a woman on her third tequila.

She stared at her glass gloomily. 'This Rohan's no better than *him*,' she spoke with distaste.

'Er...whom?' Vinay tried to follow the plot.

Mira ignored his question and rambled on, 'He left us, I was ten. Ten!' She stared cross-eyed at the bottom of her glass. 'Only ten, dammit!'

Vinay rested his hand on hers.

Mira's eyes wildly surveyed the scene. 'Where's my tequila? I want another. Waiter!'

'Mira, that would be your fourth. Don't you think you've had enough?'

Mira brushed away his hand. 'My money, my tequila.' she jabbed a finger on her chest. 'What's your problem? Waiter!'

Vinay raised his hands in surrender and slurred, 'Sure, whatever, boss.'

She snagged a passing waiter and got herself another tequila refill. 'You know the biggest irony?' Mira swirled the golden liquid in her shot glass and downed it in one go. Her eyes burned from the alcohol and the memories. 'They were in love, Vinay,' she gave a high laugh. 'Love.'

Vinay's forehead creased. 'Them? he said, jerking his thumb in Rohan and Sanya's direction.

'No, silly,' Mira giggled helplessly. 'I am talking about my parents.'

It was the first time Vinay had seen the woman before him so out of control and reckless. With all the Bitch Goddess thing going on, he wasn't sure whether it was she, or the alcohol, that was talking.

'My parents met in college—Amma says it was love at first sight. They married straight out of college when they were very young and without steady jobs. My mother's family was wealthy, his was not. The usual threats and all happened from her folks.' Mira paused and steadied her voice. 'They were so madly in love, my mother says, that they ignored her family's threats and got married. My mother's family did not talk to her for years.' She put her drink down and stared at the dark waters.

'There used to be lot of laughter in those days. A *lot*. Then suddenly, he was gone. My mother stopped laughing and grew old overnight. Just like that.' Mira snapped her fingers. She gulped down Vinay's half-finished drink and signalled the waiter for another. For somebody who was at a pub for the first time, she was behaving like a pro. She grinned maniacally and wagged her index finger at Vinay. 'That is why I am not going to fall in love. Sanya is welcome to that loser-jerk,' she finished her speech.

Though Vinay too was buzzed, he was sober enough to realize that now the topic had switched from Mira's father to Rohan, the new troublesome man in her life.

'Know why I am not going to fall in love ever? Because of *him*.'

'Rohan?' Vinay frowned.

'You are sooo stupid,' she slapped his hand. 'What does Rohan have to do with this? I am talking about *him*, my dad. Whatever Rohan has to do, he is doing with that Sanya, she said darkly, momentarily distracted.

'Huh?'

'Okay, focus. Let's go back to my dad. Know what he did?' Mira struggled to keep her voice steady and her eyes open.

Vinay's head felt like a few bricks were stacked on it. He looked at her, too dazed to speak.

'Know what he did? He found another woman, some colleague or neighbour. When Amma discovered the truth, she told him to choose between her or the Other Woman. He did just that...'

Mira laughed, a bitter and hollow sound that rolled over the water flowing beside them. 'He moved in with her...hic...and never came back.' Mira looked around bleary-eyed for a waiter. Vinay quickly shifted in his chair and blocked the nearest one from her line of vision.

'What, no waiter around....' Mira tipped her glass and tried to lick the empty base. When she couldn't reach it with her tongue, she sighed and let it drop on the table.

'He has another daughter and a son too.' Mira rubbed her eyes with her knuckles. 'It hurt that he was with them—for their birthdays, when they scraped their knees, when bullies stole their lunch...for everything. For a long time I hated my parents. My mother for being a pushover, and my dad for leaving us.'

She leaned back on her chair and stared at the stars that had started emerging in the dark sky.

'But you know what the worst was?' Her laugh was shrill. Vinay held his breath, not daring to speak.

'A few years ago, he came back. Amma let him come home, spoke to him, told him things about me. Spineless woman. Bah.' She stared at the stars silently.

Vinay tensed, his forehead creasing with worry. He expected Mira to come unhinged at any moment. But, deep down, he realized that this is what she needed to let her past demons out of her system.

'"How could you?" I asked her a few days back. "I loved him once," she replied. Years of struggling alone, so many days of loneliness, the things we had to go without because of not having enough money—because the man who loved you, betrayed you.'

'Mira, maybe we should go home?' said Vinay.

Mira banged the table. '*How* could he do this to you, to us, Amma? Then humiliate you even more by making you forget all this pain and pretend those terrible things never happened? I will NEVER fall in love. What kind of love is this?'

Mira lifted her head and gave Vinay a very strange look. 'Vinay?' her voice was a whisper. 'I think I am going to be sick.' Before he could react, she pitched her face forward onto the table and passed out.

LBD—Lousy Big Debacle

*M*ira noticed three things when she woke up the next day. One, she had a splitting headache, two, she was in someone else's room, and three, she was lying on a purple sheet that smelt of, she squinted her eyes in concentration, lemon and spice. Rohan? She flipped on her back, now wide awake and her heartbeat doing a dull gallop. She cringed when she remembered last night and slowly looked down at herself. She noticed, with a twinge of regret, that she was fully clothed.

She looked around the sparsely furnished room whose walls were painted a soothing almond, and tried to remember the events of the past night. The pub by the water front...Vinay... tequila... more tequila...Sanya...and Rohan. She rolled out of bed and stood up. This was Rohan's house and she had spent the night in *his* bed. Her stomach churned and she wanted to puke. Mira dashed through the bathroom door and tried throwing up, but nothing came out. She washed her face and rinsed her mouth vigorously with the mouthwash she found on the shelf. She looked around the bathroom that was done up in menthol blue. Seeing Rohan's toiletries lying around was oddly intimate. Her stomach churned again. She leaned against the bathroom door and gathered herself. Why was she here? How did she get here? What had happened last night? She vaguely remembered passing out.

She went back to the bedroom and sat on the bed. This was a situation worthy of her new avatar and she could use it to her advantage. Only, she couldn't figure out how. The throbbing in her head did not help; she pressed her fingers to her eyes. Think Mira, she told herself. There was only one thing to do, and that was to act, not think. *Remember Bitch Goddess. Remember Sanya*, she gave herself a pep talk. The clock on the bedside table flashed ten-fifteen. She surged to her feet.

Mira pasted a watery smile on her lips and stepped out of the bedroom. Her eyes swept over the apartment that seemed fairly spacious and posh. The living room was as minimalistic as the bedroom. A large black couch dominated the room, a matching black recliner stood at an angle to it. A Plasma TV was on the wall across. The only sign of clutter were the books and folders piled on the center glass table. It was obvious Rohan worked on this table. She picked up the picture frame kept on the small table in the corner and studied the smiling couple in the picture.

She heard the sound of somebody pottering about and peeped inside the kitchen, which was small but cheery looking. Rohan was flipping an omelette. He turned around. 'Good morning,' he smiled at her like it wasn't unusual for him to see her in his kitchen. He was wearing a pair of navy shorts and a white T-shirt. His well-toned legs and firm chest added to the dashing nautical look. She felt weak-kneed. *Remember why you are here. Think Bitch Goddess. Be Bitch Goddess.*

'Breakfast?' he asked, gesturing at the omelette he had placed on a white plate with chopped cilantro sprinkled on top. *Hmm...not bad, the man can cook, too.*

'No thanks, though I wouldn't mind some coffee,' she said, and grabbed a mug from the shelf. Rohan poured coffee for her from the coffee machine.

'Milk?' he asked.

She shook her head; she liked the caffeine to hit her hard

at the temples in the morning. She kept her smile in place and sat down on the only chair in the kitchen.

'Those are my parents, in case you are wondering,' he said, eyeing the photo she still clutched.

She flushed and hastily put it down on the counter. 'I didn't mean to pry.'

He shrugged. 'This is not prying.'

'They make a nice couple,' she said, eyeing the photograph. *They looked like decent folks. How did their son turn out to be a two-timing snake?*

She sipped her coffee and watched Rohan work around the kitchen.

'What happened? How did I get here?' she finally asked.

He raised an eyebrow but remained silent.

'C'mon, tell me.'

'Not what you are thinking, alas,' he sighed theatrically, pouring himself some orange juice in a tall glass.

She shook her head. 'Rohan!' She refused to be charmed—or worse, disarmed.

He shrugged. 'Sure you won't have breakfast?'

She shook her head.

'You, ma'am, had drunk yourself into a stupor.' He waved an admonishing spatula at her.

Mira looked away, the colour rising to her cheeks.

'I too was at the pub and saw the...the state you had worked yourself up into.'

Mira's eyes drooped to the floor in embarrassment.

'Vinay, who was a little drunk himself, had no idea what to do with you,' Rohan was scathing. 'So I offered to bring you here, and so here you are.'

Mira bit back several nasty comebacks and forced herself to smile politely. She had to be super-poised today, even if she had been a bumbling idiot last night.

'Thank you,' she said softly, looking at him adoringly.

Rohan looked surprised. 'Err...sure, it was nothing.'

'But truly, very nice of you, Rohan,' she gushed, squeezing his arms.

'Sure...' he repeated and took the omelet and toast to the circular glass dining table.

Mira sat and sipped her coffee thoughtfully. She watched Rohan spread marmalade on his toast. Vinay's words came back to her: 'Take charge, lure him into bed...seduce him.' Well, truth be told, Vinay had not exactly spoken about *seducing* him. However, after seeing Rohan canoodling with Sanya last night, Mira's mind started ticking. Her blood boiled, realizing Rohan brazenly flirted with her, kissed her, and even brought her home into his bedroom, while he had a steady girlfriend in Sanya... Mira drained her coffee. Yes, seducing him seemed like a great idea now. Her face lit up with pleasure. Be the heartless Bitch Goddess, she told herself sternly. Focus on the duplicity of this man; think of Sanya's reaction when she finds out. Mira smiled. Two birds with one stone. Three, her treacherous heart told her, if you think of the pleasure.

'What are you smiling about?' Rohan's voice cut into her thoughts.

Mira jerked back to the present.

Bitch Goddess Rule #10: A Bitch Goddess has to be quick on her feet.

'Nothing, I am just happy. I like this; sitting across from the table from you and sharing breakfast.'

Rohan's eyes twinkled. He drained his orange juice and checked his watch. 'I am sorry, I have to leave now. My university soccer team has a match in an hour.'

He clasped her hand. 'Have dinner with me tonight...here. We'll have a nice evening together.' Her mind raced. It was obvious the man had more than dinner in mind. Perfect. He was making it easy for her. Maybe the Fates wanted her to do this. Her finger trailed along his arm.

'Thanks, I would love that,' she smiled shyly. Rohan's eyes lingered on her lips.

'If we don't leave now...we won't leave ever,' he said, rising to his feet.

Mira gave a muffled giggle. 'I have no complaints with that plan, too.'

He dropped her off at her apartment twenty minutes later. Mira had plotted the evening action all the way to her home. She decided that when they would, eventually, go to bed, it would be entirely on her terms. She wanted to create an impact that night.

Rohan kissed her briefly and said he would pick her up in the evening.

She met his gaze directly. 'No thanks, Rohan. I'll take a cab and be there at eight.'

He opened his mouth to protest but she gave a Sanyaesque wiggle with her fingers and alighted from the car. She dashed into the lift and continued plotting her moves all the way to the thirteenth floor. Her fingers fumbled as she opened her door in a hurry. She walked in and paced around aimlessly, sorting things through in her mind. Her headache had vanished and she was as good as new. Revenge renewed you, apparently! Then she pulled out a pad from her stationery kit and made a list. What kind of a woman makes a list for something like this anyway? A pathetic, almost-thirty virgin, perhaps? That thought didn't stop her, though. For Mira needed a list for everything—even seduction.

When she was done with her list, she picked up her phone and made a few calls. She blew out her cheeks and exhaled loudly. Okay, she was as ready as she could ever be, for something as monumental as was going to happen tonight.

She arrived at the beauty salon for her appointment for facial-pedicure-manicure and anything-else-they-could-think-of, at exactly three. The fashionable Chinese woman at the desk checked her in. Another girl in an apron smiled, made friendly noises and led her off. There were a few other people surrendering their hair and face to the experts' hands. She changed into a blue, monogrammed robe and the girl led her off to a cubicle. She was made to lie down, had creams, lotions and gels massaged onto her face and body. Then she was gently propelled into a chair and had her arms and legs waxed. She felt like a fancy car that was being washed, cleaned, polished and painted, by overzealous car mechanics.

She stared at herself in the mirror when the salon girls finally released her. She was dismayed. Women spent hundreds of dollars…on *this*? Her hair stuck to her head like cotton wool, her eyes were puffy, and her face looked blotchy. Mira went home feeling disgruntled and broke. She prayed the women at the parlour were right and that her skin would relax into smoothness, that all this would vanish in a few hours, leaving behind a radiant glow.

The first thing Mira did when she got back was to run a Cleopatra-style bath in the bathtub. She poured eucalyptus bath salt into the running water and lit some jasmine-scented aromatherapy candles. She carefully tucked her hundred-dollar washed and styled hair under the cap. Then she quickly stripped and stepped into the bathtub. She let the warm water ebb and flow gently over her body, easing some of the tension in her muscles. She rubbed her new wheat germ bath gel all over herself and washed it off. She soaked in the water for some time, and tried to keep her mind blank of all thoughts about the impending evening. She gingerly stepped out of the tub, padded softly into the bedroom, and patted herself dry with a towel.

Her Little Black Dress was waiting for her, spread out in its satiny glory, on the bed. Mira felt a brief pang gorge itself in her chest. What if it did not look as good on her as it had on the day she had tried it on? *No, it would. It had better. Not for nothing did she blow up $250!* She pulled out the matching black thongs from her underwear drawer and slipped it on. She didn't need a bra for this outfit, just loads of attitude. Then she wore the dress that was a cool five inches above her knees. She wished the nuns, who had taught her at her convent school in Chennai, could see her now. Her new avatar would make them pull out their rosary beads in a heartbeat. She turned to face the mirror. She was becoming like Snow White's stepmother, the evil Queen— forever staring at the looking glass for reassuring answers. She narrowed her eyes. So what? A woman used whatever tools she found handy to get her way. A Bitch Goddess, even more so.

She smugly studied her reflection. Her sheer, brand new black dress stopped mid-thigh, hugging her like a second skin. The one-shoulder dress left her practically backless and skimmed the top of her breasts. She studied her slender form; relieved there were no bulges. She swung to one side, then another. She knew what was missing. She opened her jewellery case and carefully picked the pieces she wanted. The thick gold choker and matching earrings did add a touch of class to the overall look. She gently shook her hair; the freshly cut waves tumbled out and grazed her shoulders. She ran her fingers through it, satisfied with the stylishly messy look. The salon ladies were right; she looked radiant now.

Now for the make-up. She mentally repeated the instructions

the beautician had given her as she did her face: rouge goes from under the eyes, outwards to the ear; metallic shimmery grey shadow for the evenings; gloss goes over the lipstick, etc, etc. She studied her reflection in the mirror once she was done—and winced. Her red lips looked bright against her wan face, a Geisha-like effect. She wondered if she had overdone her eye shadow. She made a moue. That was the problem with not using make-up regularly; one had no idea what worked when it came to a crunch situation.

She turned away from her reflection. There was no point in starting over, she would end up looking the same. She picked up her black evening purse and arranged it stylishly on her arm. She sprayed on some fancy French perfume that she had purchased two days ago. It smelt of frankincense and violet wood. Finally, she struggled into her ridiculously thin and high black sandals, stumbling as she tried to slip the straps on. She sat down carefully on the living room sofa, picked up the phone and called for a cab. Then she went down to the foyer to wait for it to arrive. She ran into her neighbour, an elderly gentleman, at the lobby, and amusedly registered the admiring expression on his face. Though she was tempted to go back to her apartment, she tossed the idea out of her head because she did not trust herself to be alone. She might end up wondering why she was doing this and get into her Bugs Bunny pyjamas. She did not want to question her decision—the answers scared her.

Luckily, the cab arrived quickly and she was at Rohan's place before she could even say 'seduction'. He answered the door at the first chime of the bell, as though he had been standing on the other side, waiting for it to ring.

'Hi Rohan.' She dragged the syllables out, her manicured fingers playing with her damp hair.

Damn, he looked good enough to eat in his khaki shorts

and olive T-shirt that beautifully set off his dark skin. He must have just stepped out of the shower himself—she could smell the heady mix of his soap and cologne.

Rohan's eyes widened seeing her. He sputtered as he tried to form a coherent reply.

'Won't you ask me in?' she drawled, her eyes lingering over him.

He cleared his throat. He dragged his eyes away from her smooth legs and settled them on her face. He stepped back and waved her inside the apartment. Mira trailed her fingers over his face as she passed him. She sunk into the leather couch in the living room and crossed her legs to allow her dress to ride up another inch. Queen Clarisse be damned.

Rohan stood frozen to his spot, and watched her for a whole minute before he moved.

'How about a drink?' he asked nonchalantly. He held her eyes with his. He was back in control. Mira shifted in her seat and felt queasiness in the pit of her stomach. *Alka-Seltzer, please?*

'I'll have whatever you are planning on having,' she gave a seductive smile.

'I was going to have gin,' he said, pointing to the attractive bottle and the cut-glasses on the table. Then a mischievous smile formed on his mouth. 'But having seen what tequila can do to you, I think not.' She flushed but said nothing.

His eyes travelled from the tips of her toes to her hair, lingering on all the right places. 'I need you to be conscious tonight,' he said with a teasing smile. What she needed tonight was something stronger than gin, something that would make her pass out altogether, Mira thought. She stretched her arm over the back of the couch and sank farther into it.

'I think I can handle the gin, or whatever else, tonight,'

she said, her eyes never leaving his. Her voice rippled low in the room.

He held his glass up in a salute and went off to the kitchen.

He returned with a stemmed glass holding some blood-red liquid.

'I have this really nice Cabernet Sauvignon I think you will enjoy.'

As she reached to take it from him, his fingers brushed over hers. She tried not to roll her eyes; it was an old ploy. But like many time-tested moves, it worked and Mira forgot to breathe.

Strains of Tchaikovsky's *Pathétique* played softly in the background. He sat down beside her and laid his arm on hers. He watched her sip the wine, her delicate mouth matching the wine's crimson. He was close enough for Mira to smell his warm breath and catch the desire in his eyes. She was mesmerized, despite the images of Sanya and Rohan pricking her at the back of her mind.

'Allow me,' he whispered into her hair, taking the glass away from her. He nuzzled his face into her neck and hungrily caressed her. A minute later, she was in his arms, and they were kissing passionately. Mira was familiar with the love scenes from romance novels, and had even memorized some moves for future reference. But now, when his lips were on hers, her mind had completely blanked out. Strangely, her body didn't seem to have such problems. Her tongue willingly explored his mouth and she vaguely registered that his hand was on the small of her back.

Suddenly, she withdrew from him, feeling cold. Her eyes flew to her dress and realized that it was now dangerously high on her thighs. Before she could gather her thoughts, Rohan pulled her to her feet. 'Let's move to somewhere more comfortable,' he said in a low tone. He wrapped his arms around her and planted small kisses all over her body as they walked to his bedroom. Her skin tingled. She had never known one could kiss their lover as they walked—Rohan picked her up in one liquid motion—or kiss so passionately while carrying said lover in the white-knight-rescues-flaxen-haired-damsel style.

He placed her gently on the bed. Then he was beside her, sliding her dress off her shoulders, kissing her body, his hand moving down and taking off her fifty-dollar thong in a swift jerk, and casually tossing it on the floor.

'You are so beautiful,' he sighed, his tongue teasing the peaking tips of her breasts, first one, then the other. She didn't want him to stop. She tugged at his shirt. He paused and helped her take it off.

'Impatient, aren't you?' he said.

'Shut up and keep doing whatever it is you are doing,' she muttered.

He laughed and buried his face into her breasts again. He drew in a sharp breath as her fingers scraped his nipples. Lips, tongues and fingers were everywhere. She didn't know she could feel this way—so desired, so...pleasured. When he moved over her, her legs slowly parted to let him in. He shifted his body and gently moved inside her, making her moan. She wrapped her legs around him and moved with him in swift jerks. Her world spiralled out of control. 'Let go, darling,' he whispered. She did, and a minute later, they both went over the edge.

Much later, when she could finally feel her limbs again, she realized that she could lie beside him forever. He shifted slightly and she stiffened. *Don't leave me, Rohan.* She made a protesting sound and wrapped her arms tighter around him.

'Hush, baby, I'm right here,' he said, drawing her into his arms.

They lay quietly together, feeling the warmth of their bodies and their slowing pulses. The lights outside filtered in through the curtains, giving the room an unreal glow,

'Thank you,' said Rohan and kissed her closed eyelids. 'It was incredible.'

'No, thank *you*,' she remarked, savouring the taste of him on her lips. 'I never thought it would be this beautiful.' She could feel his smile on her hair. She wound her arm around him and they both fell asleep within minutes.

When she woke up in the morning, the irony of her surroundings hit her. She was in the same bed, wrapped up in the same purple sheet and she could still smell Rohan—on her. His arm was a steel trap around her, his athletic legs pinned hers down. She liked being imprisoned this way, she realized, horrified at the kinky thought. She turned and saw Rohan's generous mouth and eyes closed in deep sleep. He looked... satisfied. There was no other word for it. But was she?

Mira jerked and sat upright, pulling the sheet around her. The room suddenly felt chilly. This was ridiculous; she was disgusted with herself. One touch of his little finger and the Bitch Goddess had vanished last night. Rohan was the kryptonite to her Superman—one whiff and *bam*, the Bitch Goddess was down. There was just Mira—needy, emotional Mira. Stupid, stupid woman. Bitch Goddesses never allowed themselves to get emotionally entangled with men. They played with them and tossed them by the wayside. She looked at Rohan's calm face and felt something tug at her heart. What was she going to do now? What will happen to her grandiose plan to get back at him?

She considered her options. Wait a minute, she told herself, a sudden spurt of confidence coursing through her, feeling like Popeye after a shot of spinach. So she had turned into an emotional, needy fool. But Rohan didn't need to know that, did he? She could still lead him on. She lay back down, breathing hard as her mind raced. Fine, so that's what she would do. Play the Bitch Goddess all the way through. She had only a vague idea of how she was going to do that. But it was important that she got back in character before she and Rohan interacted again. She had to be in full control of the situation and not allow herself to go weak in the knees at the mere sight of this suave NUS professor. Damn, she didn't know professors could be so charming. All this meant was she had to get out of here before Rohan woke up.

Her mind made up, she tossed the sheet aside. He murmured and turned to the other side, and she stayed still until she was sure he was asleep again. She slipped out of bed and crawled on the floor, retrieving her underwear and the dress. She quickly got dressed, grabbed her purse, picked up her shoes and rushed out of the apartment door.

Mira fled down the stairs, not waiting for the lift; not caring that Rohan, too, lived on the thirteenth floor. She was a Bitch Goddess—she couldn't afford to feel sappy about such coincidences. She stopped at the foyer, only to put on her shoes. Then she dashed out of the building, onto the road. She waited at the curb for a taxi. Luckily, a cab came by within minutes, and she got into it gratefully. She gave the cabbie her address and the vehicle shot down the road.

Mira stared out of the window, not really seeing the passing buildings, people and trees. She had been naive, the way she had set off last night to seduce this obviously experienced man. She wasn't even sure what had happened there, except that she had lost control and let her emotions get the better of her. He had led and she had followed. Never mind that she had fun following, but that had not been the original plan. *She* should have been the one leading, making the moves and *he* should have been the one needing, wanting. She chewed on her lips. In fact, she had lost more than her virginity last night. But she couldn't put her finger on what exactly it was that she had lost.

Bitch Goddess Rule #11: Even the Little Black Dress can fail.

Blast from the Past

*I*t was a sense of loss that made Rohan wake up. He reached
out to the space beside him and found it empty. He pushed
aside his bed covers and hopped down from the bed. Where was
she? The bathroom door was open but she was nowhere to be
seen. Couldn't she have stayed put in bed till he woke up? He
put on some clothes and freshened up. He went to the kitchen,
hoping she was making them breakfast. He couldn't deny the
idea pleased him. Strip off the veneer of sophistication and
under every male, however evolved he might be, there lurked
a being that wanted his woman in the kitchen, chopping the
vegetables and grinding the spices.

He strode through the living room and entered the kitchen.
Nope, not here. He went to the balcony and the other bedroom
that served as his study. She was nowhere in the house. Why
had she run away like this?

Rohan went back to the kitchen and mechanically made
some coffee. He pondered over her behavior, both puzzled and
annoyed by it. Last night had been great; he was sure it had
been wonderful for her, too. What had happened between then
and now that had made her leave without even a 'goodbye'?
He frowned at the word; he didn't want it to be a 'goodbye'.
With a start he realized that he wanted more than friendship—
or whatever it was that they were sharing—from her. Rohan
glanced through the papers, not really reading them, and
thoughtfully sipped his coffee. Then it hit him as to why he

felt so disturbed by Mira's absence. He hadn't felt this way about any other woman before. Not that there was a history of women in his life, but he had had his share of girlfriends. Still, no woman had deserted him like this the morning after a passionate night, without even a by-your-leave. Rohan was not arrogant, but he had a healthy dose of pride; he knew he was attractive to women and smug about his prowess in bed.

Mira—after what they had shared last night—owed him an explanation. Last night had been wonderful. In fact, just being with Mira was wonderful, not just the sex. So wonderful, he realized, that he had begun thinking of something more solid than a mere fling. He wanted permanence—and that scared him.

He put the dirty cup in the sink, not in the mood to do the dishes. He was livid. How dare she run off like that? She could have at least texted him or left him a note. Rohan paced the living room. Maybe the whole experience had disappointed her. But that didn't give her the right to be so thoughtless or hurtful! She owed him an explanation, some answers. That was the decent thing to do.

Rohan showered, soaping himself savagely, all the time battling with his muddled thoughts. He fixed himself some breakfast and tried to block memories of sharing breakfast with her just yesterday morning. His first instinct was to charge over to her apartment and grab her and demand answers. But he ignored the thought. He wanted to think this through more carefully. Even at the university, he was known for painstakingly weighing his options before acting. Prof. Careful, that's what his students called him. This was no different; better to hit the brake and take a pause. He put his uneaten bagel back in the fridge and paced some more in the living room. But the anger that surged through his veins didn't subside. He wanted to go somewhere and get a grip on this. Sentosa. That would give him the distance he needed—and make Mira impatient to hear from him.

He grabbed his keys and slammed the door shut behind him.

Rohan got into the cable car that glided over the wire to reach Sentosa Island. He watched the waves below sparkle like shards of glass, already feeling more relaxed here than he had been at the apartment. He got off the cable car and shuffled in with the crowd walking towards Underwater World. It was a relief to escape the hot sun and step into such cool surroundings. He stood on the walkalator, barely noticing the fishes that swam silently in their glass cases.

Mira. He just couldn't get her out of his mind. He remembered the way her body had willingly responded to his caresses and the way she had clung to him while asleep. He remembered the way her eyes widened when he had kissed her and the flush on her face when he had complimented her body. He chuckled softly when he recalled her clumsy attempts to seduce him at the restaurant. His temper began to dissipate. Nah, she couldn't have dumped him. Knowing her, she was probably running scared. The always-in-control Mira must have felt out of her depth when she succumbed to her desire. Yeah, that was it. She must have needed to think things through and fled the scene in confusion. It was not the best way to address her qualms, but, hey, she was a little naive when it came to men, he could see. The poor girl. For all the come-hither looks and seductive charm she threw his way, he instinctively knew she had been a virgin—till last night. It must have been too much for her to handle at once.

He stepped off the walkalator and wandered into the dolphin show. He idly watched the dolphins juggle balls and leap through hoops.

Rohan frowned in contemplation. But not all was innocent

about Mira. There *was* something else going on with her. He could see it in the appraising glances she often threw his way, or the guarded look that sometimes came into her eyes when they were together. What was she hiding from him? But last night had been magic. Mira had given herself completely to him, with total abandonment. Which was why he had been surprised to find her missing in the morning.

Maybe she had fled to rebuild her defenses. Rohan clapped with the crowd as the show ended. He made his way back in the cable car to the city, lost in his thoughts.

So he would give her time, if that's what she wanted. He would gradually discover the real Mira, and not rush it. He liked the Mira he saw last night, not the guarded woman who kept her cards close to her chest. So for a start, he would knock on her door that evening. He would not confront her, if that is what she was expecting of him. He would be charming and romantic and slowly chip away at her defenses. Then he would wait and watch, and see where the road led them.

Mira was both amazingly relaxed and extremely fatigued at the same time. She savoured the quiet of the morning as she paid off the cabbie and rode the empty lift to her floor. She was glad to have the lift to herself that day. She stepped out on her floor, walked down the corridor to her apartment—and stopped. An attractive young woman was sitting on a strolley, just outside her door.

Mira was tired, filled with anger towards herself and emotionally drained. Moreover, her killer shoes were killing her. What she really wanted to do was throw away the shoes, get out of her ridiculous black dress and take a nice long warm bath. And what she did *not* want was to walk into a strange young woman sitting on some pink luggage at her door.

The girl got to her feet. The women warily sized each other up, each trying to place the other. And then recognition flickered in Mira's eyes, making her feel a bit faint. She went cold.

She straightened her shoulders and titled her chin. 'Who are you?' she asked brusquely. 'And why are you here?' But Mira already knew, looking at the girl's familiar warm brown eyes.

She walked past the girl and slid her key into the doorlock.

'I think you know who I am,' said the girl quietly, registering Mira's reaction.

'Why are you here?' Mira repeated her question.

The girl shrugged her bony shoulders, her delicate child-woman features gaunt beyond her years. 'I've run away.' Her voice was soft but had a clear, silvery quality to it.

Mira's hand paused on the doorknob before pushing the door open. She entered her apartment. and turned to face the girl.

'Good for you. But that still doesn't answer my question.' She took off her sandals and flung her handbag on the couch. She made no move to invite the girl inside.

The girl looked pointedly at Mira, her hand clutching the strolley's handle. 'May I please come in? Maybe we could talk inside?'

Mira studied the younger woman who was clad in a white T-shirt and jeans. Her hair fell in soft tendrils around her face, lending her a waif-like look. Mira was impressed at her poise, and her guts. If Mira had had that, she wouldn't be wearing the silly black dress this morning.

'You can come in, but that doesn't mean you are staying,' said Mira firmly.

The girl nodded and rolled her stroller through the door.

Mira shut the door and double-latched it, as if fearing more unwanted surprises showing up at her doorstep.

Mira sank into the couch and waved the girl to sit down. She sat next to Mira and smiled faintly at her. Mira chose to ignore such overtures.

'You are...Amita, right?' said Mira. A dim memory flickered in her mind: her mother was showing her a photograph, another of her zillion attempts to get Mira to meet her father. In the photograph, her father was sitting on an armchair, flanked on either side by two pre-teenagers. 'Your half-sister and your half-brother,' her mother had explained in a quiet voice. But all Mira could see was the protective manner in which the handsome man embraced the kids, and their happy, shining faces. Her mother had told her their names, Amita and Aman. Though Mira had feigned disinterest at the time, she had never forgotten their names or their faces.

Mira threw a quick glance at the young woman beside her. Amita had not changed much in these eight years.

The girl's eyes widened in surprise. 'Yes,' her voice was very faint. 'How do you even remember?'

Mira waved her hands dismissively. 'That's the cross we humans bear, remembering things best forgotten.'

Amita looked at Mira quizzically, but said nothing. She stared at her sneakers and muttered. 'I have run away from home.'

'I got that part. But, for the millionth time, why are you *here*?' Mira shot back, gesticulating at the apartment. She was not going to go all good-Samaritan on *this* girl.

Amita's eyes flew to Mira's face. Once again Mira was startled to see how much Amita's brown eyes resembled her—their—father's.

'I got here because this is the last place they'll think of looking for me.'

Mira's brows knit together in a frown. 'Hmm...let me see, you wanted to run away from home, which is in Chennai, for God-knows-what-reason, and you didn't want to be found. So you took a flight and came to Singapore, and walked right through my door. Smart move.'

Amita squirmed in her seat.

Mira glared at Amita. 'Now, tell me the truth. I think basic courtesy, if nothing else, demands that you tell me the truth—especially if you come barging into my home like this.' Seeing Amita made Mira remember the Other Woman. Her head hurt at the memory and she was desperate to get into the shower.

Amita swallowed hard. 'You are right, Mira. I should not have barged in like this.' She waved her hands in the air. 'But what to do? My circumstances made me come here.'

Mira cocked her eyebrows at her.

'Okay, let me explain.' I am trying to be a professional singer and am a member of a music troupe called *Desi Beats*.'

Mira remembered reading about them somewhere.

'So we got this invitation to perform at a gig at Singapore and I grabbed the chance.' Amita's voice dropped a pitch. 'I don't want to go back home, I need to fix my life. This is the one place where *they* will not look for me.' She sank back in the sofa, exhausted from her little speech.

Mira ran an appraising eye over Amita. *You don't know my mother, she can give Miss Marple a complex.*

'Let's see. You are what, seventeen?'

'Eighteen,' Amita said.

'Right, eighteen. Privileged kid of rich family, had a cushy life, one small wish thwarted and she ran away from home. What is it, boyfriend issues?' Mira bit the words out.

Amita shook her head. 'No, this is the truth, Mira. I ran

away from home...because of my singing. There is no boyfriend angle to it.'

'Your singing?' Mira was confused.

Amita nodded.

'My running away also had something to do with you...' Amita trailed, her brown eyes sliding away.

Mira sat up. 'Huh? Me?'

'Yes. Papa wanted me to become an engineer. Just like you.' Mira's skin prickled at the word. Papa? Amita and her brother called him Papa? Mira closed her eyes, the frizzy teddy bear swimming in the jetsam of her memories. She used to call him Appa when he was still, well, her father. Of late, though, she had been calling him a lot of unflattering, unmentionable things.

Mira blinked. 'Like me? Now why would he want you to be just like me?'

Amita rolled her eyes. 'Oh, you have, like, nooo idea. You are Papa's darling. "Mira is this, Mira is that, she can do no wrong... etc etc." He brags about you and your academic achievements to anybody who is willing to listen.' Amita laughed without rancour.

Mira kept her tone flat and her face emotionless. 'This, from a man, who, though my father, hasn't seen me since I was ten years old?'

Amita fell silent and waited for Mira to continue.

'Hmm...so he doesn't want you to be a singer and wants you to be an engineer,' concluded Mira.

'Yep. He wants me to join his firm and become a chip-and-code talking engineer.'

Mira mulled over this, taking her own time to digest all this information. She had always known that her father ran a successful software firm that sold some hi-end software. In fact, the company was as old as her, for he had started it the year she was born. Of late, after its tie-up with a German company, her father's firm was regularly mentioned in the media.

Mira shook her head, hoping the memories would wither away like day-old flowers. 'Alright, forget about me for a second. Let's talk about why *you* are here, in *my* house.'

Amita shrugged. 'It all has to do with my singing.'

Mira folded her hands, waiting for Amita to continue.

'I like to sing and, I am pretty good at it,' Amita said simply, without a trace of vanity.

Mira grudgingly admired her half-sister's confidence.

'But Papa doesn't like my singing,' Amita grimaced. 'He is happy as long as I treat it like a hobby. In fact he encourages me to develop it as a passtime. "Everybody needs something to help them relax," is his favourite litany. But what he doesn't get is that I am extremely serious about music. I want to become a professional singer some day.'

Mira nodded encouragingly. She was all for pursuing one's dreams—whether it was to become the most lethal Bitch Goddess or to become the next Shreya Ghoshal.

'I want to become a playback singer,' Amita said, as if reading Mira's thoughts. 'When I joined *Desi Beats* last year, Papa was unhappy. But he didn't stop me.' She rubbed her tired eyes. 'I think he hoped it would be a passing fancy. That singing with a troupe would get this…this obsession out of my system.'

'What about your studies?' asked Mira. A nagging thought at the back of her head questioned why she should even bother with so much information. Who was Amita to her, after all? An unfortunate genetic connection, at best.

'This year I am applying for colleges. I applied to engineering colleges like how he wanted but, on the sly, I also applied to some music colleges. I didn't tell anyone, not even my mom— why stir up trouble?'

Mira's eyes glazed over at the mention of the Other Woman. But she understood Amita's underhanded plans. She wished she had been so savvy in life, then Rohan may not have happened. She flinched at his name and looked down at her crumpled dress.

Amita continued, 'Then last week, I got into a music program at a university.'

Mira was getting impatient. She didn't want to know all the sordid details of this girl. It would just make her more involved with people she had spent her whole life avoiding.

'What's that got to do with you being here? Don't tell me it's the university here. '

Amita's eyes shone. 'No! It's in the UK. So I told Papa I was joining that course to become a professional singer.' She exhaled and held her head in her hands. 'And all hell broke loose. He raved and ranted and told me there was no way he would allow this. Then I argued that I would do nothing else but sing till I go to my grave. Threats, blackmail, tears and shouting—it was an explosive scene at home. I got mad, packed my bag and came here with my troupe.'

Mira held up her hand. 'Wait a minute. You've run away from home to come here? To Singapore? You should have plotted your move to the UK, instead.'

Amita shook her head. 'No, this is just a temporary escape route for me. My troupe performed last week and the rest of the members have have returned—only I stayed back.'

'Yes, I can see that,' said Mira, testily.

'What was I thinking?' Amita's voice quivered, her earlier bravado suddenly missing. She pulled her legs up and rested her chin on her knees. 'The shouting match happened last week. I was so angry, I wanted to get out. I was packing my bags with no clear idea of where I was going. Then I got this idea and just came here with the troupe.'

'But how did you find me?' said Mira.

Amita stared at the distance. 'From Papa's address book. When I got the idea of coming here, I somehow remembered you—Papa talks a lot about your success at Singapore to my brother and me. I looked through his book on a hunch, and found your address there.'

Mira felt nauseous. She didn't want to know anything more. She wanted to plug her ears and shut them—her father, the Other Woman, Amita—all out. They made her hurt. Worse, they made her *feel* things that had lain numb in her system for years. Something was slowly stirring within her, something that hadn't in seventeen years. She squeezed her eyes shut. *Bitch Goddesses should not feel pain. If there was no rule about that, there ought to be one.*

Mira raised an eyebrow and asked in a saccharine voice, 'Does that mean I can expect more...err...visitors henceforth?'

Amita considered her question, grabbing its implication. 'I certainly hope not,' she mumbled.

After a few minutes of silence, Mira asked, 'But why me? You could have sought someone else's help. I Still. Don't. Get. It.'

Amita shifted in her chair. 'I don't have much cash. The group has already left, and I had to check out of the hotel. I needed a place to stay and so I figured...' she shot Mira a meaningful look, her eyes pleading.

'And you just assumed you would be welcome here?' Mira smirked. 'So are you planning to move in with me forever?'

'Of course not,' Amita denied vehemently and then backtracked. 'Don't know, I might have to stay with you for just a week, maybe ten days. I'll pay you.'

'This is not a hotel,' said Mira in an icy tone. She was in no mood to readily embrace a long-lost half-sister in 70mm style. 'Hmm...what exactly do you plan to do next?'

Amita's face brightened. 'I have some money of my own saved up. I need to earn some more to join that music program in the UK.'

Mira looked at her incredulously. 'Find a job here? Are you out of your mind? Do you know it takes work permits and other legal formalities to find employment in Singapore?'

Amita stretched her mouth. 'Yes, of course, I know that. See, here's the thing. I will go back to India after a couple of weeks. My visa's for a whole month.' She sounded confused, defiant and lost. She faltered, taking in Mira's silence. 'Maybe I'll find a job in Bangalore? I...I have some friends there...'

Mira tried recalling how it was to be eighteen. She didn't remember cooking up any such improbable hare-brained schemes, though. Even through her bitterness, Mira realized she should do the right thing. She should probably give Amita a Big Sister lecture and put her on the next flight home. But something held her back. She was reluctant to get too involved and risk coming face-to-face with the people she most wished to avoid. Amita was technically an adult and, therefore, responsible for her own actions. It was none of Mira's business what Amita did.

'You do realize, Amita,' she said mildly, 'that you will have to come up with a better plan than this if you want to go to that college in the UK?'

Amita nodded sullenly. 'Do you have any ideas?' Her eyes searched Mira's face.

Mira rose to her feet. 'No. I am not even going to think up any for you either. In fact, I haven't yet made up my mind about what to do with you. I am going have to think about this. Right now, I need a bath and, mind you, I am going to take a really long one. We'll talk after that.' She wagged her finger at Amita as she left the room. 'Don't run away with the silver.'

Amita gave a hesitant smile, unsure whether this tough-talking elder half-sister of her's was serious or joking.

Mira gratefully soaked her tired limbs in the hot water and mulled over what had just transpired. It was a bit surreal that she had her father's other daughter in her house. 'My half-sister,' she whispered, afraid to get used to this word. She rubbed her loofah over herself and watched the foam settle over her limbs. She decided to let Amita stay, maybe for the next two weeks, not longer. An evil smile formed on her lips. Amita's family would be in a state of panic, not knowing where their precious daughter had gone. It would be interesting to watch her father and the Other Woman experience sleepless nights. What was it they said about life coming full circle?

Then Mira clenched the sides of her bathtub, her heart pounding. What if her mother got involved in the manhunt for Amita? Then all bets were off.

Girl Goes Missing

When Mira stepped out of the bath, the first thing she saw was the black dress, lying in a heap on the floor. Rohan. She had forgotten all about him in the midst of Amita walking into her life. Mira sat down on her bed with a heavy feeling, unmindful of the wet towel wrapped around her. Up until last week, the most troublesome aspects in her life had been dealing with Sanya and having a heartfelt chat with her mother. Now there was her half-sister waiting in the living room and somewhere in this city, there was Rohan, the man she had lost her virginity to. She grabbed her phone—there were no missed calls or messages from him. It was way past noon; surely, he would be awake by now? Wouldn't he have discovered that she had gone without telling him? She tossed the phone aside. Great. She must have been lousy in bed last night. He probably didn't want anything to do with her from now onwards. She shivered, the towel's dampness seeped into her skin. She gave a lopsided smile. Look at the bright side, she told herself; one problem had resolved itself, viz., Rohan. She rubbed her bare arms. Then why did she feel so bereft?

Mira slipped on a pair of shorts and a sleeveless T-shirt and walked out of the bedroom. Amita was sprawled out on the living room sofa, watching television. Mira curbed her irritation at how much the younger woman seemed at home there. She had to get into her act and couldn't afford to expend her energy on unnecessary emotions like anger.

'Amita,' she said, 'I thought about this, you can stay with me for about a week or two. But that means you should figure out in this time, whatever it is that you wish to do.'

'Yay, thank you!' said Amita. She jumped to her feet and gave Mira a quick hug. Mira stiffened, unable to hug the girl who shared a troubled past with her. She looked sternly at Amita. 'I don't want—I repeat, I *don't* people from your family barging in here or calling me and telling me to send their little girl home.'

Amita looked taken aback. 'Are you kidding? Nobody knows I am here. Nobody will even *think* of looking for me here. Why do you think I came here at all?'

Mira nodded. 'Let's keep it that way, shall we?'

'Er...' Amita paused hesitantly. 'What about your mother? She won't come to know, right...?

'Nope.' Mira crossed her fingers behind her back. '*I* definitely won't tell her.' That part was true.

She eyed Amita's strolley. 'You can take the first room on the left, down that corridor,' she said matter-of-factly, pointing to the passageway. 'It has an attached bath; let me know if you need soap or shampoo.'

Amita shot her a grateful smile.

'You are free to eat with me, of course. And you can use the spare key,' Mira added. She took it out of the cabinet near the dining table and handed it to her. 'This will ensure that we won't be in each other's way.'

Amita pulled her suitcase behind her. 'Thank you,' she said softly, as she crossed Mira to go to her room.

Mira nodded and went off to the kitchen.

'I made some coffee,' Amita called out.

Mira saw the pot warming on the machine and gritted her teeth. She was not used to anyone using her kitchen.

'And I also toasted some bagels. Be back in a bit.' Amita's voice travelled across the apartment.

Mira put the bagels on a plate, poured coffee into her mug and took them to the dining room. She took cheese from the fridge, picked up some cutlery and placed it on the table. She sat down, feeling ravenous. Amita joined her after a few minutes, her face scrubbed and her hair pulled back in a neat ponytail.

'I suppose you have eaten?' Mira asked.

Amita shook her head. 'No, no...I just thought I might make myself useful while I waited.'

Mira chewed her lips. 'What if I had been a tea drinker? What if I had meant to have the bagel for lunch?'

Amita looked stricken. 'I did look for tea, but I didn't find it. I never thought... I am sorry...' Her face fell.

Mira couldn't help being bitchy. It had become second nature to her these days. She bit into a bagel. 'Don't you want breakfast?'

Amita nodded timidly.

'What are you waiting for? C'mon, get a plate and get started.'

Amita took a plate and slathered some butter on a bagel. 'Thank you...' she began hesitantly. 'What do I call you? Didi? You are my elder sister, after all.'

Mira shot her a dark look. 'Just Mira will do. Never Didi, if you value your life.'

Amita's eyes gleamed, unfazed by Mira's frosty tone.

They both ate in silence. After a few minutes Amita asked in an undertone, 'Why did you agree to let me stay?'

Mira considered the young woman's forthright question. 'Because I remember how it is to feel helpless and angry when you are eighteen,' Mira said after a long pause. She gave a guarded smile and sipped some coffee. She could have bitten her tongue off. She didn't know where the answer had come from.

'Thank you,' Amita said again, smiling warmly.

They finished their breakfast in silence. They cleared the breakfast table, each lost in her thoughts. When Amita retired to her room for some rest, Mira was glad to be left to her own solitude. She wasn't sure if she was inviting trouble by taking the girl in. But she instinctively knew that that had been the right thing to do.

She wasn't used to another person constantly underfoot, so she was glad when Amita went off to sleep, leaving Mira to get on with her Sunday chores.

Mira and Amita were slouched in front of the TV when the door bell rang. They looked wide-eyed at each other, the same thought crossing their minds.

'Did you tell anybody you were coming here?' said Mira.

'No, even my troupe members don't have a clue.' Amita looked equally bewildered.

'Let's hope it's not the other errant member of your family,' Mira muttered, the meaning not lost on either of them. She waited until Amita disappeared into her room before she opened the door.

'Rohan!' she managed, when she saw him standing outside her door. The day was bringing one surprise after another.

'Hi Mira,' he said and thrust a glorious bouquet of pale orange and pink orchids into her hands. Mira arranged a smile on her face, feeling a bit wary and awkward. Colour rose to her cheeks when images of last night flashed in her mind.

'Come in,' she said. 'Make yourself comfortable while I find a vase for this.' She rushed into the kitchen without meeting his eyes.

Why is he here? I hope he doesn't cause a scene. Oh God, what am I going to tell him? She uttered her mantra: *Think Bitch Goddess. Be Bitch Goddess.*

By the time she had found her only glass vase, filled it with water and dunked the flowers in, she had gotten into her Bitch Goddess role. She decided to keep it casual and make it a no-strings-attached relationship that will allow her—or him—to walk out; no questions asked. Then, she made the mistake of pressing her face into the glorious flowers. She closed her eyes and breathed in their redolence. The mantra played in her head again and she snapped back to reality. No, she wasn't going to let a clutch of the most beautiful blossoms she had ever seen in her life disarm her. This time, she won't be an emotional fool. She smoothed her hand over her hair and went to the living room.

When she walked out, her mouth was curved in a smile. Rohan was in the living room balcony, leaning on the railing, and watching the scene below. She stood beside him, her hand gently brushing against his. 'Thanks for the flowers. They are beautiful,' she said shyly.

Rohan turned to meet her gaze. 'You are most welcome, they seemed to suit you.' He slid an arm around her shoulders and held her close to him. They stood like this in amicable silence for some time, watching dusk unfold in the sky.

Mira leaned on him and then started. Damn. She had been lulled. Despite herself, she was seduced by the heady combination of his aftershave cologne, his minty breath and the warmth of his body. She looked sideways at him and approved of his crisp white shirt and jeans. She was grateful he was not one of those dandy dressers like many New Age Indian men seemed to be. There were some in her office who wore purple satin shirts and bling. *Eww.*

'Penny for your thoughts?' said Rohan. He rubbed his cheek against her hair and quietly remarked, 'You could have woken me up before you left this morning. Is there something you wish to discuss?'

Take deep breaths, Mira. Choose your words carefully. First, I owe you an apology. I should not have run off like that. Sorry.'

'What was the reason?' he said.

'Nothing specific. I have no idea what is going on here,' she replied, waving her arms in the air. 'I am confused and terrified as hell. And...I am sorry for sneaking out like a thief. I was planning to message you later but never got around to doing it...I guess I just lost my nerve. I wanted to be by myself and gather my thoughts...'

He laughed softly and rubbed her back. 'And I thought you had dumped me.' He looked deep into her eyes. 'Then I remembered how you were with me last night.'

She reddened at the memory.

'I...me...I mean...' she started.

'You were confused,' he cut her off. 'Good, one is supposed to feel confused and terrified at this stage.'

Mira didn't detect any sarcasm in his tone. *Do you feel the same way?* she wanted to ask. But she was not ready for that kind of honesty. The lesser she knew about what he felt, the easier it would be for her to play her part without getting emotionally entangled.

'The only thing for us to do here is to slow down,' he said.

Mira nodded uncertainly. *What was going on here? Why wasn't he mad?*

'I thought we could start with a dinner for two tonight?' Rohan's eyes questioned her. He caught the counter-question on her face and wagged a finger. 'No hanky panky, just dinner.' His eyes danced and Mira's face flamed again.

'Let's take it easy and not rush into anything,' he added seriously, cupping her face in his hands

Take it easy? Not rush? Why was this sounding attractive to her when she had no intention of a long-term serious relationship? Think, Mira, a voice in her head said. Remember Sanya. You are being dealt a new hand.

Bitch Goddess Rule #12: A Bitch Goddess plays to win. Every time.

Mira looked into Rohan's eyes. 'Sounds like a plan. I'll just change and come.'

He checked his watch. 'Ten minutes?'

'More like thirty,' she said with a shaky smile and walked towards her bedroom. She didn't know where this was headed, but she was damn well going to find out. And the nice side benefit of this game was the time she would get to spend in sexy Rohan's company. The Bitch Goddess got the cake and the icing too.

Rohan watched her leave the room. He wore a serious look—something else was definitely going on here. It could just be nerves, as Mira claimed, or something deeper. Knowing that she had been a virgin until last night, it could well be that she was overwhelmed by the suddenness of what had happened. But then, why did he have this niggling feeling that something else was running through her formidable brain? Whatever it was, he was going to get to the bottom of it, he promised himself. Two could play the game.

When Mira reentered her building a few hours later, she was confused, puzzled and extremely frustrated. It had been a

good—no, great—evening by all accounts. Rohan had taken her to this exclusive Italian place near Holland; the food had been fantastic, the wine exceptional—she had managed to remain sober—and the tiramisu, perfect. He had outdone himself by being the perfect dinner companion. He had generously complimented her, flirted with her and made sure their bodies touched whenever he got the chance. And the kiss when he had dropped her...she was surprised the car's upholstery had not caught fire. He had been as affected by it as she had been, she could tell. Though she sensed he had already made plans for their next date, she was also astute enough to realize that they both were playing mind games with each other. She wasn't sure of what his true intentions were towards her and she would be loathe to discuss Sanya with him.

But the whole thing unsettled her; especially since the evening had gone to perfection. She was annoyed at herself. Why did she have to like the man and complicate matters in her mind? Why did she have to kiss like the devil who would have sold her soul? Arrgghh. Why, oh why, couldn't she forget that night she had spent in his bed? In the bloody Little Black Dress.

She took the elevator to her floor and heard the song even before she opened the front door. A clear, mellifluous voice was effortlessly navigating the low and high scales of a popular old Hindi film song, *Bolo re papi hara*. She knew at once that it was Amita. She was stunned at her talent and realized she could make it big, if only she got the right opportunity. She swung the door open. Anita was singing along with the song playing on an Indian TV channel.

'Hi!' Amita stopped mid-song and smiled self-consciously.

Mira barely glanced in her direction. 'Isn't it too late for errant girls to be up?'

'Um...your mother called, Mira,' said Amita.

'You spoke to her?' Mira raised her eyebrows.

'No way, I am not picking up any of your calls and letting anybody know I am here. It went to voicemail and her message came on.'

Mira switched on the machine.

'Mira, Amma here. Call me as soon as you can, even if it is late. Don't forget—okay?'

Her mother sounded anxious. Mira grimaced at the phone and opened the fridge.

'It's a nice red dress you're wearing. Hot date?' Amita asked with a big grin on her face.

'Hmm…I can't see why it's any of your business.' Mira drank some water from a bottle and put it back in the fridge.

Amita wordlessly went back to watching TV. Mira joined her on the couch. Amita turned to Mira after some time and remarked innocently, 'I remember reading somewhere that single children never learn to share their life with people.'

Mira clenched her fist. 'And I remember reading somewhere that it is rude to be nosy and ask personal questions to people you have just met.' She looked pointedly at Amita. 'I am going to bed. Goodnight.'

'You are brave, Mira,' Amita said in an appreciative tone, her eyes still glued to the TV screen.

Mira shot her a wary look.

'You are brave for not calling your mother back. She did sound worried…'

'Not right away. I like to live dangerously; why do you think I let you stay?' Mira replied breezily, with a short laugh.

As if on cue, the phone rang. Mira noted the caller ID and winced.

'Yes Amma, sure Amma,' she snivelled, ignoring the younger woman's smirk. 'I know, I know. I am sorry. I was just going to call you...' *What was one more lie in a million?*

Mira listened to her mother for some time before cutting in, 'But what happened? Why are you sounding so anxious?'

'Something terrible,' her mother declared with a loud sigh. 'You remember Amita?'

Mira bit back her smile and sat on a chair. This was going to be a fun conversation. 'Which Amita, Amma?' Mira tried to sound sincere and innocent. She cast a sidelong glance at Amita and put the phone on speaker.

'You know who I am talking about,' her mother said evenly. 'Your father—'

'What about Amita?' Mira quickly interrupted, not wishing for her mother to identify the family tree.

'She is missing! It seems she ran away from home after a quarrel with her family. They fought with her.' Her mother paused, as if searching for the right words. 'She wanted to become a singer or something. Her family didn't approve, so she ran away. At least that's why they feel she has run away. They are frantic and have been calling everybody they know...'

'Hmm...do you think she could have a boyfriend and eloped with him?' Mira asked, enjoying Amita's glare on her.

'Aiyyoo...I hope not,' her mother sounded stricken.

'Interesting, very interesting,' said Mira, distractedly playing with her hair.

'What, Mira? I know you are angry with them but this is such a big thing. Can't you say something besides "interesting"?'

'Amma, I am shocked, that's all. But how do *you* know this? Don't tell me you talk to those...those people every day.'

Her mother sighed. 'Mira, kanna, be sensible. Of course we don't talk every day. Why would we? But your father called me yesterday. I suppose he was distressed and couldn't think of any other person with whom he could share this problem.' She paused for a second. 'Anyway, don't you want to know what happened? It seems Amita sings with a music troupe and she went with them to—you won't believe this—Singapore!'

Mira gasped audibly, though she looked like she might collapse with laughter any minute. Amita made a face at her.

'Really?' Mira tried to inject concern in her voice.

'Yes, yes. The troupe got back yesterday—without Amita. It seems she didn't come home on her own, either. When the family called the troupe people, they washed their hands off the matter.'

Mira noted Amita's guilty look.

Her mother continued, 'It seems Amita had told the troupe people that she was leaving a day early to prepare for some college exams. Your father is raving and ranting at the troupe. They naturally claim that their members are all adults and the organizers are not responsible for such episodes once the show is over.' Her mother took in a breath. 'The problem is, nobody knows where she is. It is frightening.'

Mira made a sympathetic sound. She had no idea what to say.

'Mira,' her mother's voice dropped, 'Thank you, kanna.'

'Huh?'

'For not doing something like this. You have always been the good and responsible daughter.'

Mira swallowed the lump in her throat. She imagined her mother now, probably clad in one of her crêpe-de-Chine saris that she liked wearing on winter evenings, worrying the single braid she always wore, concern making her eyes drawn.

'Thanks, Amma,' she said, feeling waves of guilt washing over her.

'You know how Amita looks, right? If you want, I can email you a photo once her father sends it to me.'

'No, that won't be needed. I remember every feature of her's vividly,' said Mira curtly, her eyes sweeping over Amita.

'Then please call me in case you see someone who looks like Amita in Singapore…she is a young girl and no harm should befall her…'

Mira knew she herself could have never been as forgiving and gracious as her mother, had *her* husband abandoned her. Mira caught the admiring look on Amita's face, echoing her thoughts.

The phone went dead in her hands. Mira put the instrument down, fighting a sense of self-disgust. She refused to meet Amita's troubled eyes as she walked away towards her bedroom.

Hide and Seek

*M*ira peeped into Amita's room the next morning, just before she left for work, and immediately wished she hadn't. Amita was fast asleep, lying on her side, curled into a question mark and a hand tucked under her cheek. There was something so trusting about the whole scene that Mira felt a pang. She closed the door quickly. Mira could not afford pangs. She had to stay in character, both here and at office, where she had a plan to put into action. She was a busy Bitch Goddess, after all.

She had a quick breakfast and reached office, as she had hoped, by seven-thirty. Thankfully, there was no one else in yet—most people came in only by nine o'clock. She exhaled, dumped her things on her desk and waited for a few seconds. Then she went into Sanya's cubicle and gave a low whistle. The decor had changed. A potted bamboo occupied a corner on her desk, next to it sat a porcelain turtle, and just above that hung a mirror carved with some sort of symbols. Whoo! Who'd have thought the Resident Witch practiced feng shui!

Mira got to work. She wasn't going to let a little feng shui deter her. She booted Sanya's computer and a few minutes later, was into her files. Mira wasn't sure what she was looking for but was certain she would find something useful that she could use to her advantage. She browsed through several documents and emailed herself some, including a few pictures. The alarm in her phone went off. Her twenty minutes were up. Any longer and she could be in trouble. She quickly shut down the machine and left the cubicle. The only way anybody could know that she had been there would be if they dusted for fingerprints. There were no CCTVs and secret cameras installed inside the office—she had already ascertained this earlier.

A few minutes later, she was back at her desk, hard at work (real work), a cup of hibiscus tea steaming beside her. She enjoyed the solitude after the busy weekend that had thrown one surprise after another. Half-an-hour later, Mira heard the familiar heels click down the passage and stop near her desk. Mira continued working, a bland expression pasted on her face.

'Ah, Mira, I was hoping you would be in,' trilled Sanya. She was clad in a khaki skirt and a custard-lemon blouse. A white scarf was knotted stylishly around the neck. She towered in her six-inch tan shoes and looked down imperiously at Mira, her hands placed on her hips. Mira's gaze lingered on the scarf, fantasizing about tightening it around Sanya's neck.

Mira was normally on guard whenever Sanya assumed a friendly tone. But she was actually pleased to see her bête noire this morning. The afterglow of snooping on Sanya's computer still remained on her face.

'Good morning!' she said, with a huge grin.

Sanya blinked rapidly, as if trying to keep her wits about her. Then she did her usual straightening-of-shoulders and tossing-of-hair ritual, as if her powers lay there.

'You won't *believe* what I did over the weekend,' Sanya leaned forward over the cubicle wall, and spoke in a conspiratorial tone. As always, her recovery was fast.

'Try me,' Mira's voice was dulcet. 'I'll believe anything of you.' *And wait till you hear what I did over the weekend.*

Sanya blinked some more. 'So, anyway. I met Gerard and his wife at this club on Sunday.' She paused for effect. 'We had coffee together, the most delightful Brazilian brew I've ever tasted.'

'Hmm...' Mira said with forced interest, anticipating some bad news.

'So the group head thing came up,' Sanya gave a wily smile. 'He mentioned something about me being a strong contender.'

'Cool,' Mira nodded perfunctorily and went back to her Excel worksheet. That was a Bitch Goddess trick she had learnt along the way: to act uninterested in what your rival is saying, even if the earth is shifting beneath your feet.

Sanya ran her hand through her stylishy tousled hair. 'I know what you are thinking. Of course he—or I—wouldn't talk shop in a social meeting.' She rolled her eyes that read 'duh'. 'He just mentioned it in passing, you know how it is...'

Mira's eyes wore a blank look.

Sanya wiggled her red-tipped fingers. 'Ta, I should go now. I have tons of work to do.'

Mira once again looked longingly at the scarf around Sanya's neck and the use she could put it to.

Sanya turned on her heels. 'Oh, and I almost forgot. Do you know who I was with at the club?'

Mira looked at her warily.

'Rohan.' Sanya gave a tinkling laugh and walked away.

Bitch Goddess Rule #13: A natural Bitch Goddess is like a natural blonde. Peroxide can never compete with the real stuff and hope to win.

Why are you surprised? Mira told herself. After the pub incident, the writing on the wall was for all to see: Rohan was playing games with her. Her chest tightened and she felt uneasy. She had to get a grip on herself, and fast. She rushed to the ladies room and was relieved it was empty. She locked herself into one of the cubicles, lowered the lid and sat down. She cupped her chin in her hands. *Deep breaths, Mira.* When her breathing steadied and her mind became clearer, she was dismayed and angry that she was more upset with Rohan being with Sanya than with the conversation Gerard had supposedly had with Sanya. Mira thwacked her forehead. She was not supposed to get emotionally involved with Rohan, so why should it matter if he was two-timing her? Wasn't she too playing games with him? she thought dimly.

Think Bitch Goddess. Be Bitch Goddess. Feel Bitch Goddess. But all she felt was that she might break into hives. She had to do *something* now that would rattle Sanya's world. She remembered the stuff she had pilfered from Sanya's system. Maybe there was something there. Hmm...

Hearing female chatter outside, she stepped out. She made small talk with some of her colleagues while touching up her face. She put on some gloss, dabbed on some powder from her compact and left the restroom.

'Where were you?' Vinay asked her as soon as she stepped in. She had not seen Vinay since Wednesday, when they had been to the pub.

He had gone for an off-site training on Thursday and Friday to prep for the NUS project.

'In the loo,' she said. 'Why, what's up? You seem anxious.'

He searched her face. 'How are you? I tried to call you over the weekend, to make sure you were okay, but your phone was switched off. Are you really okay? I...I am sorry about Wednesday...at the pub...I—'

Mira squeezed his arm affectionately. 'No worries, champ. I am good. Hope the tequila has left your system?' She winked and they shared a muted laugh.

Vinay ran his finger over his forehead. 'But what happened over the weekend? You must have been miserable all by yourself...'

If only you knew, buddy. She sat back on her chair. 'I'll tell you at lunch. I need to finish something now.'

'Okay. Want coffee? I'm going to get some.'

'Thanks, Vinay. Please get me a caffè latte.'

Just then Gerard buzzed her to come to his room. He was meeting all the project heads about the quarterly earnings that had just come in. The meeting lasted about forty-five minutes, at the end of which Gerard said to Mira at the door, 'I met Stewart a few days back and he was talking about you. He is quite impressed with you and has recommended your name to some of his colleagues for future projects.' A surge of energy filled Mira; there was justice in the Universe, after all. She thanked Gerard and shot a triumphant look at Sanya who smirked and went away.

Vinay was waiting impatiently at Mira's desk. 'Where did you go? The coffee has gone cold,' he complained.

'Sorry, sorry. Gerard called us to his cabin for a recap of the quarterly earnings.' Mira picked up her coffee. 'Our team has brought in the second-highest revenue for the quarter.' They hi-fived.

Vinay cleared his throat and adjusted his glasses. He dragged his chair to Mira's side of the room and settled into it. He cleared his throat again. 'Umm...about Saturday night...' he ventured. 'You passed out and I was wondering what to do when suddenly Rohan was there beside me.'

'You just abandoned me to him,' Mira griped in half-jest, sipping her coffee.

Vinay clicked his tongue. 'Think about the scene—'

'Hold on right there. Did I or did I not puke? Tell the truth.'

'Hmm...as far as I can remember, you did not, though you threatened to do so.'

Mira nodded for him to continue.

'Okay, so there you were, lying unconscious on the table and me, half-drunk. Like in the movies, Rohan materialized, hero-like, and took charge of the situation. In my sloshed state, it made sense to follow the path of least resistance.'

'I guess so,' Mira laughed. 'What about Sanya?'

Vinay sniggered. 'She was bloody pissed off. But he wasn't listening to her. "Take a taxi back" is what I remember Rohan telling her firmly when he hauled you up and took you outside.'

Mira closed her eyes and enjoyed playing the scene in her head.

'Now *you* tell me, what happened later? I want every single sordid detail,' finished Vinay.

Mira did some very quick mental editing of the events of that weekend. She shrugged nonchalantly. 'Nothing happened. Woke up with a hangover to find myself in Rohan's apartment, with him cooking breakfast—'

'Ah, the plot thickens,' Vinay teased. Mira rapped his hand.

'Rohan told me what had happened at the pub and dropped me home. That's all.'

Vinay looked disappointed. 'That's all? No kisses or cuddles and...ahem...'

Mira shot him a dangerous look. 'Sorry to disappoint you, sir. But nothing happened, okay? Nada. Zilch.'

Vinay sulked and looked away.

Mira piped up, 'Enough about Rohan, but, hey, something else happened on Sunday.'

Vinay sat up in his seat. 'What?'

'I have a house guest...' Mira trailed, playing with her hair.

'From India? Family?'

'She is actually my half-sister.'

Vinay looked puzzled. She told him about her father and her past, at the end of which Vinay nodded sympathetically. 'Oh, this is what I think you were trying to tell me at the pub.'

Mira blinked and looked startled. 'I was? God, I made such a fool of myself.'

Vinay patted her shoulder and said in a placating tone, 'It's alright. Well, I think you *tried* talking about your dad, but we both were so drunk that I wasn't sure if you even knew what you were saying...'

Mira sighed dejectedly. 'Well, it's true. My half-sister, Amita, is here.' She looked ruefully at Vinay. 'And is probably using my shampoo and eating my Godiva chocolates.'

Mira couldn't bring herself to tell Vinay that Amita had run away from home. That would lead to more discussion—and all roads led to her father; she was not ready to open that can of worms.

Vinay rubbed his chin in thought. 'So she came with her music group and turned up at your doorstep—just like that?'

'Yes. It seems she wanted a holiday and assumed she would be welcome at my place.' Mira rolled her eyes. 'Imagine her gall!'

Vinay shook his head. 'Nope, I don't buy her story. She has come because she is curious about you, her half-sister— somebody her father talks about with pride. She came to satisfy her curiosity.' He folded his arms and sat back with a smug smile on his face—as if he had cracked a crime thriller.

Mira felt touched by Vinay's loyalty. 'Is that what you think it is?' she asked softly, feeling guilty about withholding vital information.

'Duh! It's clear as day.' He squinted at her. 'But why did you let her in? I thought you wouldn't?'

'I don't know what happened. At first I didn't want to, but there she was, an eighteen-year-old, standing at my doorstep. So I let her stay.'

Vinay stood up and hugged Mira. 'Good girl,' he said and went back to his desk.

Late that afternoon, Sanya turned up at Mira's cubicle.

'Hello, Mira,' she smiled and rested her hip against Mira's desk.

Mira stared at Sanya. Was she imagining it or had the khaki skirt and yellow blouse wilted a little?

'Hello, Sanya,' said Mira. Her voice was friendly but her eyes were watchful.

'Nice dress,' Sanya remarked, running her eyes appreciatively over Mira.

Mira now knew something was up because she was wearing a simple dress shirt and black trousers, nothing fancy.

'Thanks, Sanya, you don't look half as bad, either. So, what can I do for you?'

Sanya flicked her hair back and Mira understood she was playing for time.

'This Stewart...know him well?' she said, too non-chalantly.

Ah, so that was the deal. Gerard's words had pricked her enough to come knocking on her door. Bitch.

Mira thought on her feet. 'Hmm...not very well, a passing acquaintance. Why do you ask?' She bit back a smile, enjoying Sanya's discomfort.

'No, no, I just wondered—since Gerard mentioned something...'

Mira waved her hands dismissively. 'Oh, nothing to it, really. Stewart praised me to Gerard. You don't have to worry, Sanya. Your place is secure, unless the client decides to change their team's composition mid-stream...'

Sanya's eyes widened in disbelief.

Mira continued: 'Oh, no worries. Your team will remain intact. How can Stewart replace you with me, even if he is impressed with me?'

Sanya's good humour vanished. 'If I find you are playing games...'

'Oh, give it up, Sanya. So somebody finds my work good, finds me competent, and you think I am playing games? I never go blowing my trumpet they way *some* people do in this organization. *You* came here wanting the truth and couldn't swallow the bitter pill. I have three words of advice for you: Deal with it!'

Sanya shot her a venomous look and flounced off.

'What's going on?' Vinay approached her.

Mira grinned. 'Sanya's worried about my growing popularity with Stewart and his firm. So she came here to ferret out information from me. For some strange reason, she seems to think that I am trying to take the project from her.'

Vinay laughed. 'You are a devil.'

Mira wagged her finger at him. 'Bitch Goddess.'

Big Sister Act

*M*ira was so caught up in her thoughts that she was a little startled to find Amita lounging in front of the TV when she entered her apartment at nine-fifteen. Vinay and she had impromptu decided to have dinner at a new Mexican restaurant two blocks from their office.

'Hi,' Mira said, her eyes casually scanning the apartment; the house had been vacuumed, the bookshelves dusted and there was a delicate aroma of spices lingering in the air.

Amita flashed a warm smile that reached her eyes. 'Hi! How was your day?'

'Alright,' Mira kept her voice toneless, resisting the urge to respond to Amita's cheery greeting.

'I had a quiet day too,' Amita chattered on, 'Didn't do much. I practised music and read some of your magazines.'

Mira nodded; she did not pause in her act of putting away her shoes and hanging up her keys. She was in no mood for chitchat.

'I also did some cleaning. I thought I might make myself useful around here and not be a complete burden on you.'

Mira stiffened. 'Thank you, that's great,' she managed in a friendlier tone.

'Sure.'

'Have you eaten?' asked Mira, looking at the casseroles kept on the dining table.

'I hope you don't mind that I cooked dinner for both of us,' said Amita with a shy smile.

Mira's eyes widened. 'You did? What did you make?'

'Er. I made rice, sambar and beans-paruppu usili.'

'All of eighteen and you made a whole meal?'

Amita shrugged. 'I have always loved cooking and can whip up almost anything. My brother jokes if my music career doesn't work out, I could become a chef.'

Mira gave a small smile.

'Shall we eat?'

Mira looked at her sheepishly. 'I ate out with a colleague. Sorry, I didn't realize that you would have gone to so much trouble...'

'No issues.' Amita got off the sofa and caught her hair up in a clip. She stood there, all of five feet tall, but with poise beyond her years. She was dressed in electric-blue harem pants and a white top.

'Why don't you have dinner while I do the dishes?' Mira suggested.

'Actually, I have already done them. Umm...I thought, when you came home, we could have dinner and chat.'

Mira's face softened catching Amita's earnest, child-like expression. 'Wow, how come you are so responsible?'

Amita stretched her lips. 'I am eighteen, Mira, not eight.'

Mira remembered being that young but couldn't recall being anything like this confident young woman before her. She tried to ignore the grudging respect and even a little fondness she was developing for her half-sister

She assumed an indifferent tone, 'If there is nothing for me to do, I will go to bed. Night, night.' She started walking toward her bedroom.

'Wait,' Amita almost yelped.

The dim bulb in the passageway threw shadows on the two women.

'I thought about what I am going to do and maybe we could talk about it?' said Amita.

'Can it wait until tomorrow? I am tired,' Mira hedged. She tried to gauge the colour of Amita's eyes: warm chocolate. Yes, that seemed the most apt description.

'Okay, how about I tell you today and you can react tomorrow? Please.'

Her eyes flitted over Mira's face.

Mira frowned. *React? How was she even involved here?*

Amita dove in, 'It's obvious I can't go to that music college in the UK unless Papa pays my fees. So, I have to make him see reason.'

'Hmm...' Mira said noncommittally. She massaged the knot in her neck. The hair dresser at the salon had remarked last time, 'Too much work, eh? No more already, lah! Maybe you go on holiday, lah...' She would have loved to go on a holiday if not for Sanya's Machiavellian tendencies. Mira couldn't risk being away when so much was at stake at work.

Amita's face fell. 'I can't make him understand. I thought if somebody else, someone who matters to Papa, speaks to him, he might come around...'

Mira stared hard at Amita. 'And who is this someone who your Papa...' she narrowed her eyes. 'Do you mean what I think you mean?'

Amita fell silent but Mira could read the answer on her face. Something shifted within her.

'And is this why you are here? Supposedly on an impulse?' Mira thwacked her forehead. 'I should have known, why didn't I see this coming? So there was no music troupe—'

'No, no,' Amita sounded horrified. 'I did come with the

music troupe—you can check. But seeking your help to talk to Papa... this was not planned. I just thought of it today since I was getting desperate.' She was close to tears.

Mira walked past her to the dining room and opened the refrigerator. She was annoyed; first this girl lands up at her door and now wants to be bailed out of her personal mess. Amita hovered near her nervously. 'I know if anyone can convince Papa into anything, it's you,' she mumbled, studiously avoiding Mira's gaze.

Mira's laugh was shaky and harsh. 'I couldn't convince him to not leave me. What makes you think he'll listen to me now?' She took a bottle of orange juice from the fridge and poured some into a glass. She sat on a dining room chair.

Amita sat across the table from her. 'Remember how I told you he was so proud of your academic success? Every year you would top the class and he would brag to anybody who cared to listen. He was very happy when you became an engineer and even happier when you got this job. He talked of nothing else for days...'

Mira smirked.

'Papa was—is—so proud of you, of all that you have done so far. Not just your school scores or your job, but everything.' Amita's voice dropped a pitch. 'Like the way you took care of your mother after all...all that happened. "Learn from her, see how she handles her responsibility," he always tells Aman and me.'

Mira kept her face expressionless. She wore a closed smile wondering if her father would be proud of her latest achievement as a Bitch Goddess.

She caught Amita's eyes and said, 'The games parents play to have their way: pit one sibling against another. In our case it's even meatier—pit one half-sibling against another. These are all ploys, don't believe it.'

Amita shook her head adamantly, her bun coming undone. 'No, it's not a ploy. He really thinks you are smart and sensible. I even suspect that you are his favourite and he will listen if you talk.' Amita's face was open and vulnerable, reflecting the child-woman she was. She looked at her half-sister beseechingly.

Mira secretly admired this girl's guts and shrewdness. She sipped some juice and stared at the abstract art print that hung on the wall.

'And what made you think I would fight for your cause, pray?' she said finally, draining the glass with one long sip. She hadn't fought her own battle when she should have. And this girl thought she would go out there and fight for her? Mira suppressed the bitter laughter that rose in her throat.

'Sorry I have been selfish. All I thought about was my problem and how to solve it. But I have only two weeks to reply to the UK university. I have to convince Papa by then...' Amita trailed and chewed her lips.

The air was thick with tension. Mira tried to push away memories of long nights crying into her pillow, yearning for her father to return to her and her mother. She looked at the young girl in front of her who was spunky enough to ask her—her!—for help.

Amita gushed, 'The thing is, it's not such a big deal. Papa's argument is, who will take over the firm? That's a no-brainer. Aman can be groomed to succeed Papa. He is a geek and loves science, computers, engineering and whatever else you need to lead a software company.'

Mira wondered who Aman looked like. Did he also have brown eyes? After being an only child all these years, it suddenly felt surreal to have a half-sister and a half-brother enter her personal space.

Amita rolled her eyes. 'You know how it is—in spite of all

the ranting and the raving, it's so hard to go and do something you know your father disapproves of.' She stared at her upturned palms placed on her lap. 'More than his financial support, I need Papa's emotional support and blessings.'

Mira couldn't help nodding. She knew too well the desperate need for parental approval that clung to you even after you left home. Didn't she constantly battle her mother's dreams against her own? Worse, she also knew—despite her father's absence— what it was to be caught between two parents, where pleasing one meant earning the other's disapproval.

'The more I thought about this whole "situation" I am in, the more I felt that there was only one solution—you,' she declared theatrically.

'Well, you certainly put the cart before the horse.'

Amita ignored the snub and added cheerfully, 'If you sat down and explained to dad, talked to him, then he would agree.' She reached out and held Mira's hands. 'Please, I really need your help.'

Mira gently extricated her hands. 'Sorry, I am not going to speak to that man about this. I have nothing to do with him.'

'Please, don't say anything now. You are tired and it's not the right time to make decisions. Think about it and we can talk again tomorrow.'

Amita left the room before Mira could react.

Mira slipped on a T-shirt and pajamas. She felt like Alice going down the rabbit hole. Her world was spinning out of axis. Through her school years, she had fantasized about talking to her father and would play the images in a loop in her mind till they made her dizzy with despair. Her fantasies covered many scenarios; some in which she pleaded, some in which he begged forgiveness and many in which they were a happy family again. None, however, involved her going out to bat for any of his other children. Mira stood before the dressing room mirror and brushed her hair till it shone. It had grown a few inches since her Bitch Goddess makeover and fell in soft waves down her shoulders. She bunched her hair into a ponytail and stared at her reflection.

If anyone can convince Papa into anything, it's you.

She gave a disbelieving shake of her head. The crazy thing was, Amita really believed it. But it didn't matter what Amita believed in, did it? Mira wasn't going to talk to *him*. Not after all these years—and certainly not for this.

Mira was swamped by memories: sounds of slammed doors, of crying and more crying, the Other Woman's profile in the sleeveless blouse and the raggedy teddy bear with one of its button-eyes yanked out. It still lay in her cupboard in her old room. Mira swallowed hard and closed her eyes. She couldn't do it, and she didn't want to. She was not ready to see him or talk to him. The tears spilled disobediently down her cheeks.

Bitch Goddess Rule #14: Sometimes, even a Bitch Goddess cries. Like, really cries.

Mira tossed and turned and finally drifted off to sleep when dawn broke in the sky. She stirred awake when her alarm went off at seven.

She sat up with a feeling that something big needed to be handled that day. But what? Then she remembered last night's conversation with Amita. She lay on her bed, watching the sliver of light that shone between her curtains. Her first instinct was to charge out of the room, look her half-sister in the eye and tell her, 'Listen, there is no way I am going to tackle your father on your behalf. No way, José.'

Mira to went to the bathroom and stared at the mirror. She

should have never let Amita into her house. But the damage was done. Mira had shut the door firmly on her father and his life, a door that even the crow-bar of her mother's nagging could not open. Then Amita had turned up and Mira had unwittingly opened that dreaded door to her past with just a turn of a handle. She swore loudly at the mirror with her toothpaste-filled mouth. She rested her head against the cool bathroom wall and pondered over her situation. She didn't want to talk to her father. The very thought made her stomach feel hollow and her legs tremble. And she definitely didn't want to have any interaction with either the Other Woman or her half-brother. She disrobed and stepped into the shower.

But an insidious voice at the back of her mind whispered, 'Amita wants to study music and her father doesn't want her to. Think about it, Mira. If you support her, the father will get annoyed. Really annoyed and hurt.'

Mira grinned at the mental picture. Annoying and hurting him seemed like a plan. Even if it meant having to talk to the man.

There were possibilities here, Bitch Goddess possibilities: back the half-sister against the father. She pondered over it, weighing the odds and playing out different scenarios as she showered. If she supports Amita, that would result in a confrontation with the man, something she had often itched to do. Even her mother couldn't accuse her of being quarrelsome—it was somebody else's battle that she was fighting, after all.

She towelled herself dry and started getting dressed.

'Why not take it one step further?' the sinister voice said. 'Do something that would create tension, maybe even cause irrevocable rift between the loving father-daughter team.'

Mira pulled on her black narrow pants and paired it with a teal shirt. But what is it exactly that I must do? she mused.

'There *is* something you can do,' the voice was insistent.

Mira pondered over the matter as she ate her breakfast. If she helps Amita rebel against her father, half the battle was won! Mira stabbed a spoon into her muesli as she felt the familiar twinge of pain that accompanied memories of her father. She no longer felt hungry.

She peeped inside Amita's room; she was still asleep. Mira scribbled on a Post-it: *Thinking about what you said last night. We can talk tonight after I get home.* She stuck the note on the fridge and left the apartment.

She did not take the cab today. She crossed the overhead pass and went into the MRT station and almost ran down the steps to catch the train that would pull out any moment. She sat at a window seat and barely heard the announcements of the passing stations. The menacing voice-in-her-head was unrelenting: 'Talk to him Mira. Cause a father-daughter rift in the garb of helping Amita fulfill her dreams.'

She now wanted to return the favour to her father: for all the birthdays she had stayed up waiting for him in vain, for all the lonely and tearful nights her mother had spent, and for having innumerable nightmares through her growing years. It had been hell; all because of one man.

Sorry Amma, but sometimes a woman's gotta do what she's gotta do.

Mira did some math and was satisfied that it all added up. By the time she reached Raffles Place, she had made up her mind. Bitch Goddesses pitched family against one another to serve their own purposes, didn't they?

She picked up her bag and strode out of the station in confident steps. A smug smile played on her lips when she got into the cab. She watched the buildings slip past her as the cab navigated through the morning rush hour.

Her mind made up, she refused to accept that, perhaps, this might genuinely be a chance to help a girl she reluctantly felt a kinship with.

An email greeted Mira when she reached the office. Elcard had another project and she was heading it. She punched the air. 'Woo-hoo,' she cried.

Vinay's head popped up above the wall. 'Congrats, buddy, way to go,' he grinned and high-fived her.

Mira was just about to respond when Sanya walked straight into the moment. She looked stricken but poised like a Miss Universe finalist who didn't win the crown. Vinay darted a glance at Mira and swivelled his chair back to his desk.

Sanya smiled tightly. 'I am glad you have a project from Elcard,' she said, drumming her French manicured fingers on Mira's cubicle wall. 'Of course, it's not as big as the one *my* team got from Elcard, but still, it's a start.'

Mira ran an eye over Sanya's shocking pink blouse and skirt. Then she looked at her own teal and black outfit. She knew the grey pearls around her neck, the matching eardrops, and her grey shoes enhanced her elegance quotient. For the first time, Mira felt she looked more sophisticated of the two—maybe the confidence booster was the new Elcard project she had nabbed.

She smiled at Sanya, her eyes faintly mocking. 'I agree completely, Sanya.' Her voice was butter smooth. 'Even Stewart says the same thing—that this is just the beginning of a long association with Elcard.'

Sanya tensed. 'He spoke to you?'

Mira's eyes twinkled. 'I received the most charming email

from him.' She browsed through her Outlook and clicked on a mail.

'Ah, here it is. Let me read it: "We were keen that you head the team for the new Elcard project. Though it is not as big as the earlier one, it is more important and very critical in terms of revenue…"'

Mira looked at Sanya, who had paled. 'The mail continues, but you get the drift, don't you?' She closed her mailbox and flashed Sanya a bright smile. 'You are right, my project won't be as big as yours.'

Sanya shot her an icy look and stormed off.

Vinay's head popped up again. 'Whoa. Was that more of the Bitch Goddess stuff that's going on?'

'Yep,' Mira wore a hooded smile.

Vinay shook his head slowly. 'I am not sure I like this.'

Mira gave him a 'whatever' look and stared at her screen thoughtfully. Then she opened her personal email and systematically deleted all the mails she had sent herself from Sanya's computer a few days back, when she had hacked into it. It looked like she didn't need these after all.

Bitch Goddess Rule #15: God helps those Bitch Goddesses who help themselves.

One Phone Call Too Many

*A*mita clapped in delight. 'Really? You'll do it?'

'Yes,' said Mira, reaching for the masala tea on the kitchen shelf.

Amita bit her lower lip and shot her a glance. 'But why would you do it?'

Mira raised her eyebrows. '*You* asked me to, or have you changed your mind?'

'What I meant was, *why* have you agreed to help me?'

Mira poured the boiling water into the teapot. 'Think of it as my good deed for the year, as my Christmas present.'

'Thanks,' Amita said, her voice a little unsure.

'But we'll do it my way,' Mira said her voice firm. 'I am going to call my mom now.' She checked her watch. 'It's about seven in the evening back home.'

'I understand. You don't want your mother hearing about me from someone else.'

Mira ignored her remark and pressed the speed dial button on the phone. As she counted the rings, she rapidly edited the events of the last few days in her mind. When her mother finally answered the phone, Mira was ready.

'Mira, how are you?' her mother said. 'Sorry, I was watering the plants in the balcony and didn't hear the phone ring.'

'It's okay, Amma.' Mira took a deep breath and got battle-ready. 'Don't faint, but Amita is here with me, at my house.'

She looked sideways at Amita who was twirling the strand that had escaped her ponytail.

Mira held the phone away from her ear when her mother flung the questions: 'Amita? How did she get there? What is she doing there? How did you know…'

Mira pressed her palm to her forehead. 'Amma, please stop and listen to me. I'll tell you the whole story. Amita showed up at my doorstep suddenly. Yes, I recognized the family resemblance.' She paused to listen to her mother's excited chatter.

'How did she get here? Her father gave her my address. And I presume he got this from you…' She paused for a heartbeat and delighted in the choice of her words. 'What am I going to do? I don't know yet, she just got in. Oh, Amma, please. Of course I won't throw her out of the house. I am not the evil step-sister. Yes, she'll be here. Yes, you do that. Bye.'

'Phew,' said Mira, looking at Amita. 'The next call is going to be your family. I hope you have your little speech ready?'

'That I am going to study music whatever happens? That I won't come back unless they let me study music?'

Mira stretched her lips. 'That just sounds childish. You can't stay here forever and everybody knows that. Tell them you are going to join the UK university and that I am giving you a loan for the course.'

Amita looked surprised. 'I can't take money from you.'

'And I don't remember offering you any,' Mira replied breezily. 'But we should tell them this to make them come around.'

'Oh, and then what?' Amita looked at Mira hopefully, like she were a miracle worker.

'Then we wait for their reaction,' said Mira. 'What else?'

'But what if they still don't agree?'

'We will still find a way. There is always a Plan B.'

Just then the phone rang. Mira looked at the unfamiliar India number on the caller ID and wordlessly handed the phone to Amita. Her mother apparently didn't waste any time in flashing the breaking news.

'Hello. Yes, Mama, it's me,' Amita spoke softly. 'Yes, I am fine, don't worry. No, no. It's not boyfriend trouble; sadly, I have none.' Amita gave a short, weary laugh. She fell silent, listened to her mother and sighed heavily, 'Yes, I am very sorry Mama, I had no choice but to run away. Huh? *You* know why! I want to study music and not become a hot-shot entrepreneur running Papa's company. I'm just not cut out for it.'

Amita paused, hearing out her mother. Then she enunciated each word slowly, like she were talking to a child, 'Mama, I am not being difficult. Please understand that this is my dream. I am good in music and Papa can afford to put me through this course in the UK. No, no...I am not acting spoilt, you know it. I was desperate, so I came to Singapore. I want to find some work and pay my way through college, if possible...'

Mira heard a faint voice coming from the other end of the phone line. She wanted to shut her ears and block out the Other Woman's voice.

'No, sorry, I don't want to come there and discuss it, Mama. Not unless if you are ready to put me on a flight to London.' Amita shut her eyes and inhaled. 'No, I am not going away from here, Mama. Don't worry, yes, I will call you soon.'

She put down the receiver with a loud click.

The phone rang again. 'That's probably Papa,' Amita frowned, looking at the caller ID. Mira's mouth went dry; she had not heard his voice in ages.

'Hello Papa,' said Amita in a little girl voice that conveyed she sought her father's approval and blessings. Mira flinched, recognizing that tone as her own.

'I am sorry, Papa,' continued Amita. 'But you left me with no choice. You made it clear that you won't pay my fees. And I made it clear that music is my calling, so what choice did I have?' She sat back on the couch and listened. 'Yes, it's not easy to get a job in Singapore...yes, I am lucky Mira let me stay with her...she is even willing to offer me a loan for the music course...no, no...I didn't ask her. She has offered on her own. Huh? You want to talk to her?' Amita threw a hesitant glance in Mira's direction. 'Umm...wait a second, Papa.'

She held out the phone to Mira, who resolutely shook her head.

'She says she doesn't want to talk to you. Why is she refusing to come on line? Hmm...I think you know why, Papa,' said Amita quietly. She listened some more and added, 'No, I am not coming home. I don't want to join your firm and become your clone. I...I can't continue like this.' She ended the call and held her head in her hands.

Three minutes later, the phone rang again. Mira motioned to Amita to take the call.

'Oh, it's you, Aman,' Amita smiled for the first time that evening. 'It's true, I want to be here if Papa is not going to support my decision. Yes, I am not coming home—at least for now.'

Mira picked up her tea that had turned cold and emptied it in the kitchen sink. She pottered about the kitchen while Amita spoke to her brother. She strained her ears to hear Amita.

'Yeah, she is pretty cool,' said Amita. 'Yeah, you would like Mira. But she doesn't like us....yeah, yeah...I can understand too...Then why is she helping me? Hmm...not sure. I suppose she genuinely wants to help.'

Mira leaned into the pot of geraniums that sat on her window sill and inhaled deeply. She had been meaning to grow a kitchen garden but had never found time for it. She distracted her mind into thinking about all the herbs she could grow: coriander, basil, thyme and oregano.

Amita popped her head into the kitchen. 'Hey, you okay?'

Mira nodded briefly, her expression blank. 'Let's go to bed before we get more calls. The first may well be from my mother— tomorrow morning, if I am lucky.'

The phone rang just as Mira was drifting off to sleep. She stumbled out of bed and dashed to the living room to pick it up. It was her mother. She somehow preferred calling Mira on the landline than on the mobile.

'Mira, what is this I hear about you paying for Amita's music course?' Her mother sounded agitated.

'Don't worry, Amma. I have been working for seven years and have enough money saved up. It's just a loan that Amita will repay later.'

'But why are you doing this? I thought you didn't care about any of them?'

Mira noted her mother's half-bewildered and half-suspicious tone.

'Amma, I have my reasons for doing this,' said Mira flatly. 'I did the math and I can support her, at least initially, till she finds her feet.'

Her mother sighed heavily down the line. 'Mira, is it some sort of revenge against your father?' she enquired in a resigned tone.

Mira felt something gnawing inside her. How well her mother knew her. 'Yes, Amma, you can call it revenge or anything you want. But this man is not allowing her to chase her dreams.' She paused, knowing her mother would have flinched hearing her call him 'this man'. 'This is the best way to take out my vengeance against him.'

'Mira—'

'Please, Amma. I know what I am doing.'

'But your father will get upset—'

'Father?' Mira spat. 'I don't have a father, or have you forgotten?' Mira slammed the phone down. She never noticed her half-sister standing in the passageway and overhearing the phone conversation.

The next morning, Mira was having her breakfast when her phone rang. She was at the table, all by herself. She surmised that Amita was presumably still sleeping in her room.

'Hello,' a man spoke. She had heard this deep voice before. Seventeen years ago. Mira's skin prickled with tension.

'Mira, is that you?' the man said.

Mira froze and gripped her phone tight. Something lodged itself in her throat. 'Yes, it is,' she said a moment later, her voice a little distant.

'It's me,' the man continued. 'Appa.' Even Mira could sense the discomfort the man felt in uttering the word 'Appa', like some language he used to speak but has now forgotten.

He spoke in a measured tone, the way Mira recalled him doing when she was little. 'I am happy Amita is with you. It's nice of you to help her.' He paused. 'But what is this I hear about you wanting to fund her studies? I won't stand for it. I absolutely forbid it, do you understand?' His voice was low and clear.

'You lost the right to forbid me from doing anything a long time ago,' Mira hissed.

'Is this how you speak to your father?' he snapped. 'Put her back on the next flight home.'

Mira was surprised at how easily he slipped into the father role; he had wiped off the last seventeen years with one phone call.

'No, I won't,' Mira's tone was icy and aloof. 'I don't have to listen to you. Amita is an adult and knows what she wants from life. You ruined my dreams, but I won't let you ruin her's. If she wants to learn music, then I am going to help her. If you have any problems, talk to her, not to me. I don't owe you any explanations.'

She had felt hurt, anger and shock resonate in the silence that had flowed between them. Mira's hands trembled when she disconnected the line.

She never realized that her voice had carried through to Amita's room.

Mira dumped her empty cornflakes bowl into the sink and stepped out to face another day in her now unpredictable life.

Bitch Goddess Rule #16: A Bitch Goddess is sometimes like a nagin of Bollywood. She will wait even seventeen years to strike.

Dangerous Games

It was almost comforting to see Sanya in her cubicle after the stressful phone conversation. She was an impediment Mira had gotten used to.

'Ah, there you are!' Sanya snarled at Mira as soon as she entered. 'What did you steal from my system, you thief?'

Mira's pulse quickened. 'I don't follow you,' she said with composure.

'Don't put on the innocent lamb look. I know you have been snooping around my files. What did you take?' Sanya crossed her arms and leaned against the glass panel. Her eyebrows did a little dance on her smooth forehead.

'What rubbish! Why should I snoop on *your* system?' Mira's eyes coolly swept over Sanya. 'That's more your style, Sanya.'

Sanya ignored the remark and lifted her chin defiantly. 'Somebody's been through my files. It may or may not be you. In fact, it's probably not you; you don't have the technical skills to pull it off. But it was definitely your idea.'

Sanya turned to Vinay. 'Then *you* must have done it, I am sure. And we all know that you would do anything for *her*.'

Vinay's jaw tightened and blood rushed to his cheeks.

Mira held up a hand. 'Stop right there and start from the beginning. What's missing and why are we being accused?'

Sanya took a deep breath and ran a hand through her hair. 'I just discovered that somebody rifled through my computer files.'

'And took what?' Mira asked.

'Nothing.' Sanya shrugged. 'But that's besides the point.'

'Huh?'

'Look. Somebody's being meddling with my system—I know enough technology to understand this. But nothing seems to be missing—though it may well be. I am still figuring that out.' She looked derisively from Mira to Vinay. 'I can't think of anyone but either of you who could have done this.'

'This is such a wild charge, so ridiculous!' exclaimed Mira. 'Do you have any proof? In an office that employs around three hundred people, all of whom are tech-savvy, why should we be your prime suspects?'

Sanya's eyes skittered away. 'I still don't believe you.'

'I can't help you there,' said Mira tartly.

Sanya looked from one to the other. 'I'll get to the bottom of this,' she pointed her finger at them and strode off.

Vinay went to Mira's desk. 'What was that about? Anything I should know?'

'No clue, you know Sanya,' replied Mira evasively, settling into her desk. Vinay didn't look too convinced but went back to his desk without further questions. Mira let out a quiet sigh of relief.

It was one-thirty and the cafeteria was slowly filling up with people. Smartly dressed men and women with Network Systems IDs hanging down their necks, milled around, checking out the buffet offer for the day.

Vinay and Mira heaped food on their plates, paid the cashier and chose a corner table to sit down.

'What were you thinking, hacking into her machine?' said Vinay. Temper laced his words.

Mira paled. 'What? I didn't do it, Vinay!'

'You are such a bad liar, Mira. What did you do with the files you filched? I guess they are not on your computer any longer?' Vinay unwrapped his burger, scrunched the paper into a ball and aimed it at the nearby bin. He missed the target. Mira stared hard at him. She had never seen him so mad. 'But I didn't—'

'What was this—one of your Bitch-whatever ploys?' He shook his head. 'This is just plain stupid. What were you thinking, Mira?'

He bit into his burger and slowly thoughtfully it, his eyes fixed on her.

She wore an offended look. 'But I did *not* hack into her machine. It's just one of those wild things she says. As always.'

'That's what I also thought—at first,' said Vinay quietly, his eyes fixed on her. 'Then I saw your face.'

'But I didn't *do* anything.' Mira banged on the table, making their trays clatter.

'Don't lie to me,' said Vinay. He held up his fork like a trident. 'I don't know what you are up to. But I do hope, for your own sake, you haven't used the stuff you filched from her. Because if you have, then nobody can save you. Also, if you haven't gotten rid of that stuff, please do it right away.'

When she opened her mouth to speak, he just shook his head. 'Don't say anything.'

Mira shut up. She knew that if she spoke now, her guilt would show. She played around with her food, her appetite gone.

Vinay spoke after a long moment. 'You know what I realized today? If she had found any evidence and stuck it on me, you would have let it stay. You wouldn't have spoken in my defense. She could've have taken it to the boss and you might have just watched.'

Mira was struck by the truth in his accusation, so it was some time before she could gather the words to articulate her denial. But Vinay was already on his feet. 'You know what, I am not sure about you becoming a Bitch Goddess, but you sure are becoming a bitch.'

She watched him walk away and felt tears prickling behind her eyelids. She rested her head on the table and didn't move for a long time. When she finally lifted her head, the cafeteria wore a deserted look. She didn't think she could go back to work today.

She went to the phone and dialled an extension.

'Gerard? Mira here.'

'Yes Mira.'

'I am sick and need to go home.'

'Why? What's up?'

'Just dizzy and nauseous.'

'Off you go then. Take care.'

'Thanks,' Mira muttered and left the building. Vinay's words played back in her mind, making her feel clammy and nauseous.

The apartment was silent when she entered it. In the last few days, Mira had gotten used to being assailed by the aroma of cooking. But today, there was neither any aroma nor Amita's cheerful face to greet her. Mira gently knocked on Amita's bedroom door. Silence. She opened the door and surveyed the room. The bed was made, the carpet vacuumed and no clothes were lying around. She knocked on the bathroom door and found it empty as well.

'Amita?' Mira said loudly, her voice bouncing off the apartment walls. She ran from room to room, imagining all sorts of possibilities. She paused and tried to think through this. Don't panic, she said aloud. Had Amita gone to the market, or for a walk downstairs? Mira didn't even know if Amita had got a temporary mobile number for use in Singapore. She didn't remember Amita mentioning this. Mira went to the kitchen to get herself a drink. That's when she saw the hand-written note pasted on the fridge, under the big Sentosa magnet.

Mira gingerly pulled out the note and read it:

```
Mira, I am leaving. Thanks for the offer
to pay for my fees, but I don't want it. I
have a disagreement with my dad; I don't
hate him like you do. I refuse to be some
sort of a pawn in your revenge plan. You
want to fight him? Do it directly. You
can't use me and my situation to your
advantage. I want to pursue music and
will find a way to realize my dream—only,
in a less destructive way.
Thanks for hosting me the last few days.
Amita.
```

Mira folded the letter carefully and put it inside a kitchen draw. She went to the living room and slumped on the sofa. She had had an excess of emotions in the last few weeks and was exhausted to the bone.

Her phone pinged with an incoming message.

```
Hey, dinner tonite @ 8?
Rohan.
```

She dropped the phone beside her and stared at the wall. She wondered where Amita was. Had she gone back to India? Mira switched on the TV, hoping to catch something entertaining. Amita wasn't her problem. She was an adult, and if she was smart enough to come here, she was smart enough to go back to her folks. Why should she care? She still felt sore about Vinay but figured he will come around soon enough.

She read Rohan's message again. 'Yes' she texted back. She had made up her mind—who were the others to take over her life? She rubbed her face tiredly. But if she was so secure, then why the hell was she blinking back these tears?

Unbreak My Heart...

'Hey,' Rohan kissed Mira briefly on the lips when she answered her door a few hours later.

'Hmm…looking good, maybe we should stay home instead?'

Mira gave a listless smile and went inside.

'Hey, what's wrong?' he lifted her chin.

She shook her head. 'Family troubles.'

'Want to talk about it?'

She shook her head again. 'Just take me some place where I can forget them.'

'I can think of a place and I guarantee, you won't remember anything at all there.'

She punched him. 'I meant out of the house, idiot.'

'I don't mind if you don't mind an audience. A bit kinky, but if that's what the lady wants…'

She laughed. 'I insist on the dinner you promised.'

'I'll take it as a deferred "yes" for fooling around at home.' He slipped an arm around her and began to lead her out of the door when the phone rang. Mira let it go to voicemail.

Mira's mother's voice called out: 'Mira, call me the minute you come back. What do you mean by talking to your father like that? Don't you think it's…'

Mira's face reddened. She didn't want her mother to reveal more than she should. She avoided Rohan's questioning look and ran to pick up the phone.

'Amma,' she said tiredly.

'Mira, what took you this long to answer the phone?' her mother demanded. 'Never mind. Your father called and told me everything. What is going on, kanna? How could you speak like that to him? And why are you paying Amita's fees? Why are you encouraging her to rebel? Please stay out of it. This is none of your business.'

'Are you done, Amma? Don't forget that Amita wanted *my* help and *you* only told me to help her, so this whole thing has become *my* business, whether not I want it. Also, I felt sorry for—'

'You felt sorry for somebody from *that* family?' her mother snorted. 'I know exactly what you are up to and what you hope to achieve.' She paused and remarked quietly, 'I am sorry, kanna, but I can't help feeling ashamed of you now...'

Mira winced. 'Amma, it's not like that.'

'Where is Amita? Let me speak to her.'

'She is not here.'

'Where has she gone? Shopping? At this time of the night? Make sure she calls me the first thing when she gets back; never mind how late it is.'

'Amma, she's gone.' Mira's voice was hollow.

'Has she gone back home? Do her parents know?'

'Amma, she left my apartment when I was at work. I found her note when I got home—all it says is she has left. I don't know where she is...'

Her mother's silence was worse than her yelling. She finally spoke: 'Mira, are you telling me that your sister has left your house, nobody knows where she is, and she is out there somewhere in a strange country all alone?'

When her mother put it that way, Mira had to admit it was pretty horrifying.

'She is not my sister,' said Mira tightly.

'We are not doing a DNA test, Mira. What did you do? Why did she leave so suddenly?'

'Nothing!' Mira protested. 'I didn't do anything'.

'I suggest you find her immediately,' her mother said tersely and hung up.

Mira was left staring at the phone.

She glanced in Rohan's direction, trying to phrase an explanation in her mind. He was stretched out on the sofa and leafing through a magazine. Mira sat beside him.

'Problems?' he asked, putting down the magazine.

'Long and complicated story. Do you have a few years?' she smiled wryly and gazed at the darkening sky framed at the windows. 'My half-sister has gone missing.'

Rohan's brows knit together in a question.

'My parents separated when I was very young, and my father remarried.' Mira paused. 'So this girl turned up at my doorstep a few days ago. I discovered she is my half-sister who has run away from her home in Chennai.'

She then told him the whole story, right up to the note on the fridge.

'Wow, so this girl has been here with you for almost a week then?'

Mira nodded.

'And you never mentioned it even once...'

She shrugged. 'What does it have to do with us? And how could you have helped me?'

'Hmm...' Rohan looked out of the window thoughtfully.

'So now my mom's mad at me, the girl's missing and I don't know what to do.'

'Airport!' Rohan's face brightened.

'Huh?'

'Think about it: Strange country, short-term visa, no place

to stay, no friends or relatives, no money, one return ticket. What would you do if you were in this situation?'

Mira drummed her fingers on the arm of the sofa. She sat up. 'Where else, the airport! You must be right, Rohan.'

She picked up the landline and scrolled down the last few dialled numbers. She stopped at a familiar number. A call to this number had been made while Mira had been at work, at 2.12 p.m. It was the cab company's toll-free line that Mira often used.

She dialled the number.

'Comfort Cabs, how may I help you Miss Iyer?' a female voice spoke. She recited Mira's address.

'I had actually called a cab earlier today...' Mira trailed off.

'Yes, to go to the airport,' the woman replied. 'Hope there was no problem?'

'Oh, no, no. I seem to have lost my mobile and I thought it might have dropped in the cab. I just wanted to report it, in case you found it.'

'Very well, Ma'am. I'll let the cab driver who took you know about this and send a message to our Lost and Found department too.' She took down the phone's description and reassured Mira of helping her trace it.

Mira ended the call and looked at Rohan. 'You're right, Amita left for the airport.'

Rohan came forward and squeezed her shoulders affectionately.

Then Mira called her mother and told her.

'Thank God Amita had the good sense to go to the aiport,' her mother said. 'I'll ask your father to monitor incoming flights from Singapore. But I suppose Amita might go home on her own now.'

'Thank God she is not roaming around in Singapore,' said Mira in a small voice.

'But if she is safe, it's no thanks to you, Mira. You behaved badly and that doesn't change.'

Her mother's words pricked her. But before she could form a response, her mother hung up with a terse goodbye.

Mira blinked back her tears and smiled at Rohan. 'That's solved then. There is no point in us going to the airport now; we can't anyway enter the departures gate. Amita may well have taken off. So shall we go out for dinner?'

Rohan studied her for a few seconds. 'I called for a pizza while you were on those calls. It should be here soon.'

'Cool, sounds good to me,' she said and sidled up to him on the sofa. He got to his feet.

'What's wrong, Rohan?' Mira said, with a sense of foreboding.

'I don't know Mira, you tell me. What else have you hidden from me?'

Mira opened her mouth to speak but Rohan raised his hand.

'When you wore that gorgeous black dress and came to my place, I thought, perhaps, you were ready to take our relationship to the next level. I also tried to see your point of view when you explained why you left my apartment abruptly the next morning. I have never doubted your intentions, Mira. I thought I mattered to you; I thought *we*, as a couple, mattered to you.' Rohan took a deep breath. 'But looks like you have your own reasons for keeping secrets from me—and may continue to do so.'

Mira stared at him. She had never seen him so angry and disturbed. She wondered where his tirade was headed.

'I—' Mira began.

'I am not done,' Rohan snapped. 'We may not have been together for long, but we have invested deeply in this relationship—at least I have. I often speak to you about my family, I crib about them, tell you what makes them so special, I even showed you my baby pictures. And you also spoke to my mum on Skype that day.'

Mira nodded. Everything he said was true. She had seen his childhood photographs and had spoken to his mother who had been extremely warm. Mira began to feel miserable. First her mother accused her of being badly behaved and now Rohan was furious with her.

Rohan continued in his accusatory tone, 'But you never told me anything about your dad, or his other family. Fine, I can accept that it is a sensitive issue for you and you might have told me when you were ready. But I wish you had confided in me about your problems and considered me as a real friend.

But this thing with your half-sister? She was staying here with you all these days. Hell, she was in the house when I came here to meet you that day and you never told me?'

Mira looked away.

'You have been having all this turmoil in your life and yet you didn't tell me? That means you are ashamed of me and don't want your family to know about me. You don't want me to be a part of your life, but you just want me for sex.'

'That's so not true!' Mira almost leapt out of the sofa.

'Are you sure?' Rohan shot her contemptuous look. 'Like tonight. Your half-sister has gone missing and you didn't consider me worthy enough to take me into your confidence. You didn't want to share your personal woes but were more than willing to share your bed with me. I hope our relationship is not so shallow?'

Mira flushed.

'I'm afraid I don't want to be used just for sex. Sorry, I think this is the end of the road for us, Mira,' said Rohan.

'No, Rohan, you've got it all wrong. Please wait and I'll

explain everything to you soon.' Mira swallowed hard

'No Mira, I've waited too long and don't want to play games with you anymore.' He started walking towards the front door.

'Rohan,' Mira's voice broke.

The doorbell rang.

'That must be the pizza,' he said. He paid for the pizza amidst Mira's protests, put it on the dining table and walked down the passage of her floor. He gave Mira a lingering look before entering through the lift doors.

Mira stared long and hard at the empty passageway until the tears began to fall. She closed her apartment's door and wept loudly, giving vent to years of accumulated sorrow and regret. She turned off all the lights and fell in a heap on her bed and cried herself to sleep. The pizza lay uneaten and turned cold.

Her phone's strident ringing jerked her awake. She glanced at the bed clock. It was almost 1.00 a.m., which meant it was 10.30 p.m. in India.

It was her mother, sounding worried.

'Amma? What is it? Is it Amita...or Patti?' she said, fear making her voice high-pitched. Since her grandmother was past ninety, Mira always assumed the worst when there was a late night phone call.

'No, it's your father...'

'What happened?' Mira's heart raced.

'He just collapsed. It seems he was having dinner, had a coughing fit, became breathless, and just slumped. It happened a little while ago. They have rushed him to the hospital. The doctors discovered a clot in the brain and he is going in for surgery tomorrow.'

'Oh!' Mira blanched, feeling hollow in the pit of her stomach.

'The doctors feel some undue stress and trauma might have caused this,' Mira's mother said tightly. *And we know who would have been the cause of this.* Mira could hear the accusatory words in the silence that followed.

'Amma, please. Don't make it seem like one measly argument with me caused a blood clot. He's obviously had it all along,' Mira answered the unstated charge.

'Exactly. He might have had it, but it's obvious what triggered off the incident.'

'No, Amma, you can't put the blame squarely on me. It's so unfair! I am not the only one who exchanged heated words with him. In fact, I barely interacted with the man!' Mira bit her tongue at the word she used.

'No one's trying to blame anybody, Mira. Just telling you what the doctors are saying.'

'Yes, Amma. I am truly sorry to hear this,' said Mira gently.

'And talking about stress, it seems Amita landed in Bangalore and is staying with a friend. She called her brother to let him know.'

Mira sighed with relief. 'Thank God.'

'Yes, she told her brother that she wasn't coming home immediately. She had a vague plan about finding some job, and staying with her friend for some more time.' Mira's mother clicked her tongue with impatience. 'Oh Muruga, what has come of these modern girls these days?'

Mira shrugged. 'Amita is a gutsy one. And speaking of her, what about all the tension she caused her dad?'

'Oh well, maybe so. But that doesn't absolve you of your misbehavior towards him.'

Mira ignored her mother's admonition and asked, 'What are the doctors saying now?'

'It's a serious surgery, Mira. All we can do is hope and pray.'

Mira swallowed hard. She felt afraid for her father's life but was not ready to tell her mother so.

'When are you getting here?' her mother asked.

'Me? Why should I come there?'

'What do you mean why you should be here? Your father's in a critical condition, Mira.' Her mother sounded vexed and on the verge of a breakdown herself.

'Okay, okay, Amma. Relax.'

'What does that mean, Mira? Are you coming or not?'

'I'll look for tickets and will let you know as soon as my trip is finalized,' she replied non-committally.

'Well, hurry up. The surgery is around ten in the morning tomorow,' her mother concluded.

Sorry Amma, I am not coming. This time, no amount of emotional blackmail will work. He's got his beloved daughter back, so he'll be fine. I do understand that you are anxious that I meet him and fly down to be with him. But that's not going to happen. I am not rushing to his side, whatever happens.

Seventeen years. She hadn't seen her father in seventeen years. But his image came easily and vividly to her mind. She remembered the way he used to laugh as he scooped her up when he returned home every night after work, the way he amusedly looked at her whenever she did mischief, the way he perched her on his shoulders and took her piggy-back riding all over the house.

But it was with equal clarity that Mira remembered her parents' bitter fights and how, one day, after a major showdown with her mother, he had stormed out of the room. She didn't know it then, but that was the day her father had left them for good. It had been the middle of the night and she was fast asleep on her bed when she had heard angry voices and screams coming from the living room through the thin walls. She had crept out of bed and taken ginger steps to the living room. Her mother was sitting on the couch, weeping inconsolably. Her father was standing beside her and waving his arms agitatedly. 'Janaki, don't make me choose. I can't live like this anymore,' he repeatedly said.

Her mother had looked hard at him, through red-rimmed eyes and replied, 'It has to be either me or *her*.' She had spat out the last word like it was something that tasted foul.

'I am sorry,' Mira's father had said and walked out of the house. As he was leaving, he saw her standing in a corner, shivering in her thin cotton frock. He ruffled her hair and remarked softly, 'Shhh baby...it's not your fault.' He lifted her and held her close for a long time. 'Remember that Appa loves you and always will. He will always be there for his little princess. Okay?' She nodded and held onto him with her thin arms. He kissed her forehead and put her down. He revved up the only car they owned, the silver-grey Ambassador, and drove off into the dark night.

Mira had often wondered if he had ever known how she had blamed herself all these years for the fights her parents had had. As she tried to go to sleep now after the conversation with her mother, she played back some vestiges of her father's memories like it were a rapidly eroding LP record. In the beginning, her father used to visit them at least once a month, bringing her dolls, toys and chocolates. But as Mira grew up, she came to feel a sense of betrayal towards her mother for accepting presents from the man who left her to become a single parent. With her mother constantly weeping and turning into something of a social recluse, Mira gradually distanced herself from her father during his occasional visits. She derived a sadistic pleasure from seeing his crumpled face whenever she behaved in an aloof manner towards him. Eventually, he stopped coming and became an amorphous figure who would materialize in her recurring nightmares over the years.

Mira had felt betrayed by her mother when she had decided to resume contact with him. When she had accused her mother of not having any pride, she had philosophically explained that while she could never forgive him, she had let the anger go. Though her mother had urged Mira to do the same, remove the toxic thoughts about her father from her mind, she, Mira, had struggled to accomplish this. Mira turned on her stomach and pounded the mattress with her fist. She had reached the crossroads in her life when she began feeling betrayed by both her parents. They had had their history, but why should she have become the pawn in the process?

Mira sat up on her bed and sipped some water. She wasn't going to fly all the way home to see her father. He had made his choice and it was his karma to live with it. Just like she had had to suffer hers.

Bitch Goddess Rule #17: A Bitch Goddess is sometimes just a lost and lonely ten-year-old.

The Big Take-Off

*M*ira made sure she was at work by seven-thirty the next morning—she couldn't bear being in the apartment all by herself.

She booted her computer and heard Vinay come in and walk past her. She couldn't recall a time when he had not greeted her. She wondered how to resolve the icy situation with her best friend and strongest ally.

She was about to walk up to his desk when her mobile rang.

Mira gripped the instrument hard, bracing to hear the worst.

Her mother sighed sorrowfully. 'You are not coming, are you?'

'How is he?' Mira asked, only because it was expected of her.

Mira's mother's voice was tremulous. 'He's worse, kanna. The doctors have rescheduled the surgery for tomorrow since more tests had to be run. They have asked that the family be informed—Amita has reached...'

'Oh.'

'I am not going to keep begging you to come, kanna. You are twenty-seven-years old and it's time you started behaving your age. You are not a child anymore.'

There was an uncomfortable silence that stretched between them. Mira heard Sanya's stilettos—she could identify their owner even in a ramp crowded with high-heeled supermodels—in the periphery of her cabin.

'Just remember, whatever you decide, you'll have to live

with the consequences,' her mother ended on an ominous note and said goodbye.

Almost immediately, the phone rang again. 'Hi Mira, it's me, Amita.'

Mira was about to say something nasty but held back. Even Bitch Goddesses had mellow moments.

'Yes, Amita. Tell me,' said Mira in her most formal tone.

'Mira, look, I am sorry for abruptly leaving your apartment after all the help you gave me. But this is not about that. You really need to fly down now. Please, Papa is very sick.'

'Why should I come?' Mira said harshly. 'So that we can meet at this big melodramatic moment when he is being wheeled off to surgery? So that he and I entertain the hospital staff with our big father-daughter tear-jerking climax?'

'Mira—'

'Nope, I don't think so.' Mira's tone was hostile.

'Mira, there is a time to be petty and revengeful, but it's not when your father is on his deathbed.'

Deathbed. Mira felt an icy hand seize her heart and squeeze it.

'He loves you, Mira. He always did,' Amita sniffed. 'You know that.'

Mira pressed the mobile to her ear, idly playing with the ballerina paperweight.

'He really misses you, Mira,' Amita sounded desperate. 'He will be at peace once he sees you.'

Mira's eyes glistened with tears. She preferred being the forgotten, neglected child.

'He has all our pictures—yours, mine, Aman's—on his desk. "This is my eldest daughter", I have heard him remark proudly to so many visitors. He always goes to the temple for all our birthdays. I know yours is on February 16 because he schedules a big puja at the temple every year on that day.'

Mira took a deep breath. There was that annoying pain in the chest again—the one caused by a sense of unflappable hope. The hardened shield of hate that she had worn for so many years was melting away and she missed its comforting security. Amita was stripping her of her armour and exposing her, leaving her emotionally naked.

'I don't want to see him and I don't care what happens to him,' Mira bit the words out.

'Mira, I know you care,' said Amita.

'I don't—'

'Mira, you need to see him, make peace with him. You need an emotional closure or you will never be free of the past.' Amita paused for a moment. 'Maybe that is why you are having issues with your boyfriend.'

'What?' Mira bristled.

'Yeah, you heard right.'

'Wow, I didn't know you are such an expert eavesdropper, Amita. Singing, eavesdropping, what other talents do you possess, huh?'

'Sorry, I just happened to overhear snippets of your conversation…' said Amita.

'Right,' said Mira in a flinty tone.

'Mira, please come and meet Papa,' Amita pressed. 'Every time he opens his eyes, he asks for you.'

Mira disconnected. Her head was swimming. She sat with her head tucked into her knees and waited for the feeling to pass. When she felt steady, she got up from her chair and went to Vinay's cubicle.

'Hi Vinay,' she said. She could tell, reading Vinay's distant look, that he was still mad at her.

'What?' he snapped. He looked up, his face stony, a distant look in his eyes. Mira flinched. It was hard when dear friends turned aloof, all because *you* had screwed up.

'My dad is in the hospital,' Mira swallowed. 'I am going home for a week.'

The anger left his face and concern clouded his eyes. Vinay surged to his feet, his arms wrapped around her.

'What happened?' he asked, making her sit on his chair.

Mira told him, choking up as she did. She had thought she was done with crying, but it looked like there was a deep well of anguish buried inside.

Vinay went to his computer and opened a travel booking website. 'It's okay to cry, you know,' he said gently. 'Let it all out.'

He clicked on some links and typed out information. 'You can leave tonight on the 9.15 Air India flight.'

'Let me get my card,' said Mira, getting up.

Vinay waved her to be seated. 'Pay me when you come back.' He handed her a print out after a few minutes. 'Here's your ticket. You would have also got it on email.'

'Thanks, Vinay,' Mira smiled weakly at him. 'You still like me, don't you?'

'Don't be an idiot. Of course I do.' He paused. 'This doesn't mean you're off the hook. I am still mad at you and, frankly, quite disappointed. But that doesn't change anything in our friendship.'

He punched her shoulder gently.

'I am sorry, Vinay,' said Mira in an undertone. 'I was stupid and quite crazy to have snooped on Sanya's computer. But I never used the stuff, I got rid of the files within a few days.'

He stared at her, a small frown creasing his forehead.

'What?' she said.

He cocked his brows at her.

'Okay, okay, if it *does* come up for investigation by our company security, I will own up and take the rap. Happy?'

Vinay grinned for the first time that morning. Mira shook her head at his Darth Vader T-shirt and scruffy jeans. He was such a grubby schoolboy at heart.

'It's okay,' he patted her hand. 'Everybody is allowed to be stupid at least once in their lifetime. But you must later give me the dope about what you pilfered from Ice Queen's computer.'

'You are a good friend, thank you.'

She clutched his arm. 'Vinay! My projects, what will happen to them now?' she lamented. 'I guess they'll go to Sanya. That means the group head post is practically hers for the asking.'

Vinay shook her. 'Silly, don't fret about this, you have bigger things to worry about. A week in India is not going to do you in at work. Just go back home; that's where you need to be.'

Mira got to her feet. 'I need to talk to Gerard about applying for leave. After that I am going back to my place to pack and get ready for my trip.'

'Yes, run. Go and meet Ge-rrr-yy,' Vinay said with a Sanya inflection. 'You go on and start packing. I'll come and take you to the airport.'

Mira laughed. It was good to have her best friend back.

Gerard empathized with her situation and told her to take her time in coming back.

A few hours later, Mira was in her apartment, as ready as she could be for this trip. She was grateful Gerard had been considerate enough to allow her to take time off from work in the midst of a busy implementation period. Mira snapped her red strolley shut and number locked it. She was travelling light and wanted to return as soon as she could. Her stomach was in knots. This was going to be one emotionally charged trip.

She called her mother to soothe her nerves.

'I am glad you are doing the right thing, kanna,' was all her mother would say.

After much deliberation, her next call was to Rohan. She nervously paced the living room as the call went through.

Rohan picked up the call in one ring. 'Mira?' he said in his deep baritone.

'Hi Rohan, I just wanted to tell you that I am going home to Chennai for a week. My dad's in hospital…he is going in for a serious surgery…sorry, I didn't meant to bother you with my problems…it's just that…' her voice broke and she paused to steady herself. 'This is so hard for me and I needed to talk to you…'

'I am sure your dad will be fine, Mira,' said Rohan softly. 'Don't worry. Just stay strong and have faith.' Mira registered the concern in his voice and a part of her wondered if he still cared.

'I am leaving tonight by the 9.15 Air India flight,' she said.

'Take care, I'll see you when you come back.'

Vinay came at six o'clock and they both left for the airport in a cab. An hour later, Mira was checked in and waiting with Vinay in the Changi International Airport's swanky lounge. He thrust a sandwich and coffee at her, insisting that she get some food into her before she boarded.

'I am so angry with my father,' she said between bites, her expressive brown eyes deeply troubled. 'This just doesn't seem fair. Do you know how much of pain I've gone though, how much of hurt because of *him*? Now that he is ill, does everything become hunky-dory between us?'

'It's alright, Mira. Everything will be okay,' said Vinay, patting her arm. 'Here, have a mint.'

She glared at him. 'Are you trying to do a Gerry on me?' They chuckled.

Mira turned serious again. 'I didn't want to meet him under such circumstances—him in the hospital and I cornered into a reconciliatory stance at a time like this.'

Vinay nodded and guzzled down ginger ale from a can.

'I don't want to be forced into saying that all is forgotten and whatever he did was okay.' Mira paused and looked at Vinay.

'It was *not* okay,' she said vehemently, and put the coffee cup down. 'I don't want to forgive him. He was the reason my mother spent years crying. Do you know how many birthdays I waited for him, how many times I came back with trophies and certificates thinking that now he would come home because I had been a good girl?' She dabbed at her tears with the paper napkin that had come in her food tray.

Vinay cupped his chin in his hand and listened.

'But, of course, he never came even once! Ha! Now that he is critically ill, his first-born is expected to ooze love for him. How bloody brilliant!'

Vinay patted her arm reassuringly and made soothing sounds.

She sniffed some more and continued, 'So now he will apologize for abandoning me, just before being wheeled-off for surgery. And I will be honour-bound to forgive him. Great. This way he finds instant peace and absolves himself of all his sins. What about the lifetime of sorrows bestowed upon my mother and me...and for ruining two lives who depended on him?' Mira shook in anger, colour rising to her cheeks.

'Shh...Mira,' Vinay placated. 'You *have* to let the anger go. You have to forgive him, tell him you no longer blame him. Please do this for your sake, or you will never have inner peace.'

'I must be in a very bad shape for *you* to spout philosophy on me,' she replied with a wobbly smile. She shook her head. 'I *don't* want to absolve him. I *don't* want him to find peace. I want to hate him till Kingdom cometh.' She looked daggers at Vinay, challenging him to question her decision.

'Mira.'

She turned at hearing her name.

Rohan! She hastily wiped her face with the napkin and smoothed her hair. She fixed a smile on her face and walked up to him.

Rohan was wearing a white shirt and khakis. *The man always manages to look gorgeous.* He reached out and drew her into a hug. She didn't protest and took in the lemony aftershave he favoured.

Her mind filled with a hundred questions: What was he doing here? Was he going to throw one of those angry-does-not-mean-I-hate-you dialogues at her? She hastily squashed hopes of a reconciliation that spurted within her. He probably felt sorry for her or maybe he felt some sense of obligation for ending their romance on a more polite note. She felt like an idiot for hugging him and eased out of his embrace.

'I am sorry, I didn't mean to bother you today,' she said. 'I just felt like talking to you before I left. I didn't intend for you to take the trouble to come here and...' she trailed, unsure of how to proceed.

'From when did you become so formal with me, Mira?' Rohan grinned, a teasing glint in his eyes. 'Come on, stop thinking so much.' He held her confused gaze and tucked in a tendril of hair behind her ear. 'How are you now?' he asked softly.

'Upset, mad at my father, and...' she looked down at her feet, '...terrified as hell.' He pulled her back into his arms and stroked her back. 'He'll be fine and you'll do good,' he murmured into her hair.

'I...we...' she fumbled for words. 'I'll call later,' she finished and looked at the lengthening security check queue.

'You do that and take care,' he said and released her from his embrace.

'Mira, it's time to go.' Vinay was beside them. He nodded tersely at Rohan.

With a final wave, Mira went through the gates, wondering what Rohan meant by coming to see her off and felt tormented with scenes of her father playing in her mind.

Rough Landing

*I*t was one of the most difficult flights Mira had ever taken. She spent part of the trip wallowing in guilt over her embittered relationship with her father, and the other half in seething with rage at the unfairness of everybody demanding that she see him. She regretted all the times she had refused to meet her father and for deliberately hurting him. But she was also livid with the Fates for giving him a health crisis. This would become an opportune moment for him to try and mend fences with her. All this hurting and bitterness had exhausted her and she slept for the most part of the flight.

As the plane flew low over the dark waters of the Indian Ocean and made its slow descent into Chennai, Mira's nerves were stretched taut like steel. It was ten days since New Year and she had a feeling that her Bitch Goddess resolution was going to be severely tested.

She cleared immigration and grabbed her stroller that was the first to arrive on the conveyer belt, cleared customs and made a dash for the exit doors. Chennai's warm humid air and the faint redolence of jasmines assailed her nostrils as soon as she stepped out. She loved her city but was in no mood to enjoy the first few moments after her arrival tonight.

Taxi and auto drivers thronged the entrance even at this late hour and accosted her with 'Enga madam ponum?' Where to, Madam?' Mira was about to hail a cab when she saw a tall young man with curly hair holding a placard that read her name in bold red letters: MIRA IYER. She caught his gaze and he tentatively waved to her. She knew at once who he was.

'Mira?' he said, lowering the placard and approaching her. She was stunned by the resemblance between him and Amita. He too had the telltale brown eyes and Amita's sharp chin. She could have spotted him anywhere and known his identity.

He stood looking at her for some reaction.

'Hi, yes, I am Mira,' she said, straightening her shoulders.

'Aman,' he said, offering his hand in a firm handshake. 'Amita's brother.'

Mira rolled the stroller forward. 'You should not have bothered, I would have taken a cab.'

'Don't be silly,' he said, smoothly taking the stroller from her and wheeling it towards the parking lot.

Neither spoke as he led her to where his car was parked. Mira stilled. It was the same silver grey Ambassador that her father used to drive her around in. Mira got into it shakily and tried to blink back the tears that threatened to spill. The upholstery was no longer the dark blue velvet on which she used to sprawl across on family outings, but was now a beige leather.

'How come you drive this old relic? Don't you have a swankier car?' she asked Aman as he shifted gears. They had a very wealthy industrialist father, after all.

'I love this baby,' he grinned, patting the steering wheel and merging onto the fairly deserted highway. 'In fact it was I who dissuaded dad from selling it for a measly ₹30,000.'

Mira felt inundated by her past. Fragments of old memories were everywhere in this car; smothering her, tormenting her. She couldn't believe that the stickers of gods that her mother had stuck on the dashboard years ago were still there, albeit faded and almost gone.

She took a deep breath and tried to think of something to say to the young man who was her half-brother.

'How old are you, Aman?'

'Twenty,' he said, throwing her a look, 'seven years younger than you.'

She nodded. 'So how is he?' she asked quietly, looking out of the window and taking in the tall hoardings advertising the latest jewellery designs and the most imaginative range of silk saris for the upcoming Pongal.

Aman grimaced. 'Dad is stable as of now, but the operation is very serious.' He didn't have to explain any further; they both knew what a tricky operation it was going to be. Mira stole a sideways glance at Aman. He seemed to be straightforward and friendly like Amita, but with a mind of his own. If he could have convinced his dad to keep the Ambassador, he must have strong persuasive skills, Mira mused with a small smile.

Aman finally pulled over at the hospital car park. Mira looked at his drawn face and saw the same fear that had been reflected in his sister's eyes. He looked so young and vulnerable that Mira felt like putting an arm around him in comfort. She suddenly realized he—and Amita—were as much a victim as she was, in the decisions their father had taken. She sighed.

'Don't worry, he will be fine,' she said awkwardly.

Aman looked at her, a bit surprised. 'Thank you,' he said and walked briskly towards the hospital. They both entered the building and crossed the corridor to reach the Intensive Care Unit inside which her father lay.

Mira stopped in her tracks when she saw a woman huddled in a corner. Her stomach churned. It was the Other Woman. She was seated on one of the plastic chairs and was clad in a blue cotton sari, her hair tied in a fuss-free bun. Old memories of the woman's sleeveless blouse came back in painful waves to attack Mira. How could she forget that day in the traffic light? She felt a familiar anger course through her veins. The Other Woman suddenly looked up at her. Mira's knees almost buckled when she saw the agony written in the woman's eyes. She sucked in her breath and looked away.

Amita, in jeans and a T-shirt, was standing beside her mother, her face pensive and drawn. Aman joined them and wrapped them in a tight embrace.

'How is he?' he asked.

'Just the same,' Amita replied, biting her lips.

The three stood there, frozen in the moment, looking scared, vulnerable and lost. Mira's eyes apprised the family before her. All her life she had been fighting this—a solid family unit with her father as its nucleus. While she and her mother were two hapless women, the same man simply a ghostly presence in their lives. No wonder she had not won. But then again, didn't her mother do a fabulous job of raising her single-handedly? She looked at the three of them again. They suddenly bore a striking resemblance to her own family—both units were missing the father.

'Mira!' The most familiar voice she knew interrupted her thoughts.

Mira swung around to see her mother hurry towards her in the dimly-lit passage outside the ICU. Her mother laid a gentle hand on Mira's arm and stroked her cheeks.

Mira searched her mother's eyes. 'Are you okay, Amma?' she asked, her voice tinged with concern. Her mother had been her Rock of Gibralter all along, and she loved her despite their many differences.

'Yes, kanna. Have you eaten? There is a cafeteria downstairs…'

'It's okay, Amma. I ate in the flight, and besides, with all this going on, I've lost my appetite.'

Her mother nodded and fell silent.

'Thank God you are here, Mira,' she said. 'Your father has been chanting your name since last night. I was worried that you might not come...'

Mira sighed and leaned against the wall. 'There's no choice, is there, Amma?' she said, looking deep into her mother's eyes.

'I waited only to see you, kanna. I am going home now and will come before the surgery in the afternoon. Aman said he will drop you home.'

'But how will you go back alone? Please stay! I can't meet him without you,' said Mira, her eyes widening. She felt like a lost ten-year-old again.

Her mother shook her head. 'I have been here since the morning, Mira, and I want to go home and rest. I have hired a taxi for the day. I'll manage, you go. You'll be fine.' It was her way of answering her daughter's unasked questions and telling her that it was now upto Mira, what she made of her past.

Mira studied her mother's tired face and felt a sea of emotions surge through her. Despite what her father had done to the both of them, her mother had led a dignified and quiet life. And she was gracious enough to be by his side in his hour of need.

'Come.' Aman walked up to her and touched her hand. 'What can I call you? Didi?'

'Just Mira will do,' she replied through clenched teeth. What was with him and Amita wanting to forge ties with her? 'Come, let's go to see Papa,' he said again.

Mira shot her mother a fleeting glance.

'Go, Mira,' she said, gently pushing her towards the ICU.

Mira sighed and quietly followed Aman as he led the way.

Bitch Goddess Rule #18: In a family crisis, even a true-blue Bitch Goddess needs help from a higher power.

From Hell and Back

'Oh God!' The words were out of her mouth before she could stop them. Even though Mira knew her father was critically ill, nothing had prepared her for this frail man on the bed, hooked upto machines, his eyes closed and his breathing laboured. Although it had been years since she had seen her father, in her mind's eye, he was still the tall, broad-shouldered, impossibly handsome man who had once taken her mother pillion riding, zipping through the streets of 1960s Madras on his maroon Vespa. She knew her mother still held onto a black and white photo of the two of them seated on the two-wheeler, laughing with carefree joie de vivre at the camera. Mira flinched at seeing the shrivelled man lying in front of her. She wanted to cry but the tears refused to flow.

Aman stepped closer to the bed and touched his father's hand.

'Papa?'

Their father stirred. 'Mira? Has she come?' His voice was a whisper.

'Yes, Papa. She is right beside you.' Aman motioned Mira with a tilt of his chin. She moved forward hesitantly.

Mr Iyer opened his eyes and looked at her. Despite his poor health, his mellow brown eyes still retained their sparkle.

'You are here. Come, my dear, sit next to me,' he said. The corners of his lips twitched in a smile.

She moved near the bed and looked at him silently. The words of anger had suddenly dried up within her.

'I had hoped and prayed that you would come.' His voice was faint and he spoke with a lot of effort.

He reached out to Mira and she had no choice but to clasp his toasty hand in hers. The last time she had held this hand, her tiny palm had disappeared into his larger one and she had felt safe and secure. Her father's grip tightened. This time, it was he who was seeking strength from her, he seemed to be the one holding on.

'My baby,' he whispered. Mira flinched. He had always called her that. 'Thank you for coming.'

Her father's eyelids fluttered shut. Mira shivered. The hospital room was suddenly very cold. She looked at the man on the bed and at their joined hands. Something melted and shifted within her. She looked away.

'You'll be fine,' Mira said. She gripped his hand and leaned closer to him. His narrow-slit eyes wedged open.

'Don't worry, everything will be fine,' repeated Mira, patting his hand.

'Yes...now that you are here...' he said and closed his eyes again.

The nurse walked in and told Mira and Aman to leave.

Mira eased her hand out of her father's and stepped back from the bed.

'Mira,' her father said. 'I love you, baby, I always did.'

She met her father's gaze that managed to be resolute through his fear. And shimmering in their depths, she could read an unspoken plea for forgiveness.

'I know, I know,' she said simply.

He nodded and his eyes drooped off in sleep. The nurse showed them out and closed the door.

By mid-afternoon, her father was transferred to the operation theatre for the surgery.

A little while later, when there was nothing else to do but wait, Mira slouched on one of the plastic chairs in the waiting area and dispassionately studied her father's family. Her stomach churned again when she spotted the Other Woman. She was quietly chanting shlokas from a yellowed prayer book. Mira grudgingly acknowledged that the Other Woman was very similar to her mother, in terms of her dress sense and, perhaps, even personality. Gone was the Glam Doll who had worn sleeveless blouses and sheer chiffon sarees in the 1970s' Madras. She also seemed to be a worrywart and someone who put her family above everything else. It must be true, Mira reflected, what people said about men falling for the same kind of women. Her father certainly fell in that category.

Mira's gaze fell on Amita. She looked grief-stricken and was far removed from the vivacious girl who had stayed with her in Singapore. Aman was restless, fidgeting in his chair, and jumpy every time a nurse appeared at the ICU door.

She pictured the scene as an outsider would see it and smiled despite her gloomy mood. Her life was playing out like some melodramatic Tamil soap opera that moves from one twist to the next. A father who was battling for his life, the mandatory two wives, his multiple children—riddled with their own exaggerated sense of self-importance—and the role they played in this family crisis. And lastly, the doctor with a permanent frown and the nurse who bustled about silently.

Mira, suddenly, felt all grown-up and wise. Life was so fickle and transient. Bottling up toxic thoughts about people who were, perhaps, victims of their own desperate needs and weaknesses was so meaningless. Life was like a game of cards—it was all in the luck of the draw. The thumb rule was that you had to play with the cards you are dealt with. There was no pointing in being angry—that didn't change the hand. And one can never walk away from the table. You have to play the hand, play it wisely, play it as fairly as possible, and simply hope to win. Most importantly, play it with compassion, she concluded.

She watched Amita console her fraught mother. Aman was hurrying by with a bunch of bills in his hand to hand it over to his mother.

'Aman,' Mira called out to him softly and beckoned him. 'Please bring me all the bills from now on. Don't bother your mother about the money; she is in no state to handle such issues. Besides, it is my responsibility to take charge of the situation.'

'Mine and Amita's too,' said Aman stiffly.

Mira wordlessly took the bills from his hand. 'I'll remember that some day, when I am old and bedridden, and have my hospital bills sent to you.'

He laughed. 'You are cool, Mi—,' he broke off. 'Please let us call you Didi.'

'No! Not unless you want your bones broken,' replied Mira with a deadpan expression.

He laughed again.

'Does the hospital accept cards?' she asked.

'Yes, they do and dad is also on an insurance plan.'

'Cool, I'll settle the bills soon after the surgery. He can pay me back later.'

Aman gave her a grateful smile and went to sit with his mother and sister.

Mira settled back into her chair. Soon, exhaustion caught up with her and she fell asleep.

'Mira?' a voice floated towards her.

She woke up with a start, feeling a bit disoriented. She

looked up at Amita who was gazing at her with concern. Mira sat up anxiously. 'What happened? Hope all is well?'

'No, no, don't worry. The surgery is still in progress and it's going to be a long time before we know,' replied Amita with a sigh. 'I came to ask if you want lunch. We got something from home; you haven't eaten anything all day.'

Mira looked at the Other Woman whose eyes had puffed up with all the crying.

'How about your mother? Has she eaten?'

Amita shook her head. 'She refuses to. Aman and I have given up.'

Mira nodded and reassuringly rested her hand on Amita's lap. Then the waiting outside the OT continued for Mira and the others.

The doctor finally emerged from the OT at close to 6.00 p.m.

'Can I speak to Mr Iyer's family, please?' he called out, peeling off his gloves and cap.

Mira surged to her feet, the blood draining from her face. She was only vaguely aware of Amita and Aman trailing behind her.

'Yes, doctor? My father…' said Mira. Her throat felt parched.

The doctor gave her a faint smile. 'The surgery was successful and we have removed the clot.' He raised his hands to the heavens. 'By God's grace it worked out well. After all, this was a complicated operation.'

Relief swept over Mira and she felt too overwhelmed to even thank him. Amita and Aman embraced her.

'However, even now he is still not entirely out of danger,' the doctor cautioned. 'We will observe him—the next twelve hours are critical. So all I can say now is, let's wait and watch.'

Mira shook his hand. 'Thank you, doctor, we understand.'

'While I personally don't see any complications happening,

I would like to exercise caution, anyway. The nurse will inform you as and when your father regains consciousness. You all may visit him then.'

The doctor patted Mira's shoulder and left.

Mira looked at Aman, the last forty-eight hours of weariness settling over her. 'I would like to go home, can you please drop me?'

Mira's mother rushed out to envelope her in a hug as soon as Mira got out of the car.

'He is going to be fine,' said Mira. Her mother held her close for a few moments. 'Thank you, kanna. Thank you.'

As soon as Mira trundled upstairs to the privacy of her room, she called Vinay.

'The surgery's over, it went well,' she said in a rush of words when he picked up the phone. She ran over the events of the last two days.

'And Vinay,' she concluded on a quiet note, 'I am sorry, not just about hacking into Sanya's computer, but also about the way I have been behaving of late...'

'Hey, don't worry. No harm done—at least till now!' replied Vinay. 'Does this mean you have abandoned your new bitchy persona, or whatever you call it? Bitch Goddess, isn't it?' He sounded cheerful, even hopeful.

Mira laughed heartily, all the stress and tension of the last few months forgotten for a moment. Suddenly, she felt light and unburdened of her past. 'Let's just say I have reached equilibrium and am far more at peace with my lot than I have ever been before.'

'Hmm...' Vinay sounded a little uncertain. 'Good, good.'

'So how is our office bitch?' asked Mira.

'Sanya? According to the talk around the water cooler, she might become the group head,' he sounded gloomy.

Mira laughed. 'Now you are sounding like how I used to. Chill. I plan to be back the minute my dad moves out of the ICU. Let the best woman become the group head—or rather, the better bitch in our case!'

In the stunned silence that followed, Mira said goodbye and disconnected.

In the ensuing ten days, the family quickly fell into a familiar hospital routine. Mira, Amita, Aman and their mother took turns to visit the hospital and be in touch with the doctors. But since Mira's father was still in the ICU, the family had to mostly wait in the visitors' area, flipping through magazines and watching inane channels playing on the television. Mira's mother visited a couple of times, saw her ex-husband's sleeping profile through the ICU's circular glass windows and left.

Mira's father improved steadily and the doctors were happy with his progress. Ten days after the surgery, he was moved to a private room. One day, Mira sat on the sofa opposite to the bed where her father lay asleep. He was no longer hooked up to machines and drips, though his head was wrapped in bandage swathes. Besides the hum of the air conditioner, the room was silent. Mira worked on her office project on her laptop, while keeping a steady eye on her father.

'Mira,' a faint voice called out. Mira's eyes flew open; she had snoozed while working. She glanced at the wall clock. It was 4.00 p.m., almost five hours since she had come to the hospital.

She shut her laptop and hurried to her father's side. His tired eyes held her gaze. He reached out to her and she placed her hand on his. His grip was surprisingly firm.

'Let me call the nurse or doctor,' said Mira, reaching for the landline.

Her father's grip tightened. 'No, please, I want to talk to you.'

'But are you allowed to?'

'Please, ma,' he said. 'I am tired but not dead.'

Mira sighed and drew up a chair next to his bed.

'You are still upset with me, aren't you, baby?' His voice was soft and tinged with sorrow.

Mira inhaled sharply. 'It's somewhere in the past, Appa. Why talk about it now? You should be resting...'

Her father's eyes lit up hearing the word 'Appa'. Mira was stunned at herself for being able to utter the most difficult word in her life. But it had sat comfortably on her tongue, an old taste that reminded of her childhood years of going piggy-back riding on her father's shoulders and licking ice cream cones in Marina beach. The word rolled off her tongue easily, showing no rustiness that disuse could have caused. A lump formed at the back of her throat.

'But you still haven't forgiven your father, eh? Can you say you have?'

Mira stood up taller. 'No, I don't think I would be able to do that,' she said honestly. 'But I have tried to accept it after fighting it for so many years.' She paused, fixing her gaze on him. 'I have tried to accept what you did to Amma and me, or I wouldn't be standing here before you.'

Moments passed before her father spoke again. 'I did—and still—love you and your mother.' He stared at the ceiling, his eyes glazed with a film of unshed tears.

'I know,' Mira replied quietly. 'But you also love your other family.'

'Yes,' he whispered. 'I also love Vandana and the kids.'

Mira shook her head and frowned. 'I don't know why you are telling me all this after so many years...'

He slowly shifted his body to turn toward her. 'Now that you are a grown woman, I felt I have to explain myself. This... this surgery, our meeting...it's all like a new lease of life for me.'

'Please don't strain yourself, Appa. Maybe I should leave.' Mira got to her feet.

Her father breathed heavily and lifted a hand. 'Stay, I want to finish.'

'I agree I made some mistakes, very big ones at that,' he added. 'I did not wish for Vandana to happen. I did not go looking for another love. It happened at a time when your mother and I were having some differences in our marriage. We married young...had you soon after...and just realized we were two different individuals. I should have been stronger and walked away from Vandana...well, I didn't. I gave into temptation and paid a heavy price for it. I lost you and your mother.' He swallowed hard. 'Let's begin on a fresh note. Stay in touch with me, Amita and Aman. They respect you...'

Something pricked within her. Dark cesspools of resentment and anger rose to her throat like bile. Mira suddenly realized that by talking about the past, her father was trying to assuage his own guilt. He didn't seem to regret the choices he had made that had made her and her mother suffer all these years. He didn't understand their pain—he hadn't then, he didn't now. It was as if only his issues mattered. He wanted the best of both worlds, the love of both the families. Mira set her mouth in a firm line. Her father had to bear his own cross and lay his ghosts to rest. She couldn't forgive him more than what was necessary to move on in life and evolve as a more wholesome person.

'Let it go, Mira. Let go of the past and your bitterness. I love you, baby. I always have...'

'Appa, I don't think this is the right time to be having this conversation,' she replied crisply. 'I have told you that I have tried to accept this situation after all these years. That's all you can expect of me at the moment.' Before he could reply, her phone rang. Vinay's number flashed on the screen.

'It's my boss,' she said, scurrying to the door. 'Please rest, I'll call the nurse. See you tomorrow.'

She shut the door and fled outside the plush private hospital's glass doors.

Bitch Goddess Rule #19: Even a Bitch Goddess pauses in her tracks when the skeletons come tumbling out of the closet.

Movin' On Up

'Hey Vinay,' said Mira, as soon as she stepped outside the hospital. 'What's up?'

'Congratulations, boss,' said Vinay.

'Huh?'

'Haven't you checked your mail? Allow me to be the first to tell you that I am now speaking with the new group head.'

'Whoa! What? Wait...when did this happen? How did I...?' Mira spluttered, feeling a sort of numbness that comes from extreme good fortune.

'Because you are *that* good, silly. Now the official, and real, reason is you were found to be the most suitable person. The rumour, however, is that Sanya screwed up so badly that she put herself out of the running.' Vinay laughed.

'Why? What did she do?' Mira's heart was beating fast. This was an unreal moment—no more suffering Sanya's bitchiness.

'You aren't going to believe this. She apparently told the Elcard management that you are incompetent and that she should be the one in-charge of their projects, if they wanted the job well done.'

'What? The gall of her!' said Mira.

'I know! The top guy at Elcard, Stewart, mentioned this to Gerard, expressing his displeasure at Sanya's unprofessional behaviour,' continued Vinay. 'So Sanya's been taken to task and we don't know what will come of it yet.'

'Hmm...'

'So Gerard emailed everybody today, announcing you as the new group head. The better bitch *has* won, woo-hoo,' cheered Vinay.

Mira went silent. She sat on a bench and saw a trolley stacked with food trays being wheeled to the patients' rooms. The cool afternoon sea breeze rustled the leaves of the trees lining the driveway. A heavily pregnant woman walked slowly around the obstetrics block, the happy anticipation of motherhood evident on her face.

'What? No joyous response, no victory cry? C'mon, give me a phone high-five,' Vinay's voice interrupted Mira's thoughts.

'I don't know how to react, Vinay,' Mira said slowly. 'From what you say, I got this position *not* because of something good *I* did, but because of something bad *she* did. I am not entirely sure I like the reasoning behind the promotion.'

Vinay clicked his tongue impatiently. 'No, you are missing the plot. You got this because of simply being *you,* and not someone else.'

'Don't get you.'

'Listen. You didn't become a replica of Sanya, though your Bitch Goddess alter ego was dangerously headed that way. You stopped yourself just in time and look where that has got you.'

'How did you get to be so wise?' asked Mira after a moment.

'You ain't seen nothin' yet, baby,' he guffawed.

They chatted a little longer and then she said, 'Now let me go home and read my mail. Talk to you later.'

When Mira reached home, she ran inside to share the news of her promotion with her mother. Mrs Iyer was jubilant and hugged her daughter tight. Then she sat Mira down and gave her a tumbler of steaming filter coffee and a plate of murukku.

'Are you happy, kanna? Is this what you want?' she said tenderly.

Mira looked surprised. 'Of course, Amma. I am doing exactly what I had always wanted to in my career. It's worked out to plan so far.' She took a sip of coffee. 'Umm...this is great.'

Mira's mother affectionately stroked her daughter's cheek.

'Yes, kanna, I know. You are doing well in your career but are you happy with your personal life?'

Mira rolled her eyes. 'Oh no, is this about the highly eligible TamBram boys earning heaps and heaps of dollars in the great US of A?'

'It's not funny, Mira. Marriage is very important for women and it's time you settled down.'

'We'll see,' said Mira non-commitally and bit into a murukku.

The pressure cooker whistled. The neighbour's teenage daughter came to return the latest issue of *Femina*. Mira's mother came back after these interruptions and sat next to Mira. 'I know you are hiding something from me, kanna.'

Mira looked at her mother questioningly. 'Why do you say that, Amma?'

'There is a man in your life.' Her tone was matter of fact.

'Amma!'

'I know. A mother senses such things.'

The colour rose to Mira's cheeks.

'Mira, you might as well tell me,' her mother smiled.

Mira distractedly played with her hair and took in the minor changes her mother had made to their living room. There were new mirror-work cushion covers in bright colours and a money plant occupied the corner near the television. Her mother studied her and waited for her response.

Mira shook her head and grinned incredulously. 'Amma, how do you know?'

'Sometimes I feel I know you better than I know myself. Come on, tell me about him.'

Mira sighed. 'Alright, his name is Rohan Bhardwaj,' she began, noting the way her mother's eyes lit up. Her mind's scanner would have undoubtedly identified Rohan's correct caste and sub-caste, and even played out the wedding reception and the grandkids playing in the garden by now. Mira narrated the whole story about Rohan and Sanya, judiciously editing the scandalous bits as she went along. There are some secrets that one must guard close to the chest—Project Bitch Goddess being one of them, Mira decided.

'Hmm... so you both have been playing mind games with each other and Rohan thinks you used him to get back at Sanya,' her mother concluded shrewdly.

Mira winced. 'It's not as if I lied to him deliberately, Amma. It took me a while to figure out my own feelings, but by then the damage had been done.' Her voice was small and scared.

'Like they say, all is fair in love and war,' said Mira's mother. 'If he loves you truly, he'll come back and if he doesn't return, letting him go is the best favour you can do yourself.' She spoke with the wisdom of a woman who had experienced love at close quarters.

Mira's eyes became moist. 'Do you really think so, Amma?' She leaned on her mother's shoulder, feeling like a little girl again.

'Trust me; your self-worth is more important than finding a man.'

Mira nodded, too choked with emotion to express her gratitude to her mother.

'But if you are sure he is really the one, you must set aside your ego and pursue him. True love is worth fighting for.' Mira caught the mischievous glint in her mother's eyes and smiled.

'I will, Amma, I will,' she said. 'By the way, I need to go back to Singapore. The new group head cannot be missing for so long.'

'Yes, I agree. You must rejoin office before this Sanya girl plays further politics.'

'Oh, Amma, I don't think she can, going forward. I hope I never see her again,' Mira said with feeling.

She went to her room and logged into the Internet. Gerard's mail was effusive in its praise. He had used adjectives like 'industrious', 'efficient' and 'superior intellect' to describe her. Mira switched off the laptop and slipped in an assorted tracks CD in the player. Cyndi Lauper's powerful voice rendering *Time after Time* reverberated in the room.

Lying in my bed I hear the clock tick,
And think of you.
Caught up in circles confusion...
Is nothing new.
Flashback, warm nights...
Almost left behind.
Suitcases of memories,
Time after time...

Mira sat up. The lyrics uncannily described her state of affairs with Rohan. It was thirty-six hours since she had spoken to him, not that she was counting. What was it that her mother had said—'True love is worth fighting for.' Mira rested her chin on her palm. Rohan had been concerned, yet aloof, at the airport. She wasn't sure what was playing on his mind. Yes, if he loved her enough, he would come back. Mira switched off the lights and rested her head on the pillow.

But how long would she have to wait for Rohan to let her know one way or the other? She turned to one side and wiggled her toes. She shook her head, as if to remove the cobwebs from her mind. Her mother was right. She didn't need a man to validate her existence and self-worth. If Rohan took their relationship forward, she would welcome it. But if he didn't—so what? She curled up in a ball and hugged herself. She had survived after her father had left, and she would survive if Rohan, too, left her life. She had just got a promotion and had led the way in a family crisis. She rocked. Mira turned on her back and smiled in the darkness.

Bitch Goddess Rule #20: A Bitch Goddess doesn't need a man to fill the void in her heart; she just needs to keep the faith.

The next day, Mira shared the news of her promotion with her father. He was looking in better spirits and the nurse had just changed him into a freshly laundered powder blue hospital gown. Mira had met the doctor earlier who indicated that her father was showing signs of steady progress.

'Congratulations,' her father said. 'I am so proud of you.'

'Thanks, Appa.' Mira adjusted his pillow so that his head rested at a comfortable angle.

'But are you going to accept the role?'

'Of course! Why do you ask?' said Mira, looking baffled.

'You don't have to go back, you know…' her father trailed.

'Of course I do, Appa. Or I'll lose my job!'

'That is what I am trying to say. You don't *need* that job. Stay back, help me run the firm.'

Mira's eyes widened. 'I don't think I—'

'No, no, I am serious, Mira,' he cut in. 'You know the doctors have advised me to take things easy from now on. I also feel like stepping back a bit. We are a profitable enterprise and have established ourselves in the industry. I can be a chief mentor now, like Narayana Murthy.'

He looked at her squarely in the face. 'You are a software engineer. Take charge and succeed me in the firm. Everything is there for the asking, we are rated as the fifth best in the country.'

Mira watched him incredulously. 'You *are* serious, aren't you?'

His silence spoke volumes.

Mira spoke slowly, 'I am sorry, Appa. At this juncture in my life, it will be impossible for me to abide by your wish. I want to chase after my dreams and not be content with things given in a golden platter.'

'But this is your rightful inheritance, Mira. Amita and Aman will also have their share of the company.'

Mira considered his words. She didn't want to revisit the past by accusing him of never thinking of her—until now—in his plans regarding succession. Project Bitch Goddess had been an enlightening journey for her. She now knew what she exactly wanted—from her career and her personal life. She shook her head and smiled. 'I truly appreciate your offer, Appa. But, sorry, this is not what I want.'

Her father looked disapprovingly at her. 'Why? That's what I want to know, rather, *need* to know.'

'Appa, I have worked hard to reach a certain stage in my career on my own steam. Your firm will be safe in Aman's hands. He is a complete geek and raring to be the next young turk in town. You should groom *him* and not me.'

'You still haven't forgiven me,' her father's breath came out in faint rasps.

Mira shook her head vehemently. 'Please don't get worked up, Appa. It's not good for you.'

He looked away from her.

Mira sighed. 'You *know* I have made peace with all that has happened to Amma, to me…to us. We had that chat last week, remember? I even hosted Amita at my place in Singapore! So this decision to not join your firm has nothing to do with the past.'

'Please tell me you are not running away from me.'

Mira dragged her chair closer to his bed. She clasped her father's hands. 'I am not running away, Appa. But I have a great new role waiting for me in Singapore; something that I worked very hard to get.' She bit back a smile, remembering the day she had tried googling Bitch Goddess. It now seemed so long ago. 'I am sorry, but my heart is not in running your firm.'

'If you are not trying to punish me, then why did you offer to pay Amita's fees?'

Mira flinched at her father's hardened tone. 'I admit my motive at that point might not have been noble, but much has changed since then, hasn't it? Besides, I was also trying to support Amita in her career goals.'

'I had always dreamt of my daughters and son being groomed for the business,' Mira's father said, his voice tinged with sadness.

'But what about Amita's dream of becoming a playback singer, Appa? She should follow her passion, shouldn't she?' Mira straightened her shoulders and quietly challenged her father to oppose her legitimate request.

His silence emboldened her to continue, 'What's wrong with her studying music? She has the talent and it's a lucrative career path these days. See how huge *Indian Idol* is.'

'Study music? What good would that do? I told her she can sing her whole life as a hobby, but not pursue it as a profession. She needs a proper job that will bring in a regular paycheck.'

'Have you heard her sing?' said Mira. 'She has a God-given voice; I heard her sing in Singapore.'

'Yes, she has a good voice and has always won music competitions in school.' Her father looked increasingly agitated and waved his hands in the air. 'But that still doesn't mean she should become a...a club singer!'

'It will be such a crime to allow this talent to go waste,' said Mira with vehemence, surprised at herself for coming out in staunch support of this girl who had irked her just a few weeks back.

'Bah. She doesn't know what she wants. Studying music will be a big mistake.'

'Fine, at least give her a chance to make a mistake.'

'Not if it hurts others.'

'I remember someone making a lethal mistake that hurt two people, even shattering their lives. On that scale, this one is a mere blip,' Mira said flatly, raising her eyebrows. Her gaze lingered on her father for a few seconds.

His face turned stony and ashen. Neither spoke. The door opened and Vandana, Amita and Aman entered.

'Can you all please give Mira and me ten minutes?' Mr Iyer said. They nodded and left the room quietly. His lips curled at the corners. 'I'll make you a deal, Mira.'

Mira's brows furrowed.

'I'll let Amita sing.'

Mira grinned. 'Thank—'

Her father wagged a finger. 'Hear me out before you thank me. I'll let her sing if you stay back and take over the firm.'

'What is this?' Mira stared at him, too stunned to speak. 'A Hindi movie blackmail scene? It's a pity you are still using me as a pawn in your scheme of things. And I refuse to be party to it. Amita is a good kid with a passion for music, and is lucky enough to have the financial luxury to fulfill her dreams. If you don't give her a chance, *you*, and not her, will be the loser. Because next time round, she may not come home. And there won't be a Mira to rescue her.'

Mira's father wet his lips with his tongue.

Mira counted to ten silently to control her outburst. She spoke in a measured tone, 'It's time you stopped emotionally manipulating people to achieve your own ends, Appa. You told my mother not to make you choose. But what you ended up doing gave her no choice in the matter, did it?' Her voice rose an octave, threatening to break her composure. 'And now you are imposing your views on Amita and me. She gets to follow her dream, provided I forsake mine?' She paused to steady herself. 'Sorry, Appa, your peace of mind cannot be bought through bullying me into compliance.'

She lapsed into silence for a few moments. The air-conditioner hummed lazily in the background.

'Alright, Appa. Here's my final word on the matter,' she said, counting on her fingers:

'One. No, I don't want the firm, thank you.

Two. No, I won't stay back to run it, even if you use every possible blackmailing tactic.

And three, Aman will make a very good successor, so invest your time in grooming him instead of brainwashing and bullying your daughters.'

An icy air filled the space between Mira and her father, the warmth and bonhomie of their earlier conversation clearly undone.

'My tickets are booked and I leave day after tomorrow. If you know what's good for you, you'll let Amita sing,' she concluded with finality to her tone.

'But what about your inheritance? You are walking away from it.' She could hear her father's smirk beneath the concerned question.

'No, I am not walking away from my inheritance,' she shot him a cryptic smile.

Mira thought about the nightmares that had tormented her all these years, the long vigils she used to keep at the bedroom window, hoping for her father's return, and the incessant weeping of her mother that Mira had helplessly watched as a child. She now knew there would be no more nightmares and tears.

'You can say that I've made my peace with it.'

Her father's liquid brown eyes filled with genuine sorrow. 'I never meant to hurt you or your mother. I am sorry, Mira. Thank you for managing this crisis so beautifully. You are an asset to me and your mother.'

Mira blinked back her tears and held his hand.

'Please let Amita pursue her dream,' she gave it a last shot. His eyes glinted. 'I can, if you help me…' he wheedled.

Mira looked astonished. Despite his weak health, her father didn't want to budge from his stand. He was still using every trick in the book to get his own way. He would never give up, would he? He was a hard-nosed businessman, after all.

'I have nothing more to say,' she said and turned on her heel. She ignored the curious looks Vandana, Amita and Aman shot in her direction, blindly walked down the hospital's passageway, and straight into Rohan.

Beyond Bitch Goddess

'*R*ohan! What are you doing here?' Mira shrieked, looking at Rohan's tall, athletic frame blocking her path. He was wearing a blue plaid shirt and dark jeans, looking dashing as ever. The evening light caught his chiselled cheekbones and expressive dark eyes, making him look even more handsome. She caught a whiff of his lemony cologne. All she wanted to do was to hold him close to her and never let him go.

'I heard Chennai has become a holiday hotspot. I needed a break, and here I am!'

'Sure,' she quipped back. 'Chennai adds about three malls a day to its tourist brochure. Want to check them out?'

'Why not? There are no malls where I come from,' replied Rohan with a straight face.

They laughed. A pretty young nurse scurried past them, darting interested glances in Rohan's direction. A wheelchair clattered by, its attendant calling out, 'Make way, pliss! Make way!'

Rohan grabbed her hand. 'Come on, let's get out of here.'

He took her to his waiting cab and she gratefully got in, desperate to leave the gloomy hospital surroundings.

'Marina beach, ponga,' he instructed the driver before turning to look at her.

'Rough day?' he asked. She leaned back on the seat and squeezed her eyes shut. She was drained after the confrontation with her father.

'Yes, today was particularly bad,' she muttered. 'I wish the earth would open up and swallow me.'

'Hmm...that bad, eh? Want to talk about it?'

'It's not a sweet bedtime story, Rohan,' she grimaced.

'I think I know half the story. But I deserve to know how it ended.' He flashed a winsome smile. She was defenseless when he smiled like that.

The car pulled over in front of Marina beach. Rohan and Mira got off the car and walked past sari-clad mamis in sneakers and small clusters of youngsters chatting and laughing.

'Mood for an ice cream?' said Rohan, approaching an ice-cream vendor. They bought two orange popsicles and slowly trudged through the sand to the oceanfront. The sun was dipping into the waters and boats were bobbing in the distant horizon. The fishermen dragged their nets shorewards, their children running, half-naked, behind them.

Mira looked at the crowd around her. Coming here brought back a slew of memories—of impromptu family outings to Marina beach, of collecting sea shells while her parents settled down for a chat, of being lifted by her father each time a big wave washed over. And no trip to the beach was ever complete without her father buying her mother fragrant jasmine strings, and Mira an ice cream. There was a set pattern to their lives, a comfortable rhythm to their existence that had made her feel secure and cocooned. Then, suddenly, her familiar world had toppled, leaving her to her own devices to build a new world from scratch.

A gigantic wave crashed at their feet; the sea was rough today. Mira shuddered and clutched Rohan's hand instinctively. He shot her a concerned look and led her away. They picked a secluded spot to sit, and licked their ice creams in companionable silence.

'Are you ready to tell me now, Mira?' Rohan spoke after some time. His voice was gentle and patient, much like him. A surge of gratitude filled her; she was touched by his concern.

Mira slowly recounted the events of the last few weeks, ending with the confrontation with her father that afternoon. Rohan cupped his chin in his hand and attentively listened without interrupting her.

'Hmm...your dad is quite the despot, eh?' he said, once she had finished.

Mira shot him a laughing look. 'Amita calls him Amrish Puri,' she said, referring to Hindi cinema's favourite authoritarian father. Then she brightened up. 'But he no longer has control over my life. I've made peace with him and my past in my own way. I hope things work out for Amita, though.'

Rohan squeezed her hand reassuringly.

'Don't worry, she'll do fine. Things have a way of sorting themselves out.'

'I hope so.'

'You've been an incredible sister and an amazing daughter, Mira, and managed everything with aplomb.'

Mira blushed. 'Enough about me. Tell me, what are you doing in Chennai? Besides, of course, your penchant for its tourist attractions.'

'Like the malls...' he said.

'Yes...like the malls,' she laughed. 'But how did you know where I was?'

'I coaxed the information out of Vinay. He is very protective about you.' Mira bit back a smile hearing the jealous edge to Rohan's tone.

He chucked his popsicle stick into a bush.

'You would have got caned in Singapore for littering,' Mira said with mock severity.

Rohan held her face in his hands. 'I flew down to see you, sweetheart. That's all there is to it.' She gingerly pulled away and looked into his eyes. 'Are you still mad at me, Rohan?'

'Nah, otherwise I wouldn't have taken the weekend off to come here.'

Mira bit her lower lip thoughtfully, wondering if she should tell him about her Project Bitch Goddess. But what purpose would it serve? The bitch had had her run and the good girl had won by a hair's breath. Why should Rohan know about this now? She could tell him later, depending on what the future had in store for them.

'Penny for your thoughts,' said Rohan. He stretched out his long athletic legs.

'I wish I had trusted you more with what was happening in my life,' Mira said in a small voice. 'I wish I hadn't kept you at an arm's distance. Sorry.'

He shook his head and laughed. 'You are quite crazy—you know that, right?'

She giggled. The hazy crescent of the moon had emerged in the twilight sky. The beach was aglow with the orange light thrown from the vendors' halogen lanterns. Some brave souls waded through the choppy waters, notwithstanding the strong tides.

'But I love this crazy woman who also happens to be gorgeous, witty and intelligent—my kind of woman,' Rohan continued.

Mira punched his shoulder lightly. 'Liar.'

Rohan wrapped his arm around her and drew her closer. 'Everything changed for me when I first met you, Mira. I found you attractive right from the time I noticed you at the Quay. I pumped Sanya shamelessly for information about you that night—much to her annoyance! When we met again at the mall's food court, I thought it was serendipity.'

He paused and stared at the distant lights in the sea. The memory of that meeting lit up Mira's eyes. She remembered coming to the mall to shop for her Bitch Goddess avatar. In hindsight, the day had turned out to be momentous in more ways than one.

'But I didn't fall in love with you till you landed in my bed, drunk and unconscious,' he turned to her with a broad grin.

Mira groaned in embarrassment. 'But you were at the pub with Sanya that night,' she said, her tone accusatory. 'You were constantly spotted everywhere with her.' She shot him a sideways glance. 'Were you guys dating? C'mon, you can tell me now.'

Slow realization dawned on his face and his eyes widened. 'No. Oh God, no! I can never date Sanya. She is just not my type. Did you really think I was going steady with her? Is that why you were acting all aloof with me?' He stared at her intently.

Mira averted her gaze and drew squiggly patterns on the sand with her ice cream stick.

Rohan ran his fingers through his hair. 'Okay, you should know this. Sanya's family and my family have been close friends for many years. I have known her forever. We both moved to Singapore around the same time and since we didn't know anybody else then, we started hanging out together. You know, dinner on weekends, catching a movie, sight-seeing; casual things like that. After a while I got the sense that she wanted to take this beyond friendship. But I was not interested in her in the romantic sense—she was just the daughter of my parents' very good friends. So to me, she was—and still is—like extended family. I told her as much, though she didn't take it too well. But eventually she got the message and we now have a sort of casual friendship. Even that day at the pub, I was there with some visiting professors from Berkeley who left after a few drinks. I stayed on for dinner and she came by and joined me. I never gave it much thought, though now I realise how it might have seemed to you.'

Mira thwacked her forehead. 'And I thought you were two-timing me.'

Rohan jerked his head sharply. 'Did you really think I was two-timing you by dating you *and* Sanya?'

Mira looked away sheepishly, unsure of what to say.

'Lord!' Rohan muttered. '*Two-timing*? Am I such a cad?'

'But I fell in love with you somewhere along the way,' she said softly, almost to herself. 'I had come in my sexy little black dress with plans of cold-blooded seduction. I was annoyed that you were dating Sanya and leading me on—at least that's what I had assumed.'

'So you decided to lead *me* on, instead, by sleeping with me,' finished Rohan, his tone devoid of expression.

Mira shot him an apologetic look. 'But once we got intimate, all my plans fell by the wayside. I started developing honest, intense feelings for you...you have to believe me, Rohan.'

'Then why did you leave me that note? It just devastated me that morning,' said Rohan, his gaze fixed straight.

Mira winced. 'I'm sorry; I never meant to hurt you.'

'I was hurt *and* angry. After I had cooled down, I read your note again. That was when I sensed that something else was going on in your life...I couldn't put a finger on it, but I just knew—the way men sometimes do.'

'Even men have such finely-honed sensibilities?' Mira raised her eyebrows.

'I am in touch with my feminine side,' he drawled in an exaggerated accent.

They laughed.

Rohan shrugged. 'I gave you the benefit of the doubt, till I learnt about your half-sister. That's when I felt truly betrayed.'

Mira sat up. 'But why were you at the club with Sanya? I thought it was an act of betrayal on *your* part. But now I know better; it must have been Sanya's machinations to mislead me.'

'That Sanya woman has really screwed our budding romance,' sighed Rohan. 'I was not having a date with her at the club. I had gone for some golf practice and we ran into each other. You know her—she would have added spice and presented an entirely different picture to rub it in.'

'Thank God I won't have to deal with her nastiness when I return,' said Mira. Then she told him about the promotion and Sanya's attempt to sabotage it.

Rohan surged to his feet and pulled Mira up.

'Congratulations. You deserve this recognition darling.' He nuzzled his face in her neck and kissed her lightly. They held hands and started walking along the shore, enjoying the cool sea breeze on their faces. The crowd had thinned and the vendors had started packing up their wares.

'Rohan, I want to tell you something,' said Mira.

'Sure.'

'Even when I came to seduce you that night, it was never only about the sex for me. I was already very attracted to you and was drawn to you, despite Sanya's interfering ways.'

'Hmm...but you have to admit that the sex was mind-blowing.'

'Don't joke, listen. Do you know when I actually realized the depth of my feelings for you?' Mira stopped and wrapped her arms around Rohan. 'In the hospital's waiting area! I was feeling lost and desolate with my father's other family milling around. I longed to have you by my side, holding me, reassuring me that all will be well...'

Rohan kissed her on her forehead and smoothed her loose tendrils teased by the wind.

'Then it hit me how much I missed you and how devastated I would be if it had been *you* in the OT instead. That's when I knew that I loved you. It suddenly didn't matter whether you loved me or not...once I recognized this, the outcome of our relationship didn't terrify me anymore. The thought was so pure and sincere, something that I had never felt before. I knew I had to confess my love to you even if...if you didn't love me back.' Mira's eyes glistened with tears as she rested her head on Rohan's chest and stared wistfully at the dark waters and beyond. Transforming into a Bitch Goddess had been a cathartic event in her life. But confessing her love to Rohan had been an equally purgative moment. The realization that she had come a long way from the old confused Mira she had been at the Quay, to the confident woman she was today—all due to her Bitch Goddess persona—overwhelmed her.

'Mira, oh my dear precious Mira,' Rohan said, holding her tight. 'I love you very much.'

She looked into his eyes that were beautiful; with thick sooty lashes that women would kill for. She felt his heart pounding against hers and his warm touch made every pore in her body long for him. He leaned forward and kissed her on her lips, his tongue languorously exploring hers. She kissed him back, savouring his taste in her mouth. His hand rested on the small of her back and his fingers trailed down her neck and stopped at her shirt's top button.

She pulled away giggling. 'You'll have you wait till we return to Singapore—I don't want to put up a night show here.'

Rohan took a deep breath. 'Mira Iyer, will you be my girlfriend? Let's take it slow and easy, the way we both like it. Even my students call me Prof. Careful since I take so much time to think through things.'

She answered him with a passionate kiss that set the already hot Chennai temperature soaring. They linked their hands together and started walking back to where their cab was parked.

'I really like him,' was how her mother greeted her when Mira came down the next day for breakfast.

'Like whom, Amma?' she asked groggily.

Her mother served her a tumbler of filter coffee. 'Rohan, who else?'

Mira's eyes popped open remembering Rohan dropping her home last night. He had insisted on doing so and had behaved very charmingly in front of her mother. By the time the evening had ended, he had her mother eating out his hands. Mira sighed resignedly. He was a natural charmer. Women couldn't help being enamoured by him.

'So when are you both planning on getting married?' her mother asked, with faux innocence written on her face.

Mira spluttered on her coffee. 'I just got myself a boyfriend, Amma, and you are already hearing the nadaswarams?'

Her mother made a moue. 'Just asking, kanna. I am not getting any younger; I would love to hold my grandchildren in—'

'Amma!' Mira admonished. 'Aarrghh…are all Indian mothers filmy or only you?'

Her mother pulled Mira's cheek affectionately. 'Every single one of us, till we get our demands met.'

'Well, it will be some time before I fulfill your demands. Rohan is a nice guy, but I want to take it easy and slow…don't want more heartache in life.'

She exchanged a meaningful glance with her mother.

'Hmm...I agree, Mira, don't rush into anything.' Mira and her mother sipped their coffee and glanced through the morning's papers.

Mrs Iyer looked up from the astrology section of the Sunday magazine. 'Are you going to introduce Rohan to your father?'

Mira frowned. 'Why should I?'

'He is your father, Mira, and will be happy to see a decent young man in your life.'

'But I'm not sure where things are headed with Rohan. What is the point in introducing him at this stage?'

'The point being your father will be happy, that's all,' her mother said resolutely. 'Now that you are on talking terms with each other, please try to include him in your life, Mira. You will feel good about this many years hence.'

Mira drained her coffee, hugged her mother and went upstairs for a shower.

Rohan glanced at Mira seated beside him in the cab. 'I am excited about meeting your father,' he said.

Mira placed her palm on his and squeezed it. 'Thanks for doing this for me.'

Rohan was leaving for Singapore that evening and had readily agreed to meet Mira's father when she had asked him. The cab pulled over at the hospital's foyer and they got off.

Mira opened her father's room's door gingerly. He was propped up against pillows and reading a business magazine. He looked stronger and more vibrant now. The doctors were giving Mira positive reports about his progress. Her father's warm brown eyes radiated cheer when he saw her.

'Come, Mira, come,' he greeted her. 'What a pleasant surprise.'

'Hi, Appa, you are looking great.' She was relieved to see him cheerful despite the nasty argument they had had yesterday.

Mira took Rohan's hand and smiled, 'Meet Rohan Bhardwaj...my friend.'

Her father's eyebrows rose in surprise. 'Hello,' His voice was warm but his eyes were shrewdly assessing the young man.

Rohan stepped forward and shook hands with him. 'Very nice to meet you, sir. Great to see you recovering well.'

Mira watched them interact and saw how impressed her father already was. Happiness coursed through her. She had lucked out where Rohan was concerned.

While the two men chatted, Mira excused herself and stepped outside to complete some billing formalities. She ran into Amita enroute from the billing office. She looked pretty in a simple lavender dress, her hair tied in a neat ponytail. Mira felt a pang—that she would later recognize as affection—for the half-sister whom she was starting to like.

Amita gave her a warm hug that Mira awkwardly accepted. 'So good to see you, Mira. I've been bursting to tell you this: Papa has allowed me to pursue music. I will be leaving for the UK next week.'

'Wow,' Mira exclaimed and shook her hand. 'Good for you.'

'It's all due to you, Mira. I owe you big time for your intervention and support.'

'It's all about what a Bitch Goddess wants,' Mira muttered under her breath, high-fiving herself mentally.

'Sorry?' said Amita. 'I didn't hear you.'

Mira smiled and patted Amita's shoulder. 'Never mind, you focus on becoming a famous singer and send me free tickets to your concerts.'

Amita wore a sullen look. 'Papa's consent comes with a condition.'

'How did I forget?' Mira responded tartly. 'He *will* insert a rider; he is a businessman, after all.'

'Papa's fixed a time frame for my music career to take off. I get two years, after I finish my course, to make my singing work. If I'm unable to succeed, I should join his software company.'

'Are you fine with it?' Mira asked softly.

'There is no choice, is there? But I will make my music career work. There are plenty of opportunities out there and two years is enough time to make it happen.'

Mira admired the determined glint in Amita's eyes. 'Of course,' she said encouragingly. 'I am leaving day after tomorrow.'

'Thanks, Mira. For everything.' Amita hugged her again and this time Mira reciprocated with equal fervour. They exchanged email IDs and promised to keep in touch. Mira went back to her father's room feeling lighter—she was happy to have made a difference in Amita's life.

Rohan and her father paused in their conversation and smiled at her. *Thank God they are not at each other's throats.*

'I am sorry for compelling you to join my business, Mira,' her father said with feeling.

Mira studied him closely, sceptical if this was another one of his ploys. But all she saw was genuine regret in those warm eyes that held her gaze intently. She felt like a five-year-old again, tugging at those sturdy hands to take her to the toy shop. Her eyes turned misty as sepia-tinged memories flooded back in a rush.

'It's okay, Appa, let's not talk about it,' she said. It was pointless to argue over something that had already been resolved. 'I am just happy to see you recovering well.'

Mira's father clasped her hands in his. 'Thank you, Mira, for being a pillar of strength in my crisis. I am lucky to have you as my child.'

Mira grinned and nudged Rohan with her elbow. 'So how do you find my...err...friend, Appa?'

'He is a good man and will keep you happy,' he smiled.

She got up to leave.

'You are free to join my company if you decide to change your mind,' her father added as a parting shot. 'No pressure, it's just an option I am giving you.'

Mira nodded, realizing that he was simply doling out practical advice this time. She and Rohan said their goodbyes and left.

Mira's mother hugged her just before she disappeared into emmigration at the airport.

'I am very proud of you, kanna. And I am extremely happy that you have found someone as nice as Rohan.' She caressed Mira's cheek. 'You are finally listening to your heart with regard to your Appa and his decisions. My little girl has grown up.'

Mira kissed her mother and said teasingly, 'Amma, I will miss my flight if you continue with your filmy dialogue.'

Her mother wagged a finger at her. 'Don't delay your marriage. I'll meet Rohan's parents if necessary.'

Mira rolled her eyes and hastened to join the security check queue. Some things never change. Thank God for that.

The flight was on time and it felt good to be back in Singapore's sparkling airport after almost a month. Her eyes automatically searched for Rohan even though she knew he would be at the university conducting the viva voce exams for post-doctoral fellows. He had regretfully told her that it won't be possible to receive her at the airport for this reason. And Vinay had called to inform her that he had been sent to a client site by Gerard. Mira rolled her stroller to the exit door and stepped out into the sultry air of the city she had come to love. She hailed a cab and gave the driver her home address.

Her answering machine was flashing urgently when she let herself into her apartment.

The first message was from Vinay.

'Hey boss, welcome home. Here's a biggie, please sit down and listen: Sanya's been moved to the Bali office. Woo-hoo! Apparently, she got a lot of negative feedback from clients. The team is eagerly waiting for you. See you tomorrow.'

Mira jumped with delight and punched the air in victory. Everybody knew that the company's Bali office was more like a tourist liaison outlet than a real software development centre. All they did was organize fancy-sounding company retreats for the top brass and key employees. Mira fantasized going for such a retreat and having Sanya serve her chilled champagne. Sanya's career was over—at least at Network Systems.

Mira pressed a button to hear the next message.

Rohan's deep baritone flooded the room: 'Hey, sweetheart. Missing you like crazy. I love you.'

'I love you too,' Mira mouthed and blew a kiss to the machine.

The message continued: 'I need you to be fresh and rested because, you, Mira Iyer, are invited to a cosy home cooked dinner for two at my humble abode. Please pack your toothbrush as there is an option of a sleepover. Your chauffeur-driven sedan will be at your place at 8.00 p.m. sharp. I will advise you not to keep the chauffeur waiting. He's a temperamental man and, if tested, is capable of changing his mind.'

Mira laughed and was about to switch off the machine when Rohan's voice concluded:

'Oh, and I forgot to add that the dress code is the Little Black Dress...'

Mira laughed in delight, her mirth bouncing off her apartment walls. Only she knew that she didn't need the Little Black Dress any more. She had achieved what she had set out to achieve—and much more. She was free, at last, of the bonds that had weighed her down for so long. And, along the way, she had discovered something important: that life shimmered with possibilities. Everywhere.

Bitch Goddess Rule #21 (the most fundamental one): It is important to know when to be a Bitch and when to be a Goddess. But it is more important to know when to be just yourself.

Acknowledgements

There are many to whom I owe thanks for this book. First and foremost, a huge and heartfelt thanks to my editor, Kausalya Saptharishi, for having faith in me, my story and my heroine— even on the days I didn't; for laughing with me through the rewrites and for converting my manuscript into a real book. Thanks also to Saritha Rao and Rochelle Potkar, my fellow travellers, my sounding boards and my writing cornerstones. Thanks to Nithya Krishnaswamy for throwing me a lifeline on the days I thought I would sink. I couldn't have done this without you three. Thanks to S K Mukund, Sudha Radhakrishnan and Padmaja Anant for all the help. Thanks to P S Sreemathy for teaching me how to look at writing. Thanks to Sriram, Aditya and Vishaka for showing me the value of my dreams and making me write, even on the days I didn't want to. Thanks to Mahesh Sharma, Rajani Ramachandran, Natasha and Shyam for the unconditional acceptance and love. Thanks to the rest of my family for the encouragement and support. And thanks to Suchi, who was the first one to tell me that one day I would be published, and to her I say, 'looks like that day is here.' I also owe many thanks to my first English teacher (1972-1978), Ms Shobha Nair, K V Pattom, for giving me the joy of the language and the love of reading.